The Quality of Light

The Quality of Light

Modern Italian Short Stories

Edited by Ann and Michael Caesar

This book is dedicated
to the memory of
Pier Vittorio Tondelli
(1955–1991)

A catalogue record for this book is available from the British
Library on request.

Library of Congress Catalog Card Number: 92-83758

First published 1993 by Serpent's Tail, 4 Blackstock Mews,
London N4 and 401 West Broadway #1, New York, NY 10012

Typeset in 10/12½ Times Roman by Contour Typesetters, Southall,
London
Printed in Great Britain by Cox & Wyman Ltd., of Reading,
Berkshire

SC
QUALITY

Contents

Introduction

In this anthology, we hope to reflect something of the variety, and the quality, of Italian story-telling of the past two decades. The twenty-two stories collected here are by writers who differ enormously in age, background and literary purpose. They are no less divergent in style and subject-matter. They combine, for example, the keen anthropological sensitivity of Primo Levi's 'The Witch-Doctors' and the expressionist brutalism of Pier Vittorio Tondelli's first novel; or the underlying sadism that pervades the stories by Paola Capriolo and Susanna Tamaro, and the interweaving of the personal and the political in the ironically observed past of Rosetta Loy and Nico Orengo's stories; or the politically aggressive avantgardism of Balestrini and the narrative restraint of Veronesi and Rasy. But together they confirm that the tradition of short fiction writing, with a pedigree in Italian literature that goes back at least to Boccaccio, has if anything been reinforced in recent years. Leading writers in the seventies and eighties gave influential preference to the fragment or episode (Calvino) or the novella (Sciascia); magazines and newspapers regularly offer a space to short stories; and most Italian writers, even those who are relatively young, have a considerable stock of short fictions to their credit, many of them already published in volume form. In general, the short fiction—the tale, the novella, the short novel, or the novel that is made up of 'detachable' parts—appears to offer a narrative space in which it is possible to exploit an intensity and precision of insight that is more akin to a certain kind of lyric poetry than it is to the novel.

'The quality of light' is not only the environmental issue which, as it happens, is taken into the metaphor of Gianni Celati's story—though those of us accustomed to praising the quality of Italy's light may well wish to start here; nor does it refer only to the light evoked in the titles of other stories or books: Consolo's 'The Photographer', for instance, or *La violenza illustrata*, the novel from which the Balestrini extract is taken. That the quality of light recurs so often in these stories as the medium through which some aspect of reality is observed and recounted is testimony not so much to a peculiarly pictorial way of seeing on the part of the writer (though this is true in some cases, as in Parise or Tabucchi) as to the dominance of consciousness, or intelligence. This is a writing of the thinking imagination, which entrusts to language one of two tasks: that of focusing and holding an event, an experience, an episode in view (frequently either transitional encounters or memories of the dead as in Piersanti or Petrignani) or that of making sense, even simply imposing order upon the ambiguous signs of which everyday life is composed, in Ortese or Fontana or Del Giudice. The quality of light is a quality of intelligence. But it is an intelligence that discovers that it has recourse only to language, more specifically only to writing. The meaning of what is seen is forthcoming only in the writing, and it comes naturally to speak of these fictions, in very many cases, as possessing their own luminosity, their own glow. They are entirely self-sustaining. At the risk of isolation and solipsism, they refuse to rely on any discourse external to themselves; the event or episode is self-contained (though it may occupy fictionally a span of many years) and is not placed or explained by reference to any rule or institution, or system. Neither history, nor physical science, nor psychoanalysis has any part to play in the illumination of the world. The writing provides the story with its own light.

The intelligence of the writer is undoubtedly also a political statement. In the seventies, many writers turned their backs with a kind of tired disgust on the public arena which internationally had become increasingly sclerotic and dangerous, and nationally was strung out between violence and despair, terrorism and oppression. The decade did not mark, as is often thought, a 'return to order'. It was a period of messy, often bitter skirmishing, characterized at the level of interpersonal relations by a loss of trust, or the search for a new contractual basis. The return to order came after, in the eighties, under the aegis of a revitalized consumerism, a moneyed confidence, that already, only a few years later, begins to look distinctly tatty. The boom of the eighties was good economically for writers: publishers formed larger conglomerates and became part of multi-media empires which guaranteed publicity, Umberto Eco showed others more cynical than he how to 'package' a product and make it sell, the 'made in Italy' label was a plus in the world market, and biology lent a hand by clearing the way for a new generation of 'young novelists' with the rapid succession of deaths which struck the ranks of senior writers between 1985 and 1990 (Morante, Calvino, Parise, Levi, Sciascia, Moravia). As had happened twenty years earlier, there was considerable pressure on writers, especially younger ones, to 'produce', in order to justify their presence in the literary market. Aware of such pressure it has become more necessary than ever for writers to determine for themselves what they want to say, and not only young writers but also many who are already established but in the process of being 'rediscovered'. Indeed, paradoxically, it may be that the presence of a consumerized literary market will lead to a greater individualism, to a more determined effort to defend a subjective space, to seek, however briefly and however illusory, her or his own moment of clarity.

In compiling an anthology of this sort, one has to make many hard choices and omit of course far more than can be included. In the end, we have made decisions based on our judgement of the quality of the works in themselves and in the interests of the range of the collection as a whole. But we make no apologies for preferring, in general, writers who are unknown or little known in English-speaking countries to those who are already very firmly established, and stories which have not been translated to those which are already available elsewhere.

Ann and Michael Caesar

Rosetta Loy

The Wet-Nurse

'**S**how me your teeth.' The doctor had two enamelled cuff-links at his wrist and there was a gold chain across his waistcoat. 'From the teeth,' he had said, turning towards the lady, 'you can tell right away if a woman is healthy or not.' He had coughed, his beard round and greyish-blue on his chin.

The girl's lip, held up by the doctor's fingers, had shaken slightly; the teeth were very beautiful even if one or two were missing at the side. 'But this is inevitable,' the doctor had said, 'in the country there are only people who pull teeth . . . Now let's see the bosom.' He had taken his fingers away and was drying them with a handkerchief. The girl had not moved, swallowing the saliva which had formed in her mouth. 'Come on, undo your things,' the doctor had ordered but the girl had remained motionless. 'I told you,' he had repeated brusquely, 'open up here' and his finger had pointed at her chest, the cuff-link gleaming on the immaculate white of the cuff.

The lady was young and that was her first baby. A difficult birth that lasted from dawn to dusk and when the little girl was born she felt indifferent, so exhausted was she; if they had told her she had given birth to a puppy it would have been all the same to her. Now she was sitting in an armchair wrapped in a blue dressing gown of Pyrenean wool and felt as if her body were in pieces, still damp with a sweetish smell. The girl had undone her bodice, not sure if she was right to do so, and at each button she had looked at the doctor with his blue-grey beard which was so well cut. She was married but no one could have defined her other than as a girl. At each buttonhole undone the material seemed to pull itself back and the bosom to emerge like one of those Chinese flowers that open up on contact with water. But after the bodice there was still the shift and a kind of cloth sash; the doctor waited patiently while the lady watched all these movements as if they had nothing to do with her. At last the breast slipped out, full of light, enclosed in the delicate network of veins; and the doctor squeezed one of the nipples. The milk, squirting high, struck him on the shirt and the lady had laughed. Even the girl had laughed and her teeth had shown themselves in all their splendour. 'All the better,' the doctor had said, cleaning himself with his handkerchief.

Through the elegant curtains the brief, weak light of the afternoon was filtered and the girl's skin was burning, she was not used to central heating, just as she had never seen a telephone before that afternoon nor a radio. Nor had she ever seen such a big mirror, a mirror which was able to reflect, besides herself and the doctor, the lady as well, sunk in the armchair. Through the half-open door the maid was peeping at her. 'She's a good-looking girl,' she had said to the cook standing in the glass door that led to the servants' quarters, 'but she looks like a real country lass.'

In the bedroom the little girl slept in the cradle and the wallpaper was pink with peach tree boughs; on the white-painted furniture vividly coloured, funny dolls were painted with their heads exaggeratedly big in comparison to their bodies. 'This is the nursery,' the lady had said, using the English word. The girl had run her fingers over the fluff on the baby's head and the baby had twitched and then gone back to sucking its finger, its little face wrinkled with sleep. 'You had better wash first,' the lady had said but she was smiling and the girl looked at her hand and blushed.

That afternoon the girl had for the first time come across a bath and had sat gingerly in the bath-tub, amused at the water that rose tepidly between her legs. The maid sent to help her (really to make sure that no part was missed by the soap, not even the most intimate ones) had been able to admire her smooth, white, compact body, a body with an adolescent's long back. And yet the girl, too, had given birth not even three months before.

Afterwards they made her put on a loose white shift and she had sat down beside the cradle to wait for the baby to waken to suckle. Her neck emerged round and erect from the tremendously loose material while her glance—that of a Byzantine empress—roved diffidently, aggressive and melancholy at one and the same time: a drawing in red crayon emerging from the clumsiness of the clothes. 'But what are extraordinary are the *attaches*,' the woman had said to her husband. And by *attache* she meant the girl's ankles, which were so slim that one could circle them with two fingers.

Properly dressed, the girl had begun to go out with the pram, pushing it up and down the pavement. Her shawl, her kerchief, her apron and the stripes in her skirt all shone, and her face, taking colour from the air, seemed to reflect in its seriousness a distant point of light of springtime yet to come. But she did not like that dress or that shawl, not even the kerchief she had to put on her head. Now that she had washed her hair it slipped lightly through her fingers and in the evening she looked at it in the mirror as it lay loose on her shoulders. 'Keep looking,' the maid said to her, 'you'll end up by seeing the devil.'

The maid was nearly fifty but when she went out on Sundays she put on silk stockings and her coat with the fox-fur collar and on her return told of the men who had followed her and wanted to take her to the cinema. But even on Sundays the girl went out with the pram and took with her the knitting for her baby who had remained in the village. Sometimes she got as far as the Lake Garden and looked at the boats suspended on the water, the ducks that fanned out to cut the surface, which was full of shadows. Girls of her own age sank their oars in the water and if the boat rocked, laughed in fear; when they came out they had muddied shoes and the soldiers held them round the waist. Sometimes one of them would come up and lean over the pram; but the lady did not like her to talk to anyone for fear of contagious diseases and gave her long talks about the dangers of whooping cough and diphtheria.

She was a modern lady and explained the existence of

microbes to her. Each time she came in to see the little girl she asked if the room had been 'aired sufficiently' and some days sat to watch as she suckled the child, quick to make suggestions. She herself weighed the little girl every week and then entered the increase with satisfaction in a little notebook with a flowered cover. Her round head with its permanent wave recalled the heads on show in the hairdressers' windows with the two thin lines of the lips and the staring eyes in the long eyelashes. She had quickly recovered and had forgotten the torture of the birth; sometimes at night the girl woke up to suffocated cries, then she lit the light and the dolls painted on the wardrobe, with their bodies that were too short and their eyes that were sunk in the fat of their cheeks, kept her company. Like that tram that screeched on the curve or the gurgle of the water when at dawn it began once more to flow through the pipes of the radiator.

In spring, in connection with a trip her husband had to make to Austria, the lady had spoken for the first time of war. 'I am worried,' she had said, 'I don't feel it is the right time to make such a long trip.' Her husband had one leg shorter than the other (a piece of luck this, said the lady, because whatever happened he would be excused military service) and he dangled it nervously, sitting on the terrace among the geraniums, which were beginning to flower. He was an engineer and smoked French cigarettes, taking them from a leather case; he too was very modern and sat there without a tie, his shirt unbuttoned at the neck. Every so often his glance rested on the wet-nurse, acute, penetrating, and for a moment it looked as if he were trying to size up both her aura of holiness and her dramatic and dazzling beauty; then with a certain effort he turned back to smile to his wife.

The nurse did not notice anything, it was hot already and she took off her shawl, rolled her stockings down below the knee. The baby kicked its legs in the air with bare feet and the lady picked the first rose to place in the house on the dining room table.

She wore dresses of printed silk, this lady; she was once more as she used to be and she liked it when her husband took her in the car to Ostia. On her return she always said that the autostrada to the sea was 'a marvellous piece of work' and then seemed no longer to be afraid of that trip he had to make to Austria. 'I don't believe,' she would say, 'that there are autostradas like that there . . . .' She took up the baby girl and held it high. 'Next year,' she said, 'we'll take you to the sea too!' Her voice bubbled in her throat and the scent of the geraniums along the windowsill mixed with that of the sun-tan oil on her skin hot from the sun.

The young nurse had a bad dream. One of those dreams that mean death. With the cook they tried divining with oil in the bowl of water but the result was unclear. 'Maybe it's to do with the oil,' said the cook. 'If it isn't pure it doesn't work.' But that dream gives the girl no peace, now when she is working on the little blue jumper she keeps thinking back to it. It seems to her that in that dream there is a voice, the contact of a skin. She has not seen her little boy for months and is not even sure if she would be able to recognize him. She would like to go and visit him, at least once. 'But it's not possible, nurse, you do understand?' the lady turns away her smooth round head, she doesn't want to see those eyes in which death emerges from the depths as if in a telescope the wrong way round. Big, transparent eyes, like membranes over the darkness. 'It just is not possible, believe me,' the beautiful pointed lips shut on the words, forced them into a smile; soon they will take her into the mountains with the little girl, she will see so many new things and her bad thoughts will go away. 'Dreams, nurse, are only dreams,' something sounds unnatural in her voice, she is hardly any older than the girl and sometimes it happens to her that she wakes with a start because of a bad dream. On the floor below a new neighbour has come, he is called Pompei and they say he is a Secret Police spy, but they have nothing to fear because her husband has a timber business. The new race laws have come into force, but what has that to do with her? So why be frightened . . . She knows that the nurse's baby is already dead, the parish priest wrote to say so but added that the husband is anxious for nothing to be said, otherwise the girl would loose her milk from sadness and with the milk her post as wet-nurse.

The lady takes her out on to the terrace, the swallows are crisscrossing a sky shot through with gentle airy lights, the jasmine is beginning to flower along the wall, it will bloom all summer. The house has been built on the new lines, has big windows, a lot of sun, and from that terrace you can see the Pincio and the water that seems to explode from the mouths of the marble lions. 'That is the dome of St Peter's,' says the lady, 'have you ever been inside St Peter's?' The girl shakes her head. 'Tomorrow we'll take a trip in the car,' the lady has plucked a jasmine flower, she puts it through the pin of her décolleté, 'we'll take you to St Peter's and to the Piazza dell'Esedra.' The girl looks at the dome which is pale grey, almost pink. Perhaps the lady is right, dreams are only dreams, she is well off in this house, the little girl has grown fond of her, everyone looks at her when she takes her for a walk.

One morning she was stopped by a gentleman with a homburg and a striped brown suit. The gentleman had soft tapering hands, good manners, a dark car was waiting for him in the street with a chauffeur at the wheel. He had leant over the pram then smiled to her affably, 'A pretty baby, how old is it?' She had laughed—this gentleman who was so elegant had forgotten to close his flies. 'If you wanted,' said the gentleman, 'I could help you earn money, a lot of money.' He stared at her with protruding eyes shot through with streaks of blood, eyes like the inside of a chicken, its inside plucked out with a hooked finger. Her laughter has frozen on her lips. 'Yours,' the gentleman had said, 'is a hundred thousand dollar smile.'

That is what he said, 'A hundred thousand dollar smile.' 'But do you at least know what dollars are?' the maid asked her. She had turned red, of course she knew what dollars were (but meantime that morning she had almost run off stumbling on the pavements, sweating all over as she pushed the pram, and turned round again to see if that man was following her with his black car which slipped silently over the tarmac, the chauffeur impassive at the wheel).

But the real dream in all its ferocious clarity, she has once she arrives in the mountains. She wakes up and cannot manage to turn on the light because everything around her is different and her hands grope in the dark for a long time before finding the switch, they touch the chill of the marble on the bedside table, the brass of the lamp. Outside she could hear the splash of cascades and stones falling in the distance. He is dead, she thinks, he is dead, and I shall never see him again. Before her there are no longer the big puppets with their pink knees and laughing eyes, only a dark chest and the wallpaper patterned with Florentine lilies. The little girl began to cry but she did not stir and that crying grew till it became a scream in the starry night (a limpid July night with farmsteads scattered in the light of the meadows and gurgling brooks) and in the end the lady opened the door with her eyes narrowed by sleep. 'What is happening?' she asked, lifting up the child who was breathless from so much crying. Only then did she get out of bed and mechanically begin to suckle it. The child has a mouth like a suction cup, its hair is sweaty from crying, she holds it with rigid arms and her unbuttoned shift shows her body down to her navel, her face and hair are devastated by sleep. A witch, a feverish witch in the night and perhaps her milk is a subtle poison, as sticky as the juice of certain plants of the swamps. The lady stayed there and watched her, uncertainly fingering the tin of talcum powder, then the little pink hairbrush, the bottle of Sangemini water, her long silk nightdress which gleams among the lilies of Florence.

But July is coming to an end and shortly Stalin and von Ribbentrop will sign in Moscow the pact which will catch Poland in a vice. At Bayreuth Hitler is listening to Wagner, sitting in the box that once belonged to Ludwig of Bavaria, he applauds with a little clap of his hands the tenor who bows deeply, Isolde has long tresses of yellow silk (for him a brilliant future has been foretold, a thousand-year Reich, but some wise women have seen a violent death in the lines of his hands). In Paris the season has ended with a great masked ball given by the Polish Ambassador, President Lebrun's wife was present at the Grand Prix with a hat decorated with periwinkle-blue *aigrettes*.

The twelve-year-old princess of England went with her younger sister to meet the king and queen on their return from a trip to Canada, at Southampton they went on board the royal yacht and were given a fluffy panda. The second child of the heir to the Dutch throne is about to be born, in a few days the son of King Boris of Bulgaria will blow out the candle for his first birthday. The Kodak clicks to photograph the little princes of the House of Savoy picnicking at San Rossore, blonde and very beautiful in the green of the pinewoods. From America Tyrone Power and Norma Shearer arrive, smiling they come down the gangways of the transatlantic liner in the gleaming reflected light of the sea. Mussolini with naked torso advances over the field of wheat, which is baking in the heat. The first ears are cut for him: 'Honour bread, the good scent of the table,' is written on the house of the Fascist mayor in the village that the young nurse comes from. King Carol of Romania is cruising in the Mediterranean and General Badoglio in his shirt-sleeves is playing *bocce* at a spa, the flags are fluttering in Venice for the Film Festival and leaning on the crimson cushion of a gondola a little man who also limps slightly, father of four splendid blue-eyed children, is admiring the Grand Canal (no one has yet foreseen your violent deaths, children of Goebbels). The special trains meet in the station, carpets are hurriedly unrolled, hands are stretched out in salutes. *Sieg Heil dem Befreier* is written over the entrance to Berchtesgaden not far from Salzburg (this year at the Mozart Festival almost nothing but black Fascist uniforms, the field grey cloth of the *Wehrmacht*). But at Berchtesgaden the sky is blue, the fields are full of daisies and on the terrace facing the mountains of Tyrol someone sketches a dance step. The lake reflects the emerald of the woods and a young woman is doing gymnastic exercises, her bronzed body throws itself up, rolls over, falls gently back on the grass, the dog wags its tail, pants, splashes water. 'Schatzi, don't annoy the Führer . . .' The engineer who limps slightly—a very slight defect which might prove to be very useful in the event of war, travels through Carinthia to strike bargains over a batch of timber and from the train window looks at the peasants guiding the plough, furrows as straight as the lines of a notebook. The horses move forward slowly, their hairy fetlocks and hooves sinking into the earth. The peasants wear shapeless felt hats on their heads and have long aprons of blue material, their children with straw-coloured hair greet the train, their trousers held up by a single brace. Little lakes of malachite open up among the pines and the fishers keep the line on the surface of the water, a little hat with a feather in the hatband, toothbrush moustaches like those of Charlie Chaplin or the Führer. Some are war veterans and have scars that make themselves felt when the weather changes, they sit in a boat or on top of a rock, so intent on each slightest oscillation of the line that they do not even lift their heads at the passing of the train where the engineer thinks about the timber he has bought. The young nurse (she is only twenty and has been chosen in line with the modern criterion 'youth is health') pushes the pram along the dirt road that follows the torrent, violet flowers grow along its banks and if it rains she pulls up the waxed hood and the baby in the bottom of the pram becomes tiny, its fists clenched, its voice ready to explode angrily: it is hungry. With a gesture that has become habitual the girl touches her breast, since she had those bad dreams nothing is as before and her body has become a machine that misfires. More and more often at the moment for giving milk her breast is empty, light in the hand. When she looks at herself in the mirror she sees her face which is thinner, pointed. It has gone back to being the face of the little girl who ran barefoot among the stones and sang at the top of her voice to chase away the fear when she was alone with the sheep. She doesn't want to lose her post as wet-nurse, she needs that money. Bank notes counted and recounted in her memory, carefully smoothed out, sent off, licking the envelope and the stamp with her tongue dry from excitement.

But now she should be at peace, a letter has arrived from the parish priest in which her husband sends her the message that the baby boy has grown two teeth. 'There you are,' says the cook, 'don't be stupid, you see everything is fine.' But her body doesn't want to know, more and more often she watches the little girl sucking at nothing and falling asleep exhausted by the effort. But she has learned to be wily and when at night the baby cries because it is hungry she goes into the bathroom and soaks a corner of the towel in the water and sugar, then she gives it to the baby to suck. That way it does not cry any more. Now in her sleep the two babies become confused, they have the same desperate cry of hunger and like the horses on the roundabouts they go round and round without her being able to stop them. The August storms pelt against the windows, they soak the lawn round the house, a woman comes selling blueberries, the blueberries make your lips and teeth black, they stain her shawl of blue artificial silk. Helped by the maid she tries in vain to take out the spot, she weeps. 'What are you doing, stupid girl?' the cook scolds her. 'If you tell the lady she'll buy you a new one.'

The baby gets thin, the scales have stayed at the same place for a long time, the lady's hands run to and fro uselessly on the steel truck. Sometimes when the lady turns away she takes a cloth and throws it on to the scales to make it heavier. The little girl is weak, her head droops and from the bottom of the pram its immense eyes look at her, the blue of the irises seeming to fade in the sockets. On sunny days the lady sits by the pram and plays with the baby which is propped up against the cushions, the doctor has said not to worry, the benefits of the mountains will be seen once they have got back to the city, he has ordered boiled potatoes and an egg-yolk twice a week. The cook makes pap which it is well known brings on milk and the maid embroiders scapulars for Saint Cunnegonde, pinches the cheeks of the baby which falls asleep sucking. The lady goes away with two leather suitcases and her red-lacquered hat-box, she is going to join her husband in Vienna where they will eat Sachertorte in the cafés with their plate-glass mirrors and little tables of pink marble. She watches her go off standing on the lawn by the pram, the distance has become immense, even those letters from the parish priest take almost a week to arrive and her face has shrunk round a fixed thought, her dress, which is too big for her, hangs down from her shoulders. The lady stops uncertainly, something binds her to this figure so melancholy in her gaudy colours, not even this sunny day manages to loosen the tightness she feels in her throat as if the air was unable to pass through it. That unspoken death is now a stone that ties them together, it is a stone that pulls them down, no one knows where they will be dragged to. 'Nurse, perhaps it would be a good idea to take the baby back into the house, I think the wind is getting up . . .' She adjusts the woollen blanket, her knitting is abandoned on the pram (who will finish that little blue jumper? and for whom?). 'We'll go in now,' she says, in a few months her way of speaking has become refined; she learns speedily and only occasionally does the dialect edge return. 'Don't forget the egg tomorrow,' says the lady, she nods her head, her earrings shine in the sun. What else can they say to each other? The lady gets into the car and her back bends and disappears into the seat. The lady does not know that the trip to eat sweet things and drink Rhine wine will cost her a new pregnancy, another baby whom they will call Maria Vittoria in the hope of a victory which will not come. The chauffeur gets into the car gathering up the hem of his dustcoat, he starts the motor, the gravel spurts under the wheels. The nurse waves her hand in farewell, her eyes are one long slit in which tears are perhaps shining, then she turns and raises the front wheels of the pram to take it back into the house. The light coming in at the window is dazzling, it is reflected in gold on the floor, in the vase the long violet flowers sway in the sudden draught, in the kitchen the cook is slicing courgettes. 'She weeps, weeps too much, this girl,' she says to the woman who has come to bring the eggs, 'she'll end up having no more milk,' and shakes her head in disapproval of youth, departures, rash nights of love.

That night the girl dreams for the last time of her baby with its mouth wide open on its empty gums and its face white as wax. It is all so clear that there are no longer any doubts, she gets up and draws a cross on the glass with her finger. It is raining and the water splashes down from the gutter, it runs off over the lawn, it soaks the seats left outside, the glove the lady lost when she got into the car. In her bed the little girl is sleeping with her thumb in her mouth and the bars at the edge of the bed divide up her body like a tiny white hill. Another few days, then the first snow will appear on the crests of the mountains and the torrent will leap with new vigour among the boulders, it will rise up on the banks sucking away the overlong grass, it will submerge the islands of sand which have appeared during the summer. Soon the first sheep will come down onto the plain along the narrow tracks, the baby should be ten months and six days old, should be sitting up and testing its teeth on tin spoons and crusts of bread. She anoints the cross on the window pane with saliva, some drops of rain that have stayed suspended tremble in the light from the bedside table. The lady has arrived in Vienna and her hat-box rolls down from the train, red in the smoky lights of the station, her husband comes towards her limping a little (a slight defect which will not however help to save him, he will die like a dog killed in the middle of the street, that short leg of his a problem when one has to escape in a hurry).

The girl-nurse, will die too, of puerperal fever. She will die of having eaten dried figs, at least that is what the midwife will say, maintaining that it is not her fault, the fault lies in those figs the girl went to eat in the night, dragging herself up from the mattress of maize leaves still wet with blood. Figs that grew in a summer of great drought, the accursed figs of the summer of war.

But on the night when the young wet-nurse got up still exhausted by the birth, she no longer remembered the bad dreams of that distant summer. She had forgotten the unbroken turning of the wheels alongside the torrent. She remembered the red clusters of currants which came through the fence outside the church. She went to mass with her new shoes and there was always someone who picked these currants and offered them to her in the palm of his hands, she raised them to her lips and those currants gleamed in her smile. It was the lady who wanted to take her that time when they went in the car up to Cogne to see the Gran Paradiso. White butterflies flecked with black, *Pharnasum aedes*, flew low in great quantities. It was an unusual phenomenon, that of the summer of '39, of notable interest to entomologists. She fed the baby in the car then left it to the lady and her husband stretched on the deckchairs with their faces to the sun. Along with the cook and the others she went to eat polenta roasted in the oven with cheese, the cheese was still hot and stuck to the fork and the chauffeur sitting next to her laughed at her efforts to catch it with her tongue. The chauffeur was young and had just finished his military service, he came from the province of Udine and the nurse's way of speaking made him laugh as did her attempts to eat the polenta with her fork. 'Like this,' he said, 'this is how to do it.' He had given her his spoon. Enclosing her hand in his while with the other, with the help of bread, he pushed cheese and polenta on to it. He had a hard, hot hand and his arm went across her breast, she looked at him and in his eyes there was a great light that day, there was the Gran Paradiso and the butterflies, the currant bushes. A wind was blowing and the chauffeur had filled up her glass with red wine, then they had both climbed up along the path that led to the slopes of the Gran Paradiso, there where the meadows were more and more strewn with stones and the butterflies no longer flew while the wind blew the clouds in gusts round the white crest of the mountain. The chauffeur had offered to help her but she had refused and had kept on climbing, taking care not to scratch her shoes, with her round chin stubborn, red with the cold. From below the lady saw them going further and further up and had begun to call with her hands cupped round her mouth. She had turned her head to look at her but then had gone on just the same, the wind chilling the sweat on her neck. The grass had got shorter and invisible water wet her shoes, made that grass a carpet into which her feet sank without sound. Up there there was a great silence and the wind ruffled her hair, the chauffeur's hair gave off the scent of brilliantine. 'Have you ever been so high up?' he had asked her. She had shaken her head. 'It is cold,' she had said but she was smiling and her voice seemed to sing. The chauffeur had given her his blue jacket with a double row of buttons, that jacket smelt of cloth like the car, but of sweat as well, of the sweat of someone who is young and does not shrink from hard work.

He had an accordion, that chauffeur, and in the evening in fine weather he sat outside by the kitchen and played. He was good at it and the lady sometimes stopped her to hear him: his big strong hand went up and down on the keyboard and in the half-dark the case of imitation mother-of-pearl was like the moon. His fiancée had given him that accordion but no one knew whether he was thinking about her when he was playing. She was rich, his fiancée, and he had got to know her when doing his military service but that summer he never wrote to her. He played looking at the stars in his shirt-sleeves, it was almost always the same, the song, and sometimes he would even play it several times in an evening. A song the wet-nurse knew too and one morning the cook had heard her singing it, getting the words wrong. Every morning the wet-nurse came down to have her coffee in the kitchen while the chauffeur was busy round the stove, his chauffeur's boots making a din on the balcony where the wood was. His shoulders in the white shirt had something splendid and banner-like, so broad were they, straight, always in motion. The wet-nurse sat at the table in the kitchen and broke her bread into the coffee until she had immersed it in the cup. She came down with a shawl, without an apron, sometimes she even forgot to put up her hair. 'You have to forgive her,' said the cook, 'she is so young.'

Gianni Celati

Conditions of Light on the Via Emilia

Luciano Capelli and I often met the signwriter Emanuele Menini and often listened to his thoughts about the state of things along the road he lived on, the Via Emilia.

Emanuele Menini lived for twenty years on this road and being a landscape painter he knew very well how the light falls from the sky, how it touches and envelops things.

The road on which Menini lives passes through several cities of medium size and running through one of the least ventilated plains in the world reaches the sea. It's a dividing line between the high ground and the low ground traced I don't know how long ago, which never offers very distant horizons because it is shut off on one side by the profile of the hills and, on the other, by fields which rise up almost to the level of the eyes.

The profile of the hills rises up in eroded gullies and crests towards mountains depopulated in some parts, often bare, with woods where desolate hunters occasionally wander in search of vanished game. It is this line of mountains that blocks all the winds from the east, the rising currents of air that come from the sea, thus making these parts so little ventilated.

On certain clear days, by climbing the mountain and looking towards the long road, one can see a layer—bluish or pearly depending on the seasons—suspended almost permanently over the plain. That is the cloud in which people live in these parts, a cloud in which every kind of luminosity is dispersed in myriads of rays.

There are unbroken lines of traffic on most of the long road for many hours each day—and for a large part of its route it travels between two pieces of scenery formed by billboards, long factory sheds, service stations, emporiums selling furniture and lamps, car showrooms, car dumps, bars, restaurants, little houses in bright colours, or else districts with high blocks that have risen in the midst of the countryside.

Round about the air is almost always bright with changing tones, caused by the fine dust, by the traces of the fumes from the motors, by the layers of powdered material from the asphalt surface and from the wheeltracks, as well as by the vapours given off by the soil of chalky and clayey marl. So the light striking down from above is engulfed in a layer of atmosphere much denser and heavier than the others; and that cancels or greatly reduces the differences with the daytime shadows, because of the great dispersion of the luminous rays which are continually diverted or casually reflected, and which envelop everything in a cloud of glare and rays.

Naturally there are many differences between the ways in which the light is dispersed at the different times of day and in the different seasons. Since these parts are an extremely ancient gulf of marshes, filled for the most part with clay, where the rains run off or evaporate without being retained by the soil, they are also a zone with some of the thickest seasonal mists.

So, because of the thick mists which rise from the ground, the cloud of reflected light on the long road often seems opaque or ash-grey in humid seasons. However it is almost always iridescent in the hottest months and in summer, for instance, in the morning a field of cabbages can present itself to the eyes in a fluorescent green, a service station and a factory shed can appear as tremulous as a mirage, while the clear sky is all pearl-coloured up to the zenith.

Only when the sun is low on the horizon does it become possible to make out clearly the shadows on the ground, the contours of things, and to look at things without having the view of them obfuscated by glare in the air. And at night on the long road not many stars are to be seen, one even forgets that in other parts of the planet skies thickly populated with lights are a normal sight. Here, up high, on summer nights the light of the Milky Way and the Plough and the Pleiades are almost always lost, impossible to find, their scintillations muffled by the fog on these parts where there are so few winds.

The signwriter Emanuele Menini had often reflected on all this even if he had confined himself to observing a short stretch of that road between his house and the bar five hundred metres from this house, there and back.

Just outside the house where Menini lives you find yourself in front of a bridge over which a railway line passes. On the other side of the bridge the long road goes on between two lines of low houses and further on the space widens out towards districts made up of tall buildings all sharp against the sky.

To Menini that ring road, always crowded in the morning with motors and people going out to shop, often appeared— when seen against the light and from the other side of the bridge—merely a fog full of beams of light. And in his thoughts he saw that the lines of cars on the tar, together with the inhabitants in the streets, the bushes that had grown in a crack in the pavement, the leaves of a big plane tree next to a service station, all joined in a vast movement of convection and fluctuation of the stagnant air, through which there passed waves and whirlpools of traffic.

What he saw at that moment was a blend of air in which there moved shadows drowned in the dispersed light. Menini said: 'Light that has shattered.'

Going on beyond the bridge every morning he crossed the point where the cloud is thicker, because the road is narrower between these low houses with little shops. Here the buses which often occupied all the tarred surface, the people waiting for the bus, the people going shopping or into the bar, all were caught up in the ebb and flow with more intense whirlpools and eddies. And in the ebb and flow compressed into a narrow space, the signwriter began to detect a tremor in the air which made everything unstable, swaying around him as he himself swayed with the others.

This was the everyday tremor which comes as morning begins, something that transports you and which you can't resist, which Menini compared to a state of intoxication.

Then at the point where the road widens out and is crossed by a four-lane ring road, he often noticed that a percussive wave passes through the air as if through a combustion chamber. In fact in the larger space the tremor of the ebb and flow which was compressed at the previous point bursts out, the traffic suddenly accelerates, the vehicles go off at full speed towards the traffic lights. And when you hear those trucks with trailers accelerating, bringing to its peak the tremor which makes everything sway, you see very clearly that here it is difficult to escape from the intoxication.

According to Menini, what happened at that point was like when drunks become violent. The same went for those drunks going past in their vehicles.

Further on, at the bar where Menini went every day, the view opens out towards the perspective of a long four-lane main road. And standing at the door of his bar at various times of the year, the signwriter saw there, at the other end, a white mist on a knoll where an imposing cedar of Lebanon dominates the traffic. The silhouette of the great tree was always black, while the lines of vehicles down there were a mass of imprecise shapes with luminous contours lost in that milky fog.

Once Menini had walked as far as that knoll because the great cedar of Lebanon had made him think of God, and there an idea had come into his head.

The first time that Luciano Capelli took me to meet Menini one Sunday in January, in his usual bar, he looked me over for a long time and said at last: 'So you are someone who writes. Well done! I shall be content if you write what I say—that way my breath won't be so wasted.'

And he immediately began to tell the story of that walk to the knoll taken because the great cedar of Lebanon made God come into his mind.

When he had arrived there, turning round, he had noticed that he could no longer see the cloud that enwraps the traffic down his way, because it was no longer against the light. He had gone on beyond the knoll and had seen that even when he looked ahead he could not see the cloud on the road, because beyond the knoll there are no more obstacles and nothing screens the rays of the sun in the open countryside.

Turning back he had passed in front of a modern cemetery where they were taking the coffin of some dead person from these suburbs. He had stopped between the cars to cross himself and, just at that moment, a thought had come to him.

He had thought that to see the cloud one had to be at special points—for instance on this side of that bridge. But even at those special points there was a choice of two things: either you follow the tremor or you look at it. And in these outskirts of the town to look at and see something was almost impossible.

'Why?' he asked himself. And he explained to us why: because you look and think you have seen something, but the tremor in the air immediately carries off the thought of what you have seen. So there is only the thought of rushing on in the exploded light, and you have to rush on and that is all there is to it in the everyday bustle.

He thought this was the reason why people in his district did not seem to worry at all about the cloud in which they live, a cloud you enter without noticing it and, when you are in it, it is very difficult to observe and recognize as something unusual. That Sunday in the bar, among men playing at cards and others commenting on the sports news, he summed up his conclusions thus: 'Inside this cloud we are all bound to one another by breathing. No one can breathe differently from the others and have other thoughts. And so we are all like drunks who don't know what they are doing but hold one another by the hand. I am telling you—I'm a nobody but I have lived here for twenty years.'

We were scarcely out of the bar than the signwriter pointed out to us on the side of the road a dog mangled by the traffic and said: 'Look, that is what life is like here. So when you feel the tremor in the air you must watch out. Here we live like drunks and you never know what can happen to you. So mind you don't cross the road too often. Because hereabouts everybody respects only the vehicles and thinks only of machines. And is of the opinion that if something isn't a machine it is one of the lowest forms of life.'

Another Sunday I and Luciano Capelli went by car with Menini to visit a young industrialist—a manufacturer of spiral stair-cases who was a relation and admirer of his. It had snowed all night and as we went towards the plain where a tile-making town stands, about thirty kilometres from the axis of the long road, everything was white and blurred by the glow of the little clouds which filled the distance.

We stopped to look at a river. The noise of the water running through the snow, the barking of the dogs in the distance, the noise of the cars passing on a nearby road, reached us muffled in space. The signwriter made this comment: 'Snow resists the tremor while rain confuses it. Because with snow there comes a little immobility in things while the rain instead hammers and drums away, and nobody can stand it any longer and everyone wants only to get off home.'

A lot of cars with skiers were passing with skis on the roofs, coming out of a curve at full speed and then losing themselves in the fog on their way to that line of mountains which runs along the long road. The skiers in the cars seemed happy and Menini said: 'They are happy off skiing because the snow makes everything a little more normal. With the white the contrasts come out more sharply and then things seem clear and tranquil.'

The great plain of the tile-making town begins not far from the point where we had stopped. There, for kilometres and kilometres, they have sliced into the hills to get clay and make it into tiles. That morning as we passed we could see slices of hill still standing on the flat white ground, spurs that rose up from the earth flattened by the bulldozers. In other places we saw nothing because the hills had all been removed, and in other places, still, instead of hills, we saw immense holes dug out to get clay—big rectangular valleys surrounded by moorlands of yellowed grass.

Menini told us that when he was a child he used to go gleaning in these parts with his grandmother. They gathered heads and grains of wheat left on the ground after reaping and with them managed to make a few days' bread. Every so often during these gleaning expeditions his grandmother stopped and pissed standing up with her legs apart, scarcely lifting her wide skirt which reached to the ground. But at other times he and his grandmother went to dig clay with a spade, then with a mould they made bricks to sell to the dealers but then they stopped because the dealers only wanted industrial bricks with perfect corners.

While we were crossing a deserted spot between rows of factory sheds with courtyards in front of them all piled with tiles wrapped in nylon. Menini asked us to stop the car. In the middle of the road he pointed a finger and cried to us: 'That's where my school was,' but we only saw high buildings with windows full of US style signs which were the offices of firms making tiles in the open country. On the other side of the road a scrap heap was covered with snow and surrounded by a wire fence, further on a board warned: SHIFTING SAND.

Before arriving at the villa of the industrialist who made spiral staircases, as we passed along a little country road we saw a huge warehouse completely empty inside, all in glass, but lit up on the outside by two clusters of powerful lamps which were switched on in broad daylight. In front there was a small house in a box-like style with two Arizona cypresses on either side of the entrance.

We had stopped and Menini was looking alternately at the enormous empty and illuminated warehouse and at the two little cypresses opposite. Finally he made this announcement to us: 'These trees there are lost and dispersed because their place is on some mountain. They plant them here because they grow quickly and don't need attention. But they are lost and dispersed like me, Emanuele Menini, and almost everybody I see near where I live. You who are a writer write this in your notebook.'

That winter Sunday we arrived very late at the villa not far from the tile-making town where we were received by a woman who lived with the manufacturer of spiral staircases. The villa (since transformed) was then in the Californian style—at least such were the intentions of its owner who had had it built by a local architect.

The woman who received us was the wife of a tile millionaire, who had run away from home and come to live here in this big villa with its sloping roof and external beams of white pine, which the manufacturer of spiral staircases, according to Menini, had had built for her. He had had it built to show her his love and to convince her to leave her husband.

The young industrialist told us that day that in the vicinity there lived only millionaires—there was a millionaire every forty thousand square feet. Of himself he said: 'I made my money with spiral staircases sold all over the world—even to the Japanese. If you have an idea, making money isn't that difficult. Look at me, my father was a blacksmith and we put up the factory together. Now I'm afraid of no one, not even of the tile millionaires.'

According to Menini he was planning a trip to the United States to see if the villas in California were really made like his.

Emanuele Menini, in so far he was a landscape painter, was interested above all in understanding what things that stand still look like when they are touched by light. So every day as he went to his bar in the morning and then to the warehouse where he worked, not far from the bar, he observed how things looked on the long road where he lived.

In particular in the hot months, he noticed that not only persons and cars but also things all around—though by nature still—rarely seemed immobile.

Things appeared clear-cut and peaceful only when the wind managed to break in from time to time, sweeping the air clean. But more often they were unstable and indistinct, because of a veil of little rays of light which blurred their contours and prevented him from seeing their immobility. For example he kept an eye on an old stone post on the other side of the street in front of his bar, and he always saw it with wavering contours.

In this concentration the industrialist who made spiral staircases said to Menini: 'Menini, are you sure that isn't your eyes which see things blurred? For my part I go to the factory every morning and never see any of the things you say. Won't it be better to go and seen an oculist?'

Since others had already given him this advice the signwriter one day went to hospital to have his eyes examined. But it seems the oculist told him that he had better long sight than others because he didn't see clearly close up. When Menini explained to him that things always appeared with blurred contours because of the shining light, it seems the doctor replied: 'Well, maybe it's as you say. There is so much rubbish in the air. But if you pay no attention to it you don't notice it.'

This comforted the signwriter who therefore once again started his observation of things along the road.

One day he explained to me: 'I'll tell you why Menini isn't a great painter. Because if he doesn't see immobility he certainly can't manage to paint it. But there is another fact you must write down. If Menini or anyone else can't see it things are in a sorry state.'

Since he knew that Luciano was a photographer, one Sunday in March he asked him to accompany him on an exploration of the district with big houses in front of his bar, to photograph the immobile state of things (if they managed to see it). Because this is what Menini was always seeking around himself and within himself, in his thoughts, and hoped photography might help him.

He had never gone into that district. There, as he walked between extremely high white houses, he suddenly had the impression of being in a deserted gorge under the sun. The air gleamed against the white walls, the beams of light on the tar bothered his eyes, and those streets full of cars parked along the pavements—but empty of men or beasts—confused him.

He stopped to listen to the Sunday silence and felt a distant tremor which came right up to the shutters of these long blocks of houses and up to the blades of grass in a little lawn. He pointed out to Luciano the blades of grass which were oscillating slightly and then said: 'Dear Luciano, here too things are in a sorry state.'

At one end of the district there is a public garden with cement benches, a few dwarf firs and some magnolia trees. The two explorers sat down to watch the blackbirds flying about in the fine dust, some boys riding past on bikes, a gentleman taking a dog for a walk in the iridescent air.

Beyond the garden they found a little old church repainted with industrial paint, cream and purple. The signwriter wanted to go in and pray while Luciano stayed outside taking photographs.

They were going back to the usual bar and Menini set out his thoughts like this: 'Dear Luciano, I think we have to ask ourselves what is light and what is shadow so as not to leave things alone in their sorry state. I am coming to the point: you'll see lots of people going about who become furious if they happen to see something that doesn't move. For them it is normal for the light to be splintered, since it goes with the tremor and then everything moves and one must always be busy. Well, what can we say about those people who find no peace in the immobility of things. Remember, they are the majority. Ah what can we say?'

This is a question that Menini kept asking himself for a while. And once he asked us to go with him by car to take a trip in the countryside in order to find an answer.

Having left the long road and gone further into the countryside, we passed very many empty peasant houses whose inhabitants have gone to live in the little villas in acrylic colours scattered around. We found ourselves in places that were not places, only rows of little villas in acrylic colours surrounded by little walls of plastic clay, which in the middle of spring threw on to the tar strange summer shadows.

In front of the little villas there were always little Arizona cypresses to decorate the entrance and often little lamps in the gardens. According to Menini these lamps too were lost and dispersed because according to him everything out of place was a poor lost thing.

The over-bright colours of the flowers in front of the doors and those acrylic paints gleaming on the walls, in contrast with the dark hues of the doors and windows, made these country places modern in some prescribed way. Any twilight uncertainty having been abolished, the colours were all sharp like in a commercial traveller's book of samples. And it seemed to us that all appearances had become objects of barter with a precise model, including the shadows and the light, the silence and the noises: they are no longer depended on the time of day, on chance or fate, but solely on the model for sale.

Then we stopped in the square of a little village surrounded by polled trees and crowded by boys with mopeds parked in front of an icecream parlour. The signwriter pointed out to us things shrouded in the dispersed light of the early afternoon and showed us how everything shrouded in that light—a wall, an area of the pavement, a corner of the street invaded by beams— reminded one of buying and selling like the neon lights of advertisements.

Then he pointed out to us how these boys with their mopeds tended to gather only where there is a dispersed light full of rays which invades everything and cancels out the shadows perhaps because they are attracted by shops and by advertisements.

On the way back he wanted to stop in a little country road to reflect. This is the reflection he made: if something appears with fairly stable shadows so that the light can make the shadow breathe through the colours, instead of suffocating it in the sharp shadowless colours, that object appears to be in a sorry state. Why? He did not know why.

But he pointed to a little ditch by the side of the road. And there were fairly motionless shadows which suddenly appeared touching to Luciano.

In the car Menini said to us: 'Where do these thoughts come from? Who knows! But it comes into my head that the explosion of neon light is like a dog barking to make us run, and we run. The same with the other splintered light which looks like neon light. That is why unmoving, calm shadow seems unfortunate to Menini. For the feeling of immobility it puts into one when really one should run.'

Finally, as we went down the long road, he pointed out to us how the beautiful spring shadows in the ditches all had the air of waiting uselessly, too motionless for this world.

For many months I did not see the signwriter again because I went abroad. Menini felt my absence in that there was no one to write down his thoughts and he felt he was wasting his breath.

All the more since Luciano was now working for a company that did lagging with asbestos fibre in the industrial warehouses, and had to get up at five every morning and be out all day; then on Sunday he had to look after his little girl and so never had time to go and meet Menini in the usual bar.

At the end of the summer the signwriter telephoned him one night to ask him to jot down the thoughts that had come to him until such time as the gentleman writer came back. On the phone he said: 'Listen to me carefully, Luciano. Light and shade don't go well together these days because of the dirty air which doesn't give good shadows and then it gets into our lungs as well. And like drunks we try to make up for this by putting clear and lively colours everywhere, so that they can be seen better. But we get more and more drunk because the lively colours make you forget the shadows and the twilights and make you stupid—that's the fact of the matter.'

Towards the end of summer he tried to examine these views more thoroughly by observing a stretch of road near his house where the ebb and flow of the air produces a percussive wave like a combustion chamber. At that point the traffic accelerates and the cars go off at full speed to reach the lights before they turn red. And it was there, according to Menini, that the motorists, already drunk because of the tremor, became recklessly drunk.

But since they often did not manage to slow down in time when the lights went red and the other drunks impelled by the tremor started off too soon, there were very often accidents at the intersection.

In the case of an accident the signwriter observed the following: what the smashed cars at the crossroads looked like, in the light which was engulfed in layers of air thick with the effects of all the combustion, and what the people looked like who had got out of the cars to argue, they too standing there in the full exploded light and gesticulating like mad men, while other motorists held up at the intersection became furious too because of their immobility, which they found unbearable, and began to sound their horns in immensely long lines of cars, urged on by the spasmodic tremor that spreads through the suburbs at rush hour.

By observing these aspects he came to some conclusions. When there was an accident men and machines seemed to him to be stuck out there in the light and wrapped in reflections, in a great solitude on the asphalt.

And in his thoughts he saw that nothing renders bodies isolated in space more than does the light, showing them to be definitely isolated in the same way as a kerbstone or a vase of flowers.

One day he said to Luciano: 'In the light bodies feel their isolation and would like to run off like hares. But run off where? I am coming to the point: try to look at the horizon and then tell me if someone feeling the tremor can think of the horizon and have the wish to live in its company. Impossible! You want isolation and more and more isolation even if you are already fairly isolated. And you want to run away and shut yourself up somewhere. It is the shattered light that plays this trick because it makes you run. And you want only the things that are there, slender and lively to your eyes, and there is no question of thinking about the horizon. But everything that is there—if it stays still—you at once see what it is. What is it?'

Luciano did not know and Menini told him: 'A mere nothing in the light, a mere nothing which comes in the light. That is why no one can bear immobility, they want to be rushing along all the time, and they all get furious when something holds them up. They always want to rush along as I have already told you. Write down what I have told you and then we'll talk about it.'

At the beginning of autumn it rained a lot. Almost all the flowers of Luciano's balcony were burnt because of the acidity of the rain and because of the dirty air the balcony was covered by a layer of light-brown soft mud.

Watching the crossroads Menini saw more accidents than usual, more dogs and cats pulped by the traffic, more people coming out of their houses with little masks over their mouths, more women coming out of the hairdressers with a nylon bag on their heads to protect themselves from that deadly cloud. And his lungs began to hurt more than usual, a couple of times he woke up in the morning with his mouth full of blood and he was taken to hospital.

Then the east winds came to sweep the air clean for a couple of days and it felt like being in another world.

Emanuele Menini was not exactly a signwriter although this was the shorthand way in which he always introduced himself. His speciality was painting panels for merry-go-rounds, pianolas and also stages in theatres when they came his way. But he had learned to paint everything and in recent years he and three other partners had hired a warehouse near the Via Emilia, because their firm was commissioned to make big puppets in cardboard and comic machines with characters from strip cartoons for carnivals and American amusement parks.

It seems the Americans considered them to be craftsmen in a class of their own when it came to the creation of animated puppets. They had already consulted them over the construction of American amusement parks throughout Europe; a colossal job which would have transformed the four old craftsmen into magnates of cardboard puppets.

But Menini's real speciality always remained something else. They were landscapes, baskets of flowers, children's faces and the garlands that decorate the ring of panels at the top of merry-go-rounds, or the panels hanging at the height of the wooden horses. Above all landscapes were his passion when they had mountains covered with snow in the background, brooks meandering thorough the meadows, little pastoral figures and a lake with a big tower on the bank. Having no more orders of this kind he continued to paint landscapes for himself on wood, with hills and valleys, brooks meandering through the meadows, lakes with a big tower on the bank.

The question Menini posed to the long road where he lived also applies to the clear cut and tranquil landscapes which he wanted to continue to paint. One day he set it out in this way: 'I know that here there is a movement which can never stop when the sun is high because of business, and nothing can be motionless because the ebb and flow of the air is a great continual process of decay which we can also see with our eyes, seeing how the light confuses things rather than illuminating them. And the thicker the air is with the gas of that process of decay the less it leaves things in peace. Along with the light which distends them, along with the force of gravity which tires them by pulling at them from below, it causes them to decay continually without peace. But then I, Emanuele Menini, ask: What is this thought of immobility that comes into my head? Why do I have a desire to paint tranquil landscapes where clarity is peace? Is it because I am old and soft in the head?'

When the industrialist who made spiral staircases came back from his trip to the United States, where he had gone to find out how the real Californian villas are made, he talked to him for a long time about the air one breathes on the streets of Los Angeles. He told him that there too you can see very clearly the decaying air which you breathe, so that it is like here, and there is no difference. Menini's talk about the lack of ventilation in these plains, which makes everything unclear and shaky, seemed less unlikely to him. And on a visit to him in hospital he said to him: 'Menini, now I understand you better.'

At this time I wrote a letter to Menini from Birmingham telling him that, there too, there are suburbs and rootless people everywhere, and millions of people living in the suburbs scattered through the countryside. There too the light had become a strangely opaque filter and more visible than that which it ought to reveal outside of us, far off in the world.

Of all this Menini thought in the hospital: 'What can I do about it? I can't do anything. There is the movement which never stops. But to notice it one only has to look at the wave motion in the air. There is no need to take trips to America or England like this writer gentleman. Just look at the trees—are they going to take trips?'

In the autumn he had got into the habit of getting up very early. The first trucks had hardly begun to shake the glass in the windows as they went along the long street, than he rose and left the house to try to see the immobility of things in the dawn before the tremor arrived in the air and began the rush of every day.

During a walk we took in a park, in the month of November, he tried to tell me what he was looking for in the dawn. In the dawn he was trying to be in the company of the horizon, he was looking for a state of inner immobility—one which can only be found outside, in the space which opens out and breathes round something right up to the horizon.

Some mornings he got as far as the ring road which crosses the long street near his house, and from there on to a roundabout where cars and buses scattered in four directions. While the profile of the high buildings on the outskirts of town was swept by an uncertain light, the infrequent traffic between the big buildings of the four-lane highway looked like a liquid movement—there was as yet no bustle. Having reached the roundabout Menini waited for the rising of the sun, which came up over a mountain of rubbish which was visible at that point beyond a line of trees.

This is a mountain with a rectangular base and a track for the trucks running up along its slopes. When the peak of the mountain shone, a row of houses opposite, shaped like control towers, was directly struck by the rays of the sun and some of the windows had red gleams. Immediately after that radiant moment, the mountain of rubbish was extinguished, and Menini was sure he saw signs of something beginning out there where the skyscrapers on the outskirts had suddenly changed colour.

From the roundabout he hurried on to a park that stretches towards the line of hills—the one we were walking in that November afternoon when Menini explained the result of his researches to me. In that park, early in the morning, there was no one except young athletes running, old gentlemen taking a stroll after having gone to buy their paper, a couple of Somali women taking their masters' dogs for a walk. And none of them and no tree had a shadow because the rays of the sun, which were still very slanted, did not come over the hedge to the east which separates the park from the road.

Alongside the park there are big blocks of flats in the form of enormous cubes one on top of the other: and from them, early in the morning, Menini saw people come out and saw them make their way without shadows along the street still looking as if they were not busy. But scarcely had they reached the street, which was already touched by the rays of the sun, than they all acquired the outline of a shadow although it was still not solid on the asphalt.

Meantime the roofs of the cars began to shine, the leaves of the hedge had little gleams of light, the traffic became less fluid, moment by moment the number of people waiting for the bus increased. At this point Menini began to feel the tremor in the air, because the rush of every day had already begun.

And then, at this precise point in the day, he was able to think of a kind of immobility he had seen in the opaque light of dawn, and this thought kept alive his desire to paint limpid and tranquil landscapes.

'Why,' as he said during our walk, 'does one never see immobility? One thinks of it only after one has seen it, when the tremor is about to come over it and everything begins to move once more. But can I convince anyone that I have really seen immobility with my own eyes? No. I can only paint a landscape.'

After that walk in the month of November I never again met the landscape painter Emanuele Menini. Luciano and I often went looking for him in the usual bar and also at his house and at his workplace, but we never found him.

That winter was very hard—one of the hardest of the century. Towards Christmas there was a heavy snowfall on all the plains that the long road ran through, and on the following day the landscape painter Emanuele Menini was found dead in the snow in a ditch beside the road, near a telephone booth.

From that same telephone booth Menini had shortly before called the young industrialist who made spiral staircases to talk to him about something he had seen. He had said he had seen a little villa in the fields, close by, and that he had been able to have a good look at it because the air was very limpid after the snowfall and the snow brought out the outline of everything. He had also explained exactly where the place was.

The industrialist who made spiral staircases had got into his car at once thinking of Menini lost in that arctic cold and in a couple of hours had reached the place. He had found the landscape painter lying on his back in the snow and already dead.

He was buried in that cemetery in the suburbs in front of which he had once stopped to pray on his walk to the great cedar of Lebanon which had brought God to his mind. Apart from his three partners from the warehouse and four regulars from the usual bar, there was only the industrialist who made spiral staircases at the funeral.

His partners from the warehouse said that lately, because of the trouble with his lungs, he had always been in and out of hospital and that when he was out he spent his time on long walks for his researches. But that he should have walked in the deep snow to the place where he was found dead, sixty kilometres from home, seems rather odd.

It is also not very clear what had interested him about the little villa in the fields which he had said on the telephone he had had such a good look at.

In the spring the firm for which Luciano worked was called to replace the heating in the factory belonging to the industrialist who made spiral staircases. In this way Luciano saw the young industrialist again, talked to him often and got to know of an episode which I shall add to this brief account.

When he came back from the United States the industrialist had noticed that the woman he lived with was very interested in Menini's landscapes, as if they were the only thing that brought her a little peace. It was a very grey time for her, during which she often wept. A lawsuit against her millionaire husband who made tiles had not resolved anything, and she had been denied the custody of her little son.

The woman often sat motionless on a sofa looking at one of Menini's landscapes, paying no attention to anyone. It seemed that this was her way of calming herself and not thinking any more about her misfortunes, of the hatred she felt for her husband, the tile millionaire. Evidently the limpid colours of these landscapes were beneficial—at least for her.

Some time before the industrialist had bought a huge estate which was an abandoned farm, about forty kilometres from the long road in the direction of the sea. And one day he had the idea of building a villa there with an adjoining park, and of installing turbines in the park to make wind. Turbines like this would have had to sweep the air clean, thus making external objects always clear cut and motionless and no longer tremulous.

In the estate of the big villa he had in mind to build, he also thought of planting a wood of Canadian chestnut trees and of stocking it with racoons. He also wanted to create watercourses which would flow in meanders among grasses and reeds. The winds produced by the turbines would have rippled the water and moved the grass in a fresh breeze highlighting, by contrast, the tranquil immobility of things round about.

All this would have produced the effect of living in a landscape by Menini. And there perhaps the woman he lived with—and whom he loved greatly—would have found peace.

When the industrialist proposed the project to Menini the latter had made only one objection—that if the turbines had been strong enough to sweep the air clean like the south wind, thus giving the impression that one was living in another world, they would however have produced a tremor no less than that on the long road.

In the end the fantastic project of the industrialist who made spiral staircases came to nothing. One day unexpectedly the woman he lived with had gone back to her husband, the tile millionaire, for no sensible reason that he was able to understand. Latterly she had been indifferent to everything, and clearly she was not in the least interested in the artificial paradise he was planning.

In that vast piece of land, where he would have wished to live with the woman he loved, the industrialist had now had two hundred thousand poplars planted—trees which grow in haste and allow of notable profits.

To Luciano he had confessed to feeling very lonely in his big Californian villa, which moreover bore very little resemblance to the real Californian villas. A few days later he had left for Patagonia where he hoped to sell his spiral staircases.

Last summer Luciano Capelli and I wanted to visit the place where Emanuele Menini was found dead. We saw the telephone booth from which he had spoken and about three hundred metres from the long road the small house in which he must have noticed something that interested him for his researches.

It is a small house in a box-like style, standing alone in the middle of the fields, which one does not see very well from the road. To see it one has to go down a lane and stop in front of a hedge in which dog-roses are blooming. From there to the sea it is probably about twenty kilometres, but that landscape gives no hint of the crowds at the bathing resorts: it is quite empty. They grow tomatoes there, and further on in the middle of a field of wheat there rises the solitary tower of an electricity pylon.

The small house has a roof formed by four triangular gables and a square front with four windows, closed by rolling shutters of grey plastic which stand out against the indigo of the walls. Seen from a hundred metres or so away it looks very peaceful in the midst of the fields, with a television aerial flowering on the roof. Pots of flowers arranged near the door, a little garden wall from which there rises an ornamental laurel hedge, two little Arizona cypresses flanking the door complete its fine presence in that secluded spot.

The little house was mysterious—in itself it composed a world of images quite different from that of the Via Emilia which passes nearby. The air was clean, the afternoon shade fell exactly between the two little cypresses which frame the door, recalling the feeling of a place permanently undisturbed like that of the avenues in cemeteries.

Anna Maria Ortese

On the Neverending Terrace

In a house where I lived before, here in Liguria, strange
happenings occurred. But I must briefly describe it. Tiny, for
one thing, yet, through a peculiarity of its layout or the
structure of the premises, such as to appear quite large. Five or
six doors lining a very long, not quite straight corridor paved
with violet-coloured tiles, and two other doors, one at each end
of the corridor, but situated in such a way that they were not
directly facing, were perhaps the secret of the house's illusory
size. In the middle of the corridor was the door opening on to
the stairs, and immediately opposite, as a feature of the corridor
itself, was the little door of the lift, which thereby gave direct
access into the house. Just the two large rooms stood precisely
at each end of the corridor: one, north facing, had a yellow
floor; in the other, which was southwest facing (the house being
somewhat crooked), a fine violet-coloured floor met the eye.
The north-facing room had a narrowish balcony, and because
of its situation, it got the sun for *only* one hour in the morning.
For the rest of the day it was sunk in a sad half light. The
southwest-facing room, because of its situation, was brightened
by the sun *only* in the evening, and never in winter. And the
whole house was stretched out like an old tram, or a goods
wagon left on a disused track, in the middle of a terrace so
limitless—I'd have no way of knowing where it ended—that
I've never seen anything like it, and it seemed more akin to a
valley. Now, around it, there were mountains and more
mountains, hills so-called, but strictly mountains, and rising so
high above the room as to cast a shadow on the inner walls and

the furniture itself. This, northwards. In other directions—
south most of all—were more and more new houses, some of
them quite pretty, but all shut up tight because they were
completely uninhabited, redolent of an ancient, vast necropolis
long since forgotten in that valley. Which gave the house on the
terrace a peculiar feeling of isolation. Bearable in summer, but
in wintry weather rather sinister. The wind whistled, the rain
drummed on the roof or streamed incessantly down every wall
of the house, and a fluffy towel with a big brightly-coloured
sailor on it that I'd attached to the walls of the lift flapped
backwards and forwards somewhat foolishly, because the wind
blowing through the doors of the lift kept puffing it out and in.
And all the time, through the window panes of the balconies,
those great mountain slopes thick with vegetation, and clouds,
and the smokiness of fog and the smoke of shepherds' fires.
And, to the south, that huge great valley of empty houses,
where the sun, whenever it came out, seemed almost paler than
the fog.

Now, this is what happened. But, another thing before that, I
ought to say that the perpetual sensation of an invisible *third
presence* was a torment both to me and to the person who
lived with me in that house. This person, who for now I'll call
Trude, didn't realize it, but it cast a gloom over her, while the
thing always just put me on a knife edge of dread and
dumbfoundment.

Apart from the *presence* (just as if some uninvited guest were
living in a room or even inside a seemingly innocent wall of the
apartment, a room or wall whose *charged* atmosphere had long
since even escaped the notice of the occasional tenants, and
maybe at the time, even of the builder); apart from this
presence, there were phenomena: the first of which, more garish
than any of the others, was, one morning, a kind of immense
dawn, coloured a pink very close to cyclamen, which terrified
me more than I can say, and lasted for two hours. The
mountains were rose-pink, the valley and November storm
clouds roseate. There wasn't a gleam of sunshine, nor a single
sign of life. Trude, to whom I didn't venture a word, was equally
dismayed, thunderstruck. But since there was no janitor, nor

any tenants in the little block, nor any shops whatsoever in the neighbourhood, and not even any smallholders digging their plots, we had no idea who to ask, who to turn to for an explanation. This dawn-phenomenon had a second occurence, but its effects—in comparison with the extent and intensity of the first—were considerably less.

And then, the clocks. In the house at that time, there were a lot of little clocks in coloured wood, German made, the gift of a worker who had been for many years in Stuttgart, or rather a small town nearby, famous, it seems, for these delicate little timepieces. These toy-like clocks, decorated with birds and branches and tendrils of gold-brown wood, and little blue doors that opened intriguingly to allow a glimpse of two little figures, hadn't worked for years, but in that house they all started up again, striking the hours unsynchronized and almost without interruption, and the little blue doors would open and shut, and the two little figures would go up and down with ecstatic faces. And all of them together—fortunately not all day long—would make an artless, grating noise, as if a rapt, invisible hand had wound them up, though only so as to hear again the sound of music heard before, and to be listened to again with an urgency that came from genuine desperation; and then, abruptly, just as it had begun, the horrid little music died away. And I ought to add here the business with the house keys, which were to be found one minute on the floor of one room, the next on the floor of another; you would go to pick them up, they would fly off, and you would hear the unmistakable sound of them falling ten yards away. I won't talk about the spiders. The valley was full of them, a variety of fast, reddish-coloured spider, with a kind of curly fuzz, rather like a beard, round the head and the little legs covered in what looked like boots, reddish coloured too. Despite the house being awash with insecticide, they never went away, they were everywhere, in fact I suppose they were the worst thing. Sometimes, motionless on the walls, they seemed to be listening. The minute an eye fastened upon them, then, as people say about flying saucers, they were off. And this brings me to the pack of cigarettes.

One morning, on the table in my room, there was a pack with

red wrapping and big white lettering, bought in the nearby resort town a week before. I didn't like them in the least, I far preferred the cheap, grey national brand cigarettes. That morning, though, I didn't have any national brand. I leave the room—just long enough to answer the telephone ringing in the corridor (nobody!)—I go back, and there, on the table, *just one cigarette*—all the others had vanished—half of it a normal white cigarette, the other half entirely black.

Broken open, it was shown to be made of totally *black* tobacco, and I looked at it for two solid days, doing not a stroke of work. Then, after gathering those nasty little shreds into a piece of paper, I threw them from the top of the terrace, abetted by the gushing stream of rainwater, which whooshed them right away.

Another phenomenon, one a bit less disturbing—if you could bring any more or less into these things, their being all equally inscrutable—was the sudden cutting off of the television screen in the west-facing room in the evenings, even though everywhere else the power was still on. Then, after a few minutes, the picture came back, but with little figures moving about in the background (with their backs turned), little figures that weren't part of the programme. These had made me start to dislike the TV. However, I imagine this phenomenon was some kind of technical fault, nothing out of the ordinary, it was just that, combined with so many other things, it too had a bad effect.

Whereas there were other phenomena, like the sudden and inexplicable moving together of two *similar* objects, right before my eyes, let's say *two* nails, *two* used matches, *two* screws—even outside the room, on the terrace, and in the raging wind and rain—I didn't take much notice, they hardly seemed anything to do with me. Before my very eyes, from being essentially *motionless*, these small objects would begin to move, and after rushing together, they would stop, settle at rest. Sometimes, a day later, even so much as a month later, they would still be there, impervious to the wind and rain. Or else, *suddenly*, they'd have gone. And who's to know where these paltry objects go, and what could have been the reason either for their convergence, or for their final departure.

One autumn night—or spring perhaps? the air was so serene!— I was taking a walk on that terrace, having been sleepless for some hours. Trude was sleeping soundly, and I was going backwards and forwards along the neverending terrace, peering about among the mountains, looking out for a light, even a glimmer of one, any sign of life, Nothing, nothing! And, thinking of this, such a deep despair, such a wordless despair took hold of my spirits. I wondered whether—not just in cities, but throughout the limitless universe—the human soul is everywhere so alone and lost in such a profound silence and accursed solitude. I had been told as a child that on earth there lived, invisible, the guardian spirits of men, and I recalled that for many, very many years, I had ceased to bother with mine, I hadn't even remembered its existence. Perhaps it had grown, like me, or become, instead, very tiny? To cut a long story short: without thinking, in a sudden fit of foolishness, I called him: 'If you're there, answer, and hurry up please,' I said. 'If you're there, *creature*, or dear *angel* of mine, answer,' that's what I said.

No sooner said than done—well, let's say a moment later—a tiny little light began whirling round in front of me.

'Huh, you're a firefly!' I said laughing.

And, just as I said it, I immediately realized that there were no fireflies left in the whole world, and at that time of year, cool as it was, at night, they would never have stirred themselves.

'Well . . . do you mind telling me who you are?' I said, trembling.

And right after this:

'Oh Firefly, Firefly, pray for me.'

She gave a little whirl, as if to say: '. . . yes . . . yes . . . well . . . we'll see . . . but you'd forgotten all about me, hmm?' And with that—and a whirl or two as she went—she was gone.

First thing the next morning—it was still dark outside—there was a knock at the door.

It was the postman, with a letter bringing me wonderful news.

I can leave this house and this town of mysteries and harrowing presentiments, for the lovely life-filled, happy place where I lived before. My joy made it seem like a dream. I call Trude. She's happy too, she laughs, she can't believe it:

'So, everything'll change! So, no more wracked nerves, no more mystery! Oh, how marvellous! Oh, how could it have happened?'

She comes up to the door beside me, to give the postman a tip if he's still there. She's so delighted she wants everybody to be happy. But we can't find the key. The door hasn't been opened since the night before. The key—we see now— is in its usual place, on top of a chest.

'Oh!' cries Trude. 'So who brought the letter? So, there was nobody here! So it isn't true, the letter's a dream!'

And she bursts into tears.

But it was true! We made a telephone call, as soon as it turned nine o'clock, and had it confirmed.

Only, no news of the postman.

But a woman who was going to mass around that time says she saw a lovely little girl about six years old coming out of our house, wearing a dark cloak and carrying a lantern.

She skipped, like any schoolgirl, loose-limbed, and, the woman says, almost *flew* above the *shrubbery*.

Primo Levi

The Witch-Doctors

Wilkins and Goldbaum had been gone from the base camp for two days. They had been attempting, in vain, to record the dialect of the inhabitants of the eastern Siriono village, on the other side of the river, ten kilometres from their camp and from the western Siriono. They saw the smoke rising, and immediately hurried to get back: the smoke was thick and black, rising slowly into the evening sky, and it was coming from precisely where, with the help of the natives, they had built their huts of wood and straw. In under an hour they reached the river bank, waded across through the muddy current, and saw the disaster. There was nothing left of their camp except burning embers, bits of metal, ash, and the charred remains of their possessions. The village of the western Siriono stood in a little loop of the river, some five hundred metres further on; the Siriono were waiting for them; they were in a highly excited state. They had attempted to put the fire out by hauling up water from the river with their crude bowls, and with buckets that the two Englishmen had given them, but they had been unable to save anything. It was unlikely that this had been sabotage: their relationship with the Siriono was good, and, furthermore, the natives were not very familiar with the use of fire. It had probably been a blowback from the generator, which they had left running during their absence in order to keep the refrigerator going, or perhaps a couple of wires had short-circuited. At any event, the situation was serious: their radio was out of operation, and the nearest village was a good twenty days' hike away across the forest.

Until this particular day, the contact of the two ethnographers with the Siriono population had been scant. It had taken a lot of effort and the gift of two tins of corned beef before they had succeeded in overcoming the suspicions of Achtiti, who was the most intelligent and curious man in the village; he had condescended to answer their questions and to speak into the tape recorder microphone. This, however, was more by way of professional amusement rather than a necessary part of their work: Achtiti had understood this, and had been visibly entertained by having to teach the two of them the names of the colours, of the trees surrounding the camp, of his friends, and of his women. Achtiti had learned the odd word of English, and they had learned a hundred or so words in a guttural and imprecise pronunciation: when they tried to reproduce them, Achtiti would smack his belly with both hands, out of joy.

But now it was no longer a game. They did not feel up to having to follow a Siriono guide on a twenty-day hike through a forest that was sodden with putrid water. They would have to explain to Achtiti that he had to send a messenger to Candelaria with a message from them asking for a motor launch to be sent up the river to get them and to bring the messenger himself back to the tribe. It would not be easy to explain to Achtiti exactly what a letter was. In the meantime, they had no option but to rely on the Siriono for hospitality for three or four more weeks.

There was no problem about the hospitality: Achtiti immediately understood the situation, and offered them a straw pallet and two of the curious Siriono blankets, which consisted of intricately interwoven fibres of palm and magpie feathers. They decided to keep their explanations for the following day, and fell into a deep sleep.

The following day Wilkins prepared the letter for Suarez at Candelaria. He decided to write it in two versions: one in Spanish, for Suarez, and one in ideograms, so as to give Achtiti and the messenger some idea of the aim of the mission, so that they might abandon their obvious mistrust. The ideograms showed the messenger walking towards the south-west, along the river; there were twenty suns to represent the length of the voyage. Then there was a picture of the city, with tall buildings, with many men and women in them, wearing trousers and skirts, and with hats on their heads. Finally, there was a larger man pushing a launch into the river, with three men on board, together with bags of provisions; and then the launch coming up the river—and in this last picture there was also a drawing of the messenger, lying down and eating from a bowl.

Uiuna, the messenger chosen by Achtiti, examined the drawings attentively, and gestured for an explanation. Was the direction the same as he was pointing to on the horizon? And what about the distance? But then he loaded onto his back a kind of knapsack of dried meat, took his bow and arrows, and set off, barefoot, fast and silent, moving with the undulating gait of the Siriono. Achtiti nodded solemnly, as if to say that Uiuna was a person to be trusted. Goldbaum and Wilkins looked at each other nervously. It was the first time that a Siriono had gone so far from the village, and had travelled to a city, even though Candelaria, with its five thousand inhabitants, was hardly to be considered a city.

Achtiti had food brought for them to eat: river prawns, raw, four apiece; two japara nuts; and a large fruit which had a watery, insipid taste. Goldbaum said:

'With a bit of luck, they'll offer us hospitality and maintain us even if we don't work: in that case, which is the best we can hope for, they'll give us their rations, the same food, the same amount, and that will be hard enough. On the other hand, they might ask us to work with them, and we can neither hunt nor plough. We have nothing left to give them. If Uiuna returns without the launch, or doesn't return at all, gets sick for instance, they'll drive us out, and then we'll die in the marshes; or they'll kill us themselves, as they do with their old people.'

'By stealth?'

'I don't think so. I don't think they'll harm us either. They'll ask us to follow their customs.'

Wilkins was silent for a minute or two; then he said:

'We have provisions for two days, two watches, two ballpoint pens, a lot of useless money, and the tape recorder. Everything's been destroyed in the camp, but perhaps we could re-temper the knife blades. Oh yes, and we have two boxes of matches too:

maybe they'll be interested in that more than anything. We have to pay our keep after all.'

Negotiations with Achtiti proved laborious. He paid little attention to their watches, showed no interest in their pens and money, and took fright when he heard his own voice coming out of the tape recorder. He was fascinated with the matches, however: after a few failed attempts he succeeded in lighting one, but he was not convinced that it was a real flame until he put one finger over it and got burned. He lit another, and discovered, to his evident satisfaction, that if he held it next to straw, the straw caught fire. Then he stretched out an inquiring hand: could he have all the matches? Goldbaum promptly took them back: he showed Achtiti that the box had already been started on, and that the other one, which was full, was small. He indicated that they each needed them. Then he showed him a match, and indicated the sun and the sun's trajectory through the sky: he would give him one match for every day that the tribe kept them. Achtiti was doubtful for a long while, crouching on his haunches, humming a nasal tune; then he went into a hut, and emerged holding in his hands a clay bowl and a bow. He put the bowl on the ground; he gathered some fresh clay, moistened it with water, and showed the two researchers that the resulting dough could be modelled into the form of a bowl; then he pointed to himself. He took the bow, and caressed it affectionately: it was smooth, symmetrical, and robust. He showed the two men a bundle of long straight branches, lying a short way off, and he pointed out that the quality and the fibre of the wood were identical. He returned to the hut, and this time returned with two obsidian scrapers, one large and one small, and with a block of crude obsidian.

The two men watched him, at once curious and puzzled. Achtiti picked up a piece of flint, and showed how, with a series of precisely aimed small blows around the particular contours of the block, the whole flaked away cleanly, without splitting in two; after a few minutes' work he had made a scraping device, still in need of a further refinement, but nonetheless usable. Then Achtiti took two of the branches, each slightly more than a metre in length, and began to scrape one of them. He worked with application and ability, in silence, or humming to himself: after half an hour, the wood was already beginning to taper at one end, and Achtiti checked it at intervals, bending it over his knee to see if it was yet sufficiently supple. Perhaps he perceived a touch of impatience in the two men's attitude, or in their comments, because he interrupted his work, disappeared off between the huts, and returned accompanied by a boy. He handed him the second branch and another scraper, and thereupon they worked as a pair: as it turned out, the boy worked quite as fast as Achtiti, and it was obvious that for him too making bows was not a new trade. When the two pieces of wood had been whittled down to the required size and profile, Achtiti set about smoothing them with a rough stone, which Wilkins took to be a fragment of whetstone.

'It doesn't seem like they're in a hurry,' said Goldbaum.

'The Siriono are never in a hurry; hurrying is one of our diseases,' answered Wilkins.

'But they have other diseases.'

'Certainly. But that doesn't mean that it's not possible to imagine a civilization without diseases.'

'What do you think they want from us?'

'I think I understand what he's getting at,' said Wilkins.

Achtiti continued with his careful smoothing of the pieces of wood, turning them in his hand and checking their surface with his fingers and with his eyes, which meant that he had to squint because he was somewhat shortsighted. Then, finally, he bound them together, placing one alongside the other so that their two non-tapered ends overlapped, and between the tips he strung a cord of twisted gut. There was an air of pride about him, and he showed the two men how, when he plucked it, the cord gave out a long, resonant tone, like a harp string. He sent the boy to fetch an arrow, which he aimed and fired. The arrow struck home, quivering, in the trunk of a palm tree about fifty metres away. Then, with an emphatic gesture, he handed the bow to Wilkins, indicated that it was his to keep and to try. Then, from the already opened box, he took two matches, and handed one to Wilkins and one to Goldbaum; so doing, he squatted down, clasped his arms around his knees and waited—with no hint of impatience. Goldbaum stood there, bemused, holding his match, until he said:

'Ah, I think I see what he's getting at.'

'Exactly,' answered Wilkins. 'I think the gist is pretty clear: we poor Siriono, if we have no scraper, then we make one; and if we have no bow, we use the scraper to make a bow; and we might smooth it too, so that it looks good to feel and hold. You foreign witch-doctors, who know how to steal men's voices and put them in a box, you have no matches now—make some.'

'So?'

'We're going to have to explain our limitations.'

With two voices, or rather with four hands, they tried to explain to Achtiti that, while it is true that a match is a small thing, a lot smaller than a bow (Achtiti seemed particularly taken with this point), nevertheless the head of the match contained a power (how to explain this?) which dwelt far from them, in the sun, in the depths of the earth, beyond the rivers and the forest. They were painfully aware of the inadequacy of their defence. Achtiti leaned towards them, his lips pursed, shook his head, and told the boy things that made him laugh.

'He'll be saying that we're bad witch-doctors, good for nothing, all we do is talk hot air,' said Goldbaum.

Achtiti was a methodical man: he said something else to the boy, who took the bow and a number of arrows and went and stood twenty paces from them, with a resolute air; he went away, and returned with one of the knives that he had found among the remains of their base camp, and which the fire had distorted and oxidized severely. He picked up one of their watches from the ground and handed it to Wilkins; Wilkins, with the ashen look of somebody who has turned up unprepared for an important examination, shrugged his shoulders impotently: he opened the back of the watch, and showed Achtiti the tiny cogs, the flickering balance-wheel, the tiny rubies, and then his own hands: as if to say, 'Impossible!' The same thing, or more or less, happened with the tape recorder, although in this case Achtiti was unwilling to touch it. He had Wilkins pick it up himself, and he blocked his ears for fear of hearing the voice again. And the knife? Achtiti seemed to be indicating that this was a kind of repair test, or an elementary examination, which any idiot should be able to do, witch-doctor or not: come on, make a knife. Well, a knife isn't some kind of animal with a heart that beats; it's easy to kill it, but very hard to bring it back to life: it doesn't move, doesn't make a noise, and it's made up of only two parts, and they themselves possessed three or four, which they had bought ten years previously and had not paid much for—an armful of pawpaws and two cayman skins.

'You explain: I've had enough.'

Goldbaum was not as well equipped with gestural talents and a sense of diplomacy as his colleague. He embarked vainly on a set of gesticulations which not even Wilkins understood, and Achtiti, for the first time, burst out laughing: but there was something slightly unnerving in his laugh.

'What were you trying to tell him?'

'That maybe we would be able to make a knife; but that we would need special stones, different stones, which burn, and which you don't find in this country; and also a lot of fire, and a lot of time.'

'I didn't understand, but probably he did. He was right to laugh; he must have thought that we were just playing for time until they came to fetch us. A favourite trick of all witch-doctors and prophets.'

Achtiti called out, and seven or eight robust warriors arrived. They took the two men and shut them in a hut made of solid tree trunks; there were no windows, the light came in only through small chinks in the roof. Goldbaum asked:

'Do you think we're going to be here for a long time?'

Wilkins replied: 'I fear not, but I rather hope so.'

But the Siriono are not a fierce people. They were content to leave them there to expiate their lies, and supplied them with plenty of water and a little food. For some obscure reason, perhaps because he felt insulted, Achtiti kept away.

Goldbaum said: 'I'm a good photographer, but without lenses and without a film . . . Maybe I could make a camera obscura? What do you think?'

'At least that would amuse them. But they're asking for more than that: they want us to demonstrate, concretely, that our civilization is superior to theirs; that our witch-doctors are better than theirs.'

'The trouble is, I don't know how to do much, with my hands. I can drive a car. I can change a fuse or a light bulb. Unblock a sink, sew a button on. But there are no sinks here, and no needles either.'

Wilkins thought for a moment. 'No,' he said, 'we'd need something more basic than that. If they let us out of here, I shall try taking the tape recorder apart; I don't know much about their inside workings, but if there's a magnet in there, that should do the trick; we'll float it in a bowl of water, and that way we can leave them with a compass, and the knowledge of how to make it.'

'First, I don't think you'll find magnets in a tape recorder,' Goldbaum replied. 'And anyway, I'm not at all sure that they'll find a compass particularly useful. They use the sun. They're not navigators, and when they go through the forest, they follow well-established tracks.'

'How do you make gunpowder? Maybe it wouldn't be too difficult. Don't you just mix charcoal, sulphur and saltpetre?'

'In theory, yes. But where are you going to find saltpetre here, in this swamp? And there may be sulphur, but who knows where; and what's more, what use will gunpowder be, if they have no way of making a gun barrel?'

'Wait a minute, I've an idea. Around here, people die from the slightest scratch: of septicaemia or tetanus. Why don't we ferment some of their barley, distil the juice, and make some alcohol; perhaps they'll enjoy drinking it too, even though it wouldn't be very ethical. As far as I can see, they don't have stimulants or drugs; that would be a good bit of witch-doctory.'

Goldbaum was tired. 'We have no yeast, and I don't think I'd be capable of finding yeast out here, and you neither. And anyway I'd like to see you having to use their local pots to make a still. I'm not saying it's impossible, but it would take us months, and here we're talking about days.'

It was not clear whether the Siriono meant to leave them to die of hunger, or if they were simply maintaining them at the lowest possible cost until the launch came up the river, or until they hit on some idea of what to do with them. Their days were passed in a state of increasing torpor, in a sort of waking trance, made up of damp heat, mosquitoes, hunger and humiliation. And yet both of them had studied for the best part of twenty years; they knew many things about human civilizations both ancient and modern, they had investigated every kind of primitive technology, from the metallurgy of the Chaldeans, to the ceramics of Mycenae and the woven textiles of the Aztecs. And now, perhaps (*perhaps!*), they might have been able to flake a flint, because Achtiti had shown them how to do it, whereas they were not in a position to show Achtiti anything at all: only to indicate by gestures marvels which he had not believed, and to show him the miracles that the two of them had brought with them, manufactured by other hands under another sky.

After almost a month of imprisonment they had run out of ideas, and felt reduced to definitive impotence. The entire colossal edifice of modern technology was beyond their reach: they had been forced to admit that they were incapable of transferring even one of the discoveries of which their civilization was so proud to the Siriono. They lacked the raw materials to begin with, or, if they were available, they would not have been capable of recognizing them or picking them out; none of the arts which they knew would have been considered useful to the Siriono. If one of them had been good at drawing, he could have drawn Achtiti's portrait, and, if nothing else, given him something to wonder at. If they had a year to do it in, they could perhaps have convinced their guests of the utility of the alphabet, adapting it to their language, and they could have taught Achtiti the art of writing. For an hour or so, they discussed a possible project of making soap for the Siriono: they could have got potash from the wood ash, and oil from the seeds of a local palm; but what use would soap have been to the Siriono? They had no clothes, and it would not have been easy to persuade them of the usefulness of washing with soap.

In the end, they settled on a modest project: they would teach them how to make candles. Modest, but irreproachable; the

Siriono had tallow, peccary tallow, which they used to grease their hair, and as regards wicks there would be no problem, because they could be made from the hair of the peccaries themselves. The Siriono would appreciate the advantages of being able to light the insides of their huts at night. For sure, they would have preferred to learn to make a rifle, or an outboard motor; candles were not much, but they were worth a try.

They were in the process of trying to re-establish contact with Achtiti, to exchange their freedom for a candle-making project, when they heard a great bustling outside their little prison. Shortly after, the door was opened, amid much incomprehensible shouting, and Achtiti signalled to them to come out into the blinding light of day. The launch had arrived.

Their leave-taking was neither long nor ceremonious. Achtiti had suddenly distanced himself from the door of the prison; he squatted on his heels, turning his back to them, and remained immobile, as if turned to stone, while the Siriono warriors took the two men to the river bank. Two or three women began laughing and shrieking, and exposed their bellies towards the men; all the other people of the village, children included, shook their heads, singing '*Luu luu*', and showing them their hands, flapping them around as if they were disconnected, flapping them from the wrist, like over-ripe fruits.

Wilkins and Goldbaum had no luggage. They boarded the launch, which was being piloted by Suarez in person, and they asked him to leave as fast as possible.

The Siriono are not an invention. They really exist, or at least they existed up until about 1945, but what we know of them suggests that they will not survive long as a people. They were described by Allan R. Holmberg in a recent monograph (*The Siriono of Eastern Bolivia*): they lead a minimal existence which oscillates between nomadism and primitive agriculture. They have no knowledge of metals, they have no terms for numbers above three, and even though they often have to cross marshes and rivers, they are not able to build boats. They do know, however, that they knew how to make boats once, and a story is handed down among them, about a hero, whose name was that of the Moon, who had taught their people (who at the time were far more numerous) three crafts: how to light fire; how to make dug-outs; and how to make bows. Of these, only the last has survived: they have even forgotten how to make fire. They told Holmberg that in a not too distant past (two or three generations previously; at more or less the time when the West was seeing the first internal combustion engines, and when electric lighting was being developed and people were beginning to understand the structure of the atom) some of them knew how to make fire by rubbing a stick in a hole in a board; but in those days the Siriono lived in another part of the country, with an almost desert climate, where it was easy to find tinder and dry wood. Now they live among swamps and forests, in perpetual damp: since they can no longer find dry wood, the fire-stick method has been abandoned, and forgotten.

They have, however, succeeded in maintaining fire. In each of their villages, or their wandering bands, there is at least one old woman whose task is to keep the fire alight in a tufa brazier. This art is not as difficult as that of lighting fires with a fire-stick, but it is not simple either; especially during the rainy season, they have to feed the little flame with the flowers of a palm tree, which are dried in the heat of the flame itself. These vestal women are very diligent, because if the fire dies, then they too are put to death, not by way of punishment, but because they are considered to be useless. All Siriono who are considered useless because they are incapable of hunting, or of procreating, or of ploughing with a stick-plough, are left to die. A Siriono is already old at the age of forty.

I repeat, what I have said here is not invented. It is taken from *Scientific American*, October 1969, and it suggests something sinister: it shows that not everywhere, and not always, is humanity necessarily destined to make progress.

Vincenzo Consolo

The Photographer

The thread had already been broken with the call-up and with the flight to the hills of youths still wet behind the ears and fathers of families already getting on in years. With the escapes and the evacuation the close network of acquaintances, of customs, of hates and affections, of daily labour and of days of rest, of the echo of the deaths to the toll of bells (four for an honest man, three for someone who just got by), of wooings with the promenading and the glances up at the window, through the basil and the mint, of betrothals with the ring, of elopements and amends made at dawn in the sacristy or else with full-blown weddings with mass, of births and baptisms. It was like a single courtyard, a single alley, like one house only, one family. And everybody knew about all the others and all the others knew about everybody else. But with the bombardments, the confusion and the fear, everything had come to an end from one day to the next, the spell was broken, the babble of voices. Emptiness, silence, desert had come to the town.

Now with people coming back, with the repatriation of ex-servicemen and deserters, of prisoners escaped from Malaspina, Syracuse or Noto, with the mass entry of Saracens and Turks, of these allied hordes, it had suddenly become a Babylon, a Babel, the counterweights had fallen to the ground, the shuttle had gone mad, the threads become entangled, the carding-comb only made the knots tighter. Everything had turned foreign, in looks and in speech.

Mazzarino was invaded by the English and the Americans.

They were encamped in tents and huts with mosquito nets up at the castle in the Fiorentino district and above the belvedere of the Most Blessed Maria of the Màzzaro River. But they were always careering about the town in every street and district on foot or in jeeps, they kept coming and going from dives and cafés, being lovers of boiled beans, doughnuts and frozen almonds, and above all of 'vino', called 'wine', of any colour or kind, whether it was sweet from Noto or dry from Caltanisetta. And they queued night and day, under the eye of the MP guards, at the door of the house, near the Cemetery, of Buteresa and her daughter Concettinella.

The officer in command of the whole outfit, in command even of the carabiniere Sergeant Dessy and the Town Council, of that military administration they called Amgot, was the Scottish Major Abell, who went around with a little Scottish cap with a pompom and a little pleated skirt that left his knees bare and further down his legs clad in white knitted stockings. This way of dressing of his, half feminine and very odd, was the wonder of all the ordinary folk and a joke for the kids who—in the Corso, let's say, or else in front of the Town Hall, in Via Firriato or the steep Via degli Angeli, whether he was alone or accompanied by Donna Elisa Accatoli—stopped playing and threw themselves on the ground, flat out, to squint up the skirt to see whether under it there were rolled-up trousers, under-pants or nothing at all. Donna Elisa was quick to catch on to all this hanging about, lost her patience, and got furious at the ignorance and rudeness of the place.

'Clowns,' she shouted at them. 'Misbegotten! or go and look up the skirts of those fat whores your mothers.'

And Major Abell, totally at a loss, looked at her and did not understand the reason for her annoyance.

Everyone knew by now that Major Abell, nicknamed Signorina, had developed an overwhelming passion at first sight for this titled lady of Mazzarino, sister of the baron, Don Luigino, wife of the complacent Commendatore Alì, cousin of the Fascist ex-mayor, Don Ercole Francesco. A fine woman, yes, Donna Elisa, elegant but of such pride and so overbearing and into the bargain with such a sharp tongue that it was as if she had a couple of things down there like a man. In short, she was the one who ran things in the town. To the point where hers was the appointment of the first mayor of the *comune*, of Professor Antrònaco, hers his dismissal and hers the subsequent nomination of the lawyer Caico. In her house proclamations, ordinances, temporary laws, which Mayor Abell confined himself to giving his approval to and adding his signature and seal. And even the famous list of Fascists to be sent to camp or banished was drawn up by the jewelled white hand of the lady leaving out herself, Don Luigino her husband, her cousin Don Ercole, all her relatives, all the barons and all the landowners, and putting inside only these poor creatures—the teachers and municipal employees who had been the acolytes and slaves of her cousin the fascist mayor. Fortunately nothing was done about that list. And Peppino Pianciamòre, the anarchist shoemaker, who had been a miner in Belgium, laughed wholeheartedly along with his followers and comrades at the terror and the flight from the town of the persons who had got onto the list. He himself had refused to put in writing the names of yesterday's bosses at the official invitation of Major Abell before he got involved with his mistress. Partly out of repugnance at informing, partly because he knew that, given the link now forged between this military authority and the ever-present power of the barons by means of the diabolical glue, the magic ring, the hair of a woman which, in this case, was the perfumed hair of that cunning witch, Donna Elisa, everything would end up in a fart, a joke.

He surprised them laughing like that, Peppino and his comrades, sitting on the chairs, in the shade of the balconies, on the pavement, in front of the shoemaker's shop, with his eye on the view-finder of a Leica and with the quick click that fixed them on the film, an odd American soldier who wandered about the village, as if he were daydreaming, as if passing the time, but watchful and curious about everything, with that camera slung round his neck, quick to snap a scene, a situation, a gesture, which are swift and fleeting in the river of life as it runs past. He was a French photographer who, drafted because of his fame as a photographer into the American forces, had been dropped days before from a Flying Fortress on to the plain at Gela and had arrived here in Mazzarino on a jeep. He had to photograph the war, this war in Europe on the Italian front, on the soil of Sicily.

But Andrey (his real name this, along with the Hungarian family name Friedmann, which—as an exile in Paris—he had changed to Robert) hated war, the disgusting nature of war, the disgusting nature of the various forms of fascism and of the dictatorships which cause wars. He had still before his eyes the war in Spain, the dead and wounded of the Sierras, that militiaman above the Guatarrama, a libertarian gypsy caught at the moment when the enemy bullet went through him, the international volunteers and the republicans of the battles of Madrid and Saragossa, the patriotic boys and peasants from all over, the Andalusian and Catalonian anarchists. And the people of Spain were on his mind, the innocent people, the women, the old people and the children, with terror in their eyes under the bombardments, on the roads in the shelters, refugees in the suburbs and the countryside. The war was that small boy dead against a dry wall, face down on a heap of trunks and stones, a poor white pair of overalls and *zapatos de lona*, his little arms wide open like wings, as if he had fallen from the skies on to these black stones, a frail sparrow, a frozen finch. The war was his Gerda, his intrepid comrade, dead, crushed under a tank on the Brunete front.

The stalling of the American advance (General Eisenhower was sleeping in the villa Bertolone outside Mazzarino) due to the counter-attack by the *Goering* and the *Livorno* divisions, which had withdrawn along the valley of the Gela, up towards the Erei, and had halted to reform near Niscemi and Ganzeria, forced the photographer to do an about-turn from the front to the village. With his jeep he went up hill and down dale across the infinite flat lands, yellow naked sun-beaten, with columns of smoke from burning stubble-fields, yellowish mounds of spoil from sulphur mines, a few skeletal trees here and there, a few tufts of thorn, nettle tree, tamarisk, chickling vetch or some other skeletal vegetation, a few sheep-folds or solitary farmhouses, just like those in Spain and Tunisia, he photographed shepherds and peasants. Motionless, with staffs in their hands, as worn as the earth on which they stood, or bent over their heavy hoes breaking the hard soil, they seemed indifferent to the troops which passed along the sheep-tracks bordered by the agaves and blackberries, to the photographer's jeep, indifferent to this war which went on around them. Indifferent and motionless they looked, there for centuries, spectators of all the conquests and reconquests, invasions and liberations that had been played out on that stage. And it was as if their real war was another one, age-old and unending, with that land which belonged to others, estates of barons and overseers, avaricious and hostile, against that impassive and mocking sky.

Robert had been taking photographs on these plains, had photographed with amusement and sympathy one of those peasants or shepherds, a man who stood scarcely a span above the earth, an ageless goblin, an elfin creature of an earthy rust-brown, in trousers and vest of worn corduroy, a ragged shirt patched a thousand times, shoes of canvas and sheep-skin, a handkerchief on his head knotted into a kind of cap. Next to him, on his hunkers, his arms on his thighs, wedding ring on his finger and gold bracelet on his wrist, a lanky American soldier, a smooth and handsome Gary Cooper, blond, healthy, smiling. The peasant, one hand on the soldier's shoulder, with the other in which he held his long stick was pointing at something in the distance, a road, a village, perhaps the mirage of a well or a fountain. Behind them the countryside, arid, flaming, rose up in hillocks of gypsum and silicates.

So here I present you, reader, with this little image dense with meaning, an image which from now on you will see reproduced everywhere in magazines and books, right up to your children's history textbooks, hoping that the Hungarian photographer, blown up by a mine at Thai Binh in Indochina, one afternoon in 1954, may from his heaven and with his ironic look approve this gesture of mine.

And perhaps here with these photographs by Robert, a man of thirty-three on Sicilian soil, as on that of Spain and China before that, the age of the word begins to draw to a close and that of the image to be launched. But they will then little by little be images void of meaning, one like the other and impassive, set down without understanding and without love, without pity for the suffering human beings. And so you will pass before your eyes as if they were normal and everyday matters, in their thousands, scenes of war and of disasters, of deaths and massacres, of intimacy violated, of sufferings exposed to indifference and scorn. As we know habit—a tannin that encrusts, a soot, a cancer that devours and transforms—covers up, dowses reason, and idiocy is the mother of degradations and cruelty.

    . . . Monsieur Guy de Maupassant va s'animaliser . . .

After these photographs Robert felt the need to write, to make notes in his diary:

    'I didn't know a word of Italian and it is in bad Spanish that I tried to communicate with the Sicilians I met. One of them kept repeating to me a strange word (Broccolino, Broccolino) which I at last identified as Brooklyn; perhaps he was trying to tell me that he had relations in that district of New York. I immediately made it clear that I too came from that part of the American city; immediately our relations and general understanding improved . . .'

Seeing themselves being photographed like this, taken by surprise, by that American soldier photographer, Peppino Pianciamòre and his comrades stopped laughing and stiffened in their chairs, quick to be suspicious and distrustful because of being communists or anarchists. But Robert smiled and was amused and smiled above all at Pianciamòre because of his singular face, his serious but benevolent look.

    'Allo,' said one of the young men to break the silence and the embarrassment.

    'Hello,' Robert replied. 'Do you speak English?'

Silence on the other side.

    'Habla español?'

Silence.

    'Parlez-vous français?'

    'Moi, je parle français,' replied Pianciamòre.

    'Êtes-vous allé en France?'

'Non, je suis allé en Belgique, à travailler, dans les mines.'

'. . .'

'Et vous, êtes-vous américain?'

'Non, non, je suis hongrois, mais j'habite en France.'

'Ah, la France, le pays de Proudhon et de Victor Hugo,' exclaimed Pianciamòre.

'Oui, de Proudhon, de Hugo et bien d'autres . . . .' replied Robert smiling widely. But he understood at once who he was facing and thought, looking at the face of his interlocutor, of Durruti's Catalan peasants and of the tough miners of the Asturias.

'Dîtes-moi, était-il de ce pays le cardinal Mazzarin?' asked the Frenchman.

'Bah, ici il n'y a jamais eu un cardinal, mais seulement des prêtres, des religieuses et des capucins. Nous en avons déjà assez!'

Robert held out his hand with a smile and the other shook it. 'Au revoir,' he said, 'au revoir.'

'Au revoir,' replied Pianciamòre. 'Vive la France.'

'Oh . . . Vive le monde tout entier!' said Robert.

Susanna Tamaro

The Big White House

The two of us lived in the big white house on our own, along with my dog and an unspecified number of other animals which came to see us only in order to be fed. The house stood at the edge of the upland plain, just at the point where the wind, having travelled all the way across the mountains and plains of western Europe, hurls itself to oblivion on the sea below, in the same way that they say happens in Russia. How many years did we live there together? I don't know, because I never felt like counting them, but I do know that without those years my life would have been very different.

We first met on a train, more or less by chance, when we found ourselves sitting opposite each other, both reading the same book. She was the first to smile at the coincidence. Then, over a period of about two years, I used to go and see her every week. We would take tea in the garden in summer, and in winter in front of a fire in the sitting room. Of the two of us, she was the one who had the sense of humour.

Then one day, unexpectedly, I found myself without a place to live. As if it was the most natural thing in the world she said: 'Why don't you come to live here?' And that was how my dog and I came to be living in the big white house.

My room was on the ground floor, and my window opened on to a fine-looking apricot tree. I've never had a stable job, and that period was no exception, so I spent most of my time either around the house or in the garden. At a certain point the local people started gossiping about us, so I bought myself a peaked cap, and we used to go around together with me pretending to be her chauffeur. 'Where does madame wish to go today?' I would say as I opened the car door for her each morning. And she would say things like: 'To see the Shah of Persia,' Or, 'To the moon, if you don't mind.'

I was twenty-five years old and she was eighty. And the way we enjoyed ourselves together was like two children playing in a garden shed far from the gaze of grown-ups.

These days people have a mania for classifying relationships into types. The inside pages of the mags are full of questionnaires and tests. 'How would your life be with a man who's younger than you?' 'Are you the dominant or submissive type? Do you think you're perverted? Tick the questions in the following boxes to find the answer.' One day I overheard two girls talking in a store. 'I had a terrible dream last night,' one of them said. 'All night long I dreamt I had a great big steaming pot resting on my stomach.' 'Didn't you know?' replied the other, 'it's your subconscious . . . .' In my relationship with Marta I suppose I could have put ticks all over the place. We were a case of an unresolved Oepidus complex; a bad case of gerontophilia; a sado-masochistic relationship; or maybe I was a gold-digger. All kinds of things like that. In the eyes of the outside world I'm sure our relationship must have looked either inexplicable or downright sordid. And in fact during the early days of our eventful life together, I even found myself thinking that this was what it was all about. It's very easy for people's thinking to become like driving a car down a motorway—you just push on, carried by inertia, obediently following the road signs without ever actually seeing anything. In the same way, those tests and questionnaires never include the possibility of simple basic human generosity.

One afternoon when it was raining and we were sitting in the lounge, I said: 'When I was little, I used to love hiding under tables and in cupboards.' She laughed happily. 'It's nice to see things from an unusual angle.' That's the way we were together. We saw things more or less the same way, and we travelled down a bit of life's road together.

There were other things too—like the fact that she had no children, and I had no one else in the world; the way that I used to mistreat her, and she would put up with it; the fact that she was rich and I wasn't. There was all this in our relationship, but there was something else too. Perhaps if we want to understand love, the only way is to be naked, with nothing around you, stretched out on the bare earth as if you're dead. Or at least that's how I came to see it. But I came to this realization too late, when things had already gone too far to be changed.

The wind around these parts hits without any kind of warning, and then it blows furiously for three days at a time. Scientists say that the human body contains a kind of barometer which is able to sense coming changes in the weather, and I think that must be true, because whenever there was a strong wind due I'd find myself rampaging round the house like a wild animal. We'd get into arguments, or rather, I'd be the one arguing, and she would simply defend herself, or try to defend herself, with silence. I would wake up grinding my teeth, and I'd pace up and down the house kicking doors and lashing out at the curtains. If she decided to make rice for lunch, I'd push my plate away saying that I wanted fish; if she'd prepared fish, I'd say I wanted rice. She'd go along with this for a while, but then her arms would drop by her side, and she'd bow her head and withdraw to her room. When this happened, Dik, my dog, and I would go for a long walk in the country.

We would walk on the high plateau for hour after hour; the ground would be parched, with not a sign of movement, and the trees and plants looked as if they'd been painted, all yellow and brown. Dik would follow me with his tail between his legs, and the minute I sat down he would come up and put his square muzzle on my leg and look up at me as if to say, 'What's the matter? What can I do to help?' And I would scratch his head: 'You don't know how lucky you are, being a dog . . .' Then he would walk and walk, and the more I walked through that hot, static air, the more something began to grow inside me, something that I couldn't give a name to. It was growing in my stomach, somehow, compressed between my ribs and my hips. Sometimes it was cold and sometimes red-hot, and it would drive me forwards as if pulling me towards it like a magnet, although I had no idea where the other pole was—perhaps somewhere way beyond the Urals. As I walked on an idea began to develop and fixed itself in my head: I found myself wishing I had a butcher's knife in my hand—broad, flat, vaguely obscene—so that I could whirl it round my head, slashing and ripping at the air in the way that madmen rip at curtains, to find out whether there's anything behind them, or just empty nothingness. Then I would find myself wanting this knife not just to dash around in the air but to use on myself, and at that point something in the surrounding landscape would suddenly begin to move restlessly—a blue-green thistle, perhaps, or a branch of a tree, or a tuft of grass—and then, after a bit, slowly, gradually, the wind would pick up, and everything would start waving about as if moved by invisible threads. At that point I would sit down. I'd look up at the tops of the oak trees and the hornbeams, and it was only when they too began moving noisily in the wind that it would end, and when it finally ended, I'd slump back on the grass, with my eyes shut and my hands spread open.

On our road back to the house, Dik would forge ahead with his long ears streaked back in the wind. I would pull my jacket round me and I used to sing at the top of my voice. It was only when you came round the last bend in the road that you saw the big white house. As I came in she generally didn't lift her head from her book. She would just sit there, looking engrossed and hurt. There would be a moment's pause during which absolutely anything could have happened, but in fact nothing usually did happen, because the minute I said a cheerful word the spell would almost always be broken. I say 'almost' always, because one day, as I came down from a particularly violent crisis, instead of laughing at my pleasantry, she burst into tears. 'What do you want from me?' she said. 'Why can't you leave me alone? Don't you understand, I'm a poor old woman . . .?!' When she said that, I sat on the arm of her chair and hugged her. 'I'm sorry,' I said. 'Forgive me, I don't know what came over me.'

I kissed her on the forehead and stroked her hair and her

shoulders, and it was only then that I realized how fragile she was, how really old she was.

For a number of years, even though this would have been contrary to nature, I was convinced that I was going to die before she did. And in my moments of anger, as the wind brewed up beyond the mountains of the East, I would often shout out loud: 'There ... Right ... I'm going to kill myself, I'm going to die!' She would smile gently. 'I'm sorry, but I think it's my turn first.' On the rare occasions that she spoke of death, she showed no sign of fear. She would say 'When I die' like somebody saying 'When I put my coat into mothballs'. Her only regret was at not knowing what would become of me if she left me alone in the world.

One evening, after a particularly tiring day, she left a note under my pillow. In her trembling hand she wrote: 'One day I'll come back as a big, buzzy house-fly, and you'll always find me buzzing around you.'

The next day the wind was blowing again. It was gusting violently and sweeping leaves and petals up into the air. She had just finished reading a book about Japan. 'How absolutely marvellous,' she said. 'Do you know that the Japanese go on long journeys just to see cherry trees in blossom?' I immediately went and got the car out of the garage. For the whole of the afternoon we drove to and fro across the upland looking for something worth seeing. Every now and then we'd stop and get out of the car, and with one hand she'd hold my arm tightly, and with the other she'd pull her coat round her, and she'd be like a young girl with her cheeks glowing red with the wind.

On our way back, as well as the wind we had to contend with a rainstorm. It was raining so hard that the windscreen wipers couldn't shift it all. Even though it was April, ice was beginning to form on the surface of the road and every time we went round a bend we risked going off the road. By the time we arrived home I was extremely jumpy. As we went from the garage to the house, Marta said something she should never have said.

'Your dog is digging too many holes in the garden.'

It was just not the right moment for a comment like that. I blew my top. I kicked open the front door and went storming off to my room, locking the door behind me. A short while later, I heard the sound of her slippers shuffling down the corridor. She stopped outside my door, and stood there in silence. Was she coming to shout at me, or to apologize? At that moment I hated her. I ran my hands through my hair and said to myself: 'Go away, old woman, because otherwise I'm going to kill you.'

Is there such a thing as telepathy? Maybe there is. I hadn't said a word, but she had heard me. After a minute's silence I heard the sound of her slippers moving off slowly in the opposite direction.

It's hard to describe the sound of the wind. A lot of people think that the wind only howls, like it does in films. You have to live immersed in the wind for month after month to know that it's not like that at all. The wind makes a different noise every time. It depends on its speed, and the angle at which it hits the house; it depends on whether there are trees around, or open fields, or fruit hanging off the branches, or a weather-vane on the roof, or tiles and chimneys, and whether there's rain or not . . . When the wind blows, you need a well-tuned ear to understand its different noises. And the wind makes for restless nights. Houses don't have deep roots like trees; they're just placed there—bricks on the ground, a roof on the bricks—and it would take nothing to pluck them up, rip off the roof, and whirl you away like a piece of rag into the night. When it blows like that you hang onto your bed, but you wonder what there is on your bed to hang onto.

That's how it was on this particular night. The house was creaking like a sailing ship; there were hissing sounds, and sudden cracks and crashes. I was half asleep and half awake, and became aware of the sound of a window-shutter splintering. I could clearly hear it as it banged to and fro. Then there was a brief pause. The wind has to stop for breath too, every now and then. Before it explodes, it has to wind itself up somehow, like a spring. During this pause, something happened, or at least I think it did, because Dik had been asleep at my feet, but he suddenly got up and began whining and pacing up and down the room. Dogs know things that we humans don't know. I listened carefully for a moment, but I couldn't hear a thing, absolutely nothing at all. By then he was howling and scratching at the door with his paw. I lay down again and pulled the blanket up over my head, but I wasn't like that for long, because he came up and grabbed the edge of the blanket with his teeth. What did he want? Was he trying to play? Meantime the wind had started blowing again. It was blowing hard and angrily, and in its howling I seemed to hear the sound of a feeble voice, the sound of somebody calling. This lasted for just a fraction of a second and then it was over. But as we know, the wind can be treacherous; like a ventriloquist, it speaks with a thousand voices, and all those voices are false. Dik was still barking, and I couldn't get back to sleep. I got up, gave him a kick, and then went back to bed and turned over the other way.

By the time daybreak came, it was all over. There was a chill in the air and long purple clouds were streaking the sky. I dressed in a hurry, and without even stopping for a coffee I took Dik and we went out of the house. He was acting as if he didn't want to go. Every two steps he would turn round as though he wanted to go back to the house. We passed through the village. The bakery was just opening, so I bought a couple of rolls, one for me and one for him. Then we headed out towards the open countryside. We walked without stopping until we reached the slopes of Bear Mountain. It was called that not because there were bears there, but because some prehistoric skeletons had once been found in a nearby cave.

This was the high point of the plateau. From the top, with one sweep of your eye you could take in everything from the sea to the Alps. I slowed down a bit. Big drops of rain were still falling from the trees, and the ground was covered with freshly fallen leaves and broken branches. I pointed out to Dik some fresh fox's droppings on a stone; he sniffed at them in the manner of an over-fed man sniffing at a delicious meal. Instead of rushing frantically about with his nose to the ground, he kept close to me. Old age comes early for dogs, I thought to myself, and I stroked his head.

At the start, the path took us through a wood of black pines. On the ground there was nothing but white rock and a carpet of yellowing pine needles. These woods are gloomy places; partly because of the kind of soil, and partly because of the acidity of the leaves, nothing ever grows under the trees. Instead of relaxing you, they just make you feel nervous. They look like a landscape that has survived some chemical disaster. Then we emerged into an open stretch of grassland. The grass was glistening with the rain, and so were the low white-stone walls. Around the juniper bushes there were signs of rabbits having been there. A thought came into my head. I decided that I was rather like the pines in that wood: all bony and lanky, I reach towards the sky, in vain. Nothing ever grows around me. And strangely enough, the thought of this didn't disgust me at all, but came as something of a relief. A goshawk flew low in front of me. It had a beakful of twigs to make its nest.

Things change, I told myself; everything changes. By now I was close to the summit, and on my face and in my hair I could feel the gentle, constant breeze which always blows across the heights. It was incredibly different from the wind of the night before. Instead of bringing fury, it brought calm. I sat down next to the marker stone that showed the height above sea level. Far away to the south, the sea was glistening like a little ceramic tile and the last of the dark, swollen clouds was scudding off seawards. Behind me, stretching away to infinity, barren and irregular, lay the successive contours of the plateau; half hidden among the bushes you could see the sentry boxes at the border, and a soldier with a rifle on his shoulder, marching wearily from one box to another.

I lay down, and Dik crouched at my side. Above our heads two goshawks were doing their morning hunting and using the updraughts of air to soar and then to settle again. I closed my eyes, and in the darkness behind my eyelids Marta suddenly appeared. At first it was just her slippers shuffling down the dark corridor; then she was there in her entirety, sunk into her armchair in the sitting room, with a book in her hand. Then I saw an image of her pulling a cake out of the oven and exclaiming 'Look at that!' like a child who's just done something special. Then everything went dark and I seemed to feel just her hands, small and bony as they were, holding my hands tightly, and I heard her saying: 'You shouldn't worry. Youth passes. Everything passes.'

It was as though Marta were right there, sitting next to me on the mountain. In a flash I realized that she was the only true thing in my life. And that thought led to another. I thought: in the same way that there are some people in this world who can't read, there are some who don't know what love is. And that was me. I'd thought a lot, and I'd read a lot, and I thought I knew everything. But instead I was just blind, deaf and dumb. Without my realizing it, her stubborn persistence had succeeded in opening my eyes and my ears, and one by one had loosened the knots by which my tongue was tied.

A whistling sound suddenly made me open my eyes. It was one of the hawks, with its wings swept back, diving from the sky like a rocket. I got up. Dik barked joyously, and went streaking off down the path. I began running too, and before too long the terrain in front of us transformed into a scrubland with low-growing bushes.

As I picked my way between the rocks and the roots I thought that in real life love does not just come; it wedges itself in, and breaks things, so that parts that were previously ordered get shattered into the wonderful confusion of a kaleidoscope. Gentleness and rigour. That was the secret of love. All of a sudden I felt cured, and in the euphoria of my cure I told myself that the time had come for a change of roles. I was going to take care of her, in her old age, just as she, up until that moment, had taken care of me in my youth.

As we ran onwards without stopping, we emerged from the wood. We had almost reached the village when I felt a sharp, painful twinge around my heart and I was forced to stop. I wasn't used to that kind of running any more. I shouted for Dik with as much voice as I could muster, but either he didn't hear me or he didn't want to hear me, and with his tail held high he disappeared into the village. I bent over with my hands on my thighs, like an exhausted footballer standing at the edge of the pitch. As I stood there getting my breath back, I found myself thinking back to how the dog had been so restless the night before. Had something really happened? Or was it only my imagination? I began to breathe faster, even faster than when I had been running. I remembered back to the feeble sound that I had heard when the wind had dropped, and as I listened I realized what it must have been. It must have been the sound of Marta calling. Perhaps she'd got up and taken a fall; something must have happened to her; maybe she'd died, or perhaps she had been lying groaning at the foot of her bed for many, many hours. Ignoring the pain, I set off again, I cursed as I was forced to duck this way and that in order to avoid people and objects. It was only when I reached the last bend in the road, as the big white house suddenly appeared, that my curses suddenly turned into prayers. 'Please, let her still be alive, let her still be alive,' I murmured to myself like a child. In the meantime the sky had descended on the surrounding countryside with a mantle of opaque uniformity.

What would have happened to the prodigal son if he'd found nobody waiting for him when he returned home? Who can say? Perhaps he would simply have re-embarked on his life of pleasure, with a free head and a happy heart. But on the other hand maybe he would have just sat there, for year after year, for his whole life, waiting for somebody to arrive whom he could ask to forgive him. This is how life inflicts its punishment on us: to understand something, and then not be able to live it.

If Marta really had died during the night, I would have been able to weep and to curse the cruelty of fate. But the only untoward thing that morning was that when I came out I'd forgotten my keys, so now I had to ring the bell at the gate.

At the first ring the house stayed dark and still. At the second ring, too, there was no sign of life. The tears were already rising in my eyes as I rang a third time. At that point, unexpectedly, the miracle happened. The light on the staircase came on, and after a minute or less the light came on in the hallway too. I was overcome with the kind of happiness that dogs show, a pure bodily happiness. I waited for the click of the electric lock on the gate—but it never came. Maybe, I thought, she's got the radio on too loud, or maybe she's in the bathroom with the taps running. So I rang again and waited. I must have waited there, ringing at the bell, for over half an hour. I kept my finger on the bell-push for minutes at a time. I pushed aside the ivy hanging over the gate and peered through.

Various lights were still going on and off around the house. When I thought I spotted her figure passing behind the curtains in the hall, I began calling her name loudly, and banging and kicking at the gate. And meanwhile Dik was barking and trying to dig a tunnel under the fence. I don't know how long we stayed there like that. Eventually it began to rain great drops out of the skies, and I realized that my fists were covered in blood. The dog shook the water from his fur; then, instead of starting to dig again, he crouched on the ground, placed his head on his paws, and sighed deeply. At that point I sat down too, slumped to the ground like a puppet. Icy drops of water from my collar dripped down my back. Dik's warm tongue was licking my knuckles. And as I sat there in a puddle, with my hair sticking to my head, all of a sudden I gave up. I realized what had happened.

My suspicions were confirmed the following morning. Outside the front gate I found all my things, packed into two huge boxes.

For a year now I've been wandering the uplands with Dik. Every night I come down to the big white house, and I wait. The children in the village call me the 'Madman of Bear Mountain', and when they see me they start laughing loudly. And when the icy wind comes down from the East, instead of going out to meet it as I used to do in the old days, I seek shelter, and block my ears with my hands. I don't want to hear anything any more. Nothing at all. It's as I said. If we want to understand love, the only way is to be naked, with nothing around you, stretched out on the bare earth as if dead.

Nanni Balestrini

Let a Thousand Hands Reach Out to Pick up the Gun

At 10.45 the coroner begins the autopsy will finish at about 1 o'clock with the following result the young woman had been hit by two bullets one hit her in the left shoulder and the other the fatal one went through her chest. The officer comes down tells his men to keep at a distance he goes towards the farmhouse which was supposed to be abandoned according to information received previously. Three hours of tension pass while doubts questions hypotheses proliferate at 4.30 the two sisters arrive at the carabinieri barracks in a police car they reach the hospital shortly before 5 o'clock. The attempt to escape in a red Fiat 127 and a white Fiat 128 was blocked by the carabinieri but while the women had dived to the ground coming out of the driver's door the man had inexplicably exited by the right-hand door in other words on the side most exposed to enemy fire.

A corpse with no name it is that of a woman between thirty-five and forty with curly red hair she is dressed in a beige jumper faded jeans and red sandals with a raised cord heel. The lieutenant goes up to the farmhouse to peer through a groundfloor window it is at this moment that an SRCM-type hand grenade is thrown from the floor above. They stand up and proceed slowly towards the morgue at the door the public prosecutor is waiting for them they betray no emotion remain impassive before the photographers' flashguns the door closes behind them. The doors of the criminals' car spring open and suddenly a hail of gunfire explodes because they have two pistols and a sten gun with them.

Her face looks strange in death one might say surprised she is wearing very tight jeans and a beige sweater but it is all stained red so you guess the colour rather than see it. He went on and banged on the door saying carabinieri here at this point a first-floor window opened out of which a woman appeared who replied what do you want the officer demanded entry and from another window the first hand grenade was thrown. It was not a long wait at 5.15 the public prosecutor comes out nods his head it's her he says they recognized her at once they only had to look at her face. They were cut off and the red Fiat 127 collided with the 128 these were the last moments of violence the robbers again leapt out and ran off across the grass heading downhill. In the area of the shoot-out a fierce battle that lasted more than half an hour a young woman was killed who belonged to the kidnappers' gang. The lieutenant called up support there's someone there come out in reply a window was flung open on the first floor and two hand grenades thrown at the same time explode the splinters lacerate the officer's arm and face. There would anyway have been other elements that would have made identification easy a small ring the sisters had a similar ring the mother had given to all three ten years previously. Still in the 127 and the 128 the woman had her accomplice fire at the officer then seeing that escape is impossible the way out is also blocked by the blue Fiat 127 patrol car the gangsters start running towards the woods across the grass around the farmhouse.

The body lying on the slope of the hill the red hair splayed across the green the face disfigured this was the end of her short life in the din of gunfire of exploding grenades of a desperate bid for freedom broken off by a hail of bullets. At that moment from a window on the first floor a hand grenade is thrown which explodes a few yards from the lieutenant taking off his arm and injuring his eyes. The woman terrorist killed yesterday in the shoot-out at the farmhouse finally has a name. The carabiniere officer seeing that the criminals are not accepting defeat himself fires a first hail of bullets that seems to scare the two out in the open.

The central nucleus of the inquest is represented by the few square metres of the morgue in which the still nameless woman's body lay. The explosion tore the officer's arm off the grenade splinters blind him he falls headlong while a pool of blood extends around his body. It seems it was not easy to establish the woman's identity on her was found a fresh identity card coming from a stock of stolen documents. As they came round the corner of the farmhouse they found our 127 in the way in the attempt to get round it they went off the road then they got out raising their hands we surrender they were ten yards from me in the grass I raised my gun the man was sheltering behind the woman.

Who is the dead woman the question had no answer until this morning but in fact she was identified almost at once. The sergeant and the private run up but they are forced to throw themselves flat because a second grenade is thrown from the farmhouse wounding both of them. The identikit pictures in the possession of the carabinieri however did not bear much resemblance to the victim at the farmhouse in order to avoid recognition the woman had cut off her long black hair. All of a sudden the man turned back OK we surrender he shouted and almost at the same time a series of gunshots was fired in the direction of the sergeant and the private was also wounded.

There is a tense wait it is an important moment because it can make a decisive contribution to assisting the police inquiries enabling them to construct an identikit of the gang's members. This was the start of a fierce exchange of gunfire single shots and series of shots from inside two men and a woman are firing and perhaps another man too who had come out and who had managed to escape. She had dyed her hair red also her features were lined by the hardships endured during the long period of years that she had been in hiding. Finally the others shouted that they were surrendering pointing his gun the carabiniere told them to come forward slowly the woman in front and the man behind.

Central command confirms that the four carabinieri of the patrol had come under fire from a man and a third person the woman had then been killed while her accomplice although wounded had managed to reach the bushes. The door is thrown open and a man and a woman come running out into the yard they throw another grenade they are holding sub-machine guns they fire wildly the sergeant and the private fall to the ground. Formal identification was made possible once the name had been established for the first time at 5.10 today at the hospital morgue. They put their hands up and shout we surrender but instead of standing still or walking forward the girls are holding guns the other man still has a sten gun the gangsters back off. How many accomplices two men and a woman two women and a man one man and a woman yesterday the second version was given as the official one. There is also a series of shots from the machine pistol and one of the bullets hits the private in the head the sergeant was wounded too in the leg. She was identified by her sisters who had not seen her for five years on the basis of various identifying marks a small scar on one lip some moles and a ring with the same setting which the three daughters had in common with their mother. The woman and her accomplice came down and the officer instructed them to put their hands up the gangsters raised their hands and the man shouted OK that's enough I've been hit but at the same time his hands went down towards his belt.

The carabinieri who were engaged in a gun battle with the people in the farmhouse state that they had seen only one man and one woman there was talk of two women of another individual who had been seen or heard escaping after the shoot-out. Immediately afterwards this same woman had thrown the second grenade it is not known how many of them there were but it is known that the woman got into the orange Fiat 127 and her accomplice into the white 128 and then the two cars collided and ended up in the ditch. The official identification was carried out by the woman's two sisters they had not seen her for five years they said but they identified her at once thanks to particular marks, especially a number of moles. Suddenly the man stops turns round puts his hands up and shouts OK I give up I'm wounded I surrender but he immediately puts his hands down again takes a grenade from his belt and throws it at the carabiniere.

Up at the farmhouse the branch of a cherry tree torn off by a burst of gunfire testifies to the violence of the bloody clash between the carabinieri and the bandits. A man and a woman were the people who came out of the farmhouse after throwing the grenade which had knocked the lieutenant to the ground shooting wildly and mowing down the private they had reached and started the 127 and the 128. Before arriving at the lying-in room at the hospital already at the carabinieri headquarters they had identified the identical ring their mother had given them. Suddenly no sooner had the officer lowered his gun they made a break for it in his left hand the gangster has a second grenade once again an SRCM and he throws this one too this time at the lone officer.

Other evidence of the battle can be seen in the shattered glass of the windows in the window shutter blown off its hinges by the blast from an SRCM on the grass where the woman was shot down the blood looks like rust. Then the gangsters having hit the private too with a burst of gunfire tried to get away trying to get away in their car in order to get round the blue 127 carabinieri patrol car they dived towards the ditch running alongside the path. The identification happened at 5.10 in the morgue of the general hospital at that time the two sisters arrived they came into the room together with the public prosecutor. He seemed to be intending to use her as a shield I saw him put one hand inside his jacket I thought he was going to pull out a gun instead he pulled out another grenade he threw it in my direction.

On the bodywork there are bullet holes the 127 has a shattered windscreen the sidelight of the 128 is blown out and it has a big 9mm bullet hole in its left side. There is a moment's pause in the jeep the driver takes the radio mike and makes contact with his patrol few words hurry I am here he repeats the phrase three times. Seeing the naked body of the woman marked by the cuts made during the autopsy more than by the facial resemblance they had not seen her for five years. I threw myself forward it exploded behind me I had run out of bullets I leaned over the private's body I took the magazine from his gun I put it in mine. There are still the two cars which were to be used for the gangsters' final getaway they are a red 127 and a white 128 it appears they crashed and ended up half in a ditch. Meanwhile with his other hand he takes his service pistol and in turn rushes towards the farmhouse while two women and a man are running towards a car. They were able to identify her on the basis of a number of moles and a cut on one lip one detail which convinced them was a small ring on the ring finger of the left hand. When one of the pair suddenly pulled out a grenade and threw it in the direction of the officer he dived to one side then threw himself forward keeping low and escaping the effects of the blast.

Here a number of different-coloured wigs used by the young woman as disguises in her exploits. The driver runs over he is a soldier married fifty years old with four children calm thoughtful brave he takes the 9mm gun with seven bullets in it he sees his colleagues on the ground shot up his nerve steady he has not a moment of uncertainty. A gold ring with three small black stones it was a memento of her mother she had given an identical one to each of the daughters also getting one made for herself the flurry of confusion about her identity was thus resolved. The man had shouted enough I'm wounded I surrender but almost simultaneously he had thrown another grenade and the driver of the patrol car ducking in order to avoid it had fired at the woman who was killed while the man succeeded in escaping.

She is the head of the bandit group which breaks into prison she is the one who rings the bell at the front gate and who runs towards the cell a short-barrelled machine pistol under her arm while her colleagues immobilize the warders. The officer fires a shot but over their heads to indicate that they should stop as regulations require the fugitives do not stop they reach a 127 parked under the trees and try to make a getaway. The identification of the woman was carried out at about 5.30 in the morgue where the body had been taken by the two sisters. He took out a grenade and threw it at the soldier he realized what was happening he threw himself forwards avoiding the blast of the grenade which went off behind him and he fired his gun hitting the woman.

On that day in mid February the trail went cold it re-emerged again on Thursday concluding in the image of the young woman stretched on the ground dead after the grenade battle with the carabinieri. Between the gangsters and the carabiniere who in the meantime had taken his pistol and had thrown himself to the ground to the left shielding himself behind the car there was an exchange of gunfire. The identifying features which made the identification possible were a series of moles that the woman had on her back a scar mark on one lip and a ring which she was wearing on her hand. The officer dives forwards and while the grenade flies over his head and explodes behind him he shoots with his issue 9mm pistol the woman is in the line of fire and falls hit by two bullets which go through her chest and her right arm.

Women with guns at their side women who rob who kidnap who attack prisons who shoot representatives of the law and of the state women who have followed their road to the end going from the role of support and consoler of their male colleagues to that of protagonists. The man and the woman he relates in a low voice barely marked by the emotion which has taken hold of him since the tragedy they got into the 128 and the 127 parked on the grass they left in a hurry perhaps because they thought they had killed the whole patrol. This latter detail was decisive it was a ring with three mounted stones which had been given by the mother to all three sisters. There followed another shoot-out in the course of which the woman was hit at this point according to the false version provided by headquarters the carabiniere ran out of ammunition and the other man took advantage of this to escape.

In the yard of the farmhouse at the point where she had been struck down this morning there were found six red roses. Immediately afterwards he saw the bandits' two cars which were trying to get past the carabinieri's car which was blocking their way but they got onto the road ending up in a ditch. Yes it's her the two sisters told the magistrate it's been five years since we last saw her standing arm in arm they looked at the dead woman weeping in silence the body of the woman was stretched out naked on the marble bench. From the man's sub-machine gun came the series of shots that hit the woman and also hit the man who even though with a bullet in his body managed to reach the first line of trees and disappear into the woods.

Naturally nobody knows who left the bunch of red roses nobody has seen anything and none of the local farm people have seen strangers. However their line of escape is blocked in front of them is the carabinieri's 128 across the middle of the road the bandits have no time to go into reverse. A patch of blood in the centre of the chest another on the left arm the fingers of the right hand blackened and contracted as if frozen in the act of gripping the earth the left hand wearing a gold ring with three small stones. And I started shooting again and downed the girl who was screaming wildly the man also started shouting I'm wounded and he ran off into the fields and disappeared.

Then for the whole of the day the searching of the woods continued an operation in which three hundred carabineri eighty policemen twenty security guards six helicopters and a number of dog-handler units are still involved. The carabiniere fires a second shot which one assumes hit the man who was on the back seat of the 127 a bloodstain was found afterwards. The black hair in the subdued light of the morgue not red as it had appeared at a distance yesterday in the sunlight between the trees on her lip a small scar. It was found the bullets still in the magazine one of the girls ended up killed while the soldier tries to reload his weapon the accomplices manage to escape on the young woman's chest there are three holes the demonstration.

Antonio Tabucchi

A Hunt

It's a herd of six or seven, Carlos Eugénio tells me, his satisfied smile showing off such a brilliant set of false teeth it occurs to me he might have carved them himself from whale ivory. Carlos Eugénio is seventy, agile and still youthful, and he is *mestre baleeiro*, which, literally translated, means 'master whaler', though in reality he is captain of this little crew and has absolute authority over every aspect of the hunt. The motor launch leading the expedition is his own, an old boat about ten metres long which he manoeuvres with deftness and nonchalance, and without any hurry either. In any event, he tells me, the whales are splashing about, they won't run away. The radio is on so as to keep in contact with the lookout based on a lighthouse on the island; a monotonous and it seems to me slightly ironic voice thus guides us on our way. 'A little to the right, Maria Manuela,' says the grating voice, 'you're going all over the place.' *Maria Manuela* is the name of the boat. Carlos Eugénio makes a gesture of annoyance, but still laughing, then he turns to the sailor who is riding with us, a lean, alert man, a boy almost, with constantly moving eyes and a dark complexion. We'll manage on our own, he decides and turns the radio off. The sailor climbs nimbly up the boat's only mast and perches on the crosspiece at the top, wrapping his legs around. He too points to the right. For a moment I think he's sighted them, but I don't know the whaleman's sign language. Carlos Eugénio explains that an open hand with the index finger pointing upwards means 'whales in sight', and that wasn't the gesture our lookout made.

I turn to glance at the sloop we are towing. The whalemen are relaxed, laughing and talking together, though I can't make out what they're saying. They look as though they're out on a pleasure cruise. There are six of them and they're sitting on planks laid across the boat. The harpooneer is standing up though, and appears to be following our lookout's gestures with attention: he has a huge paunch and a thick beard, young, he can't be more than thirty. I've heard they call him Chá Preto, Black Tea, and that he works as a docker in the port in Horta. He belongs to the whaling cooperative in Faial and they tell me he's an exceptionally skilled harpooneer.

I don't notice the whale until we're barely three hundred metres away: a column of water rises against the blue when some pipe springs a leak in the road of a big city. Carlos Eugénio has turned off the engine and only our momentum takes us drifting on towards that black shape lying like an enormous bowler hat on the water. In the sloop the whalemen are silently preparing for the attack: they are calm, quick, resolute, they know the motions they have to go through off by heart. They row with powerful well-spaced strokes and in a flash they are far away. They go round in a wide circle, approaching the whale from the front so as to avoid the tail, and because if they approached from the sides they would be in sight of its eyes. When they are a hundred metres off they draw their oars into the boat and raise a small triangular sail. Everybody adjusts sail and ropes: only the harpooneer is immobile on the point of the prow: standing, one leg bent forward, the harpoon lying in his hand as if he were measuring its weight. He concentrates, hanging on for the right moment, the moment when the boat will be near enough for him to strike a vital point, but far enough away not to be caught by a lash of the wounded whale's tail. Everything happens with amazing speed in just a few seconds. The boat makes a sudden turn while the harpoon is still curving through the air. The instrument of death isn't flung from above downwards, as I had expected, but upwards, like a javelin, and it is the sheer weight of the iron and the speed of the thing as it falls that transforms it into a deadly missile. When the enormous tail rises to whip first the air then the water, the sloop is already far away. The oarsmen are rowing again, furiously, and a strange play of ropes, which until now was going on underwater so that I hadn't seen it, suddenly becomes visible and I realise that our launch is connected to the harpoon too, while the whaling sloop has jettisoned its own rope. From a straw basket placed in a well in the middle of the launch, a thick rope begins to unwind, sizzling as it rushes through a fork on the bow; the young deckhand pours a bucket of water over it to cool it and prevent it snapping from the friction. Then the rope tightens and we set off with a jerk, a leap, following the wounded whale as it flees. Carlos Eugénio holds the helm and chews the stub of a cigarette; the sailor with the boyish face watches the sperm-whale's movements with a worried expression. In his hand he holds a small sharp axe ready to cut the rope if the whale should go down, since it would drag us with it under the water. But the breathless rush doesn't last long. We've hardly gone a kilometre when the whale stops dead, apparently exhausted, and Carlos Eugénio has to put the launch into reverse to stop the momentum from taking us on top of the immobile animal. He struck well, he says with satisfaction, showing off his brilliant false teeth. As if in confirmation of his comment, the whale, whistling, raises his head right out of the water and breathes; and the jet that hisses up into the air is red with blood. A pool of vermilion spreads across the sea and the breeze carries a spray of red drops as far as our boat, spotting faces and clothes. The whaling sloop has drawn up against the launch: Chá Preto throws his tools up on deck and climbs up himself with an agility truly surprising for a man of his build. I gather that he wants to go on to the next stage of the attack, the lance, but the *mestre* seems not to agree. There follows some excited confabulation, which the sailor with the boyish face keeps out of. Then Chá Preto obviously gets his way; he stands on the prow and assumes his javelin-throwing stance, having swapped the harpoon for a weapon of the same size but with an extremely sharp head in an elongated heart shape, like a halberd. Carlos Eugénio moves forwards with the engine on minimum, and the boat starts over to where the whale is breathing immobile in a pool of blood, restless tail spasmodically slapping the water. This time the deadly weapon is thrown downwards; hurled on a slant, it penetrates the soft flesh as if it were butter. A dive: the great mass disappears, writhing underwater. Then the tail appears again, powerless, pitiful, like a black sail. And finally the huge head emerges and I hear the deathcry, a sharp wail, almost a whistle, shrill, agonizing, unbearable.

The whale is dead and lies motionless on the water. The coagulated blood forms a bank that looks like coral. I hadn't realized the day was almost over and dusk surprises me. The whole crew are busy organizing the towing. Working quickly, they punch a hole in the tail fin and thread through a rope with a stick to lock it. We are more than eighteen miles out to sea, Carlos Eugénio tells me; it will take all night to get back, the sperm-whale weighs around thirty tons and the launch will have to go very slowly. In a strange marine rope party led by the launch and with the whale bringing up the rear, we head towards the island of Pico and the factory of São Roque. In the middle is the sloop with the whalemen, and Carlos Eugénio suggests that I join them so as to be able to get a little rest: under enormous strain, the launch's engine is making an infernal racket and sleep would be impossible. The two boats draw alongside each other and Carlos Eugénio leaves the launch with me, handing over the helm to the young sailor and two oarsmen who take our place. The whalemen set up a makeshift bed for me near the tiller; night has fallen and two oil lanterns have been lit on the sloop. The fishermen are exhausted, their faces strained and serious, tinted yellow in the light from the lanterns. They hoist the sail so as not to be a dead weight increasing the strain on the launch, then lie anyoldhow across the planks and fall into a deep sleep. Chá Preto sleeps on his back, paunch up, and snores loudly. Carlos Eugénio offers me a cigarette and talks to me about his two children who have emigrated to America and whom he hasn't seen for six years. They came back just once, he tells me, maybe they'll come again next summer. They'd like me to go to them, but I want to die here, at home. He smokes slowly and watches the sky, the stars. What about you though, why did you want to come with us today, he asks me, out of simple curiosity? I hesitate, thinking how to answer: I'd like to tell him the truth, but am held back by the fear that this might offend. I let a hand dangle in the water. If I stretched out my arm I could almost touch the enormous fin of the animal we're towing. Perhaps you're both a dying breed, I finally say softly, you people and the whales, I think that's why I came. Probably he's already asleep, he doesn't answer; though the coal of his cigarette still burns between his fingers. The sail slaps sombrely; motionless in sleep the bodies of the whalemen are small dark heaps and the sloop slides over the water like a ghost.

Nico Orengo

The Grand Council

At nine Her Highness refused bread sprinkled with oil. Bice said: 'Dear, you must eat—love comes later.'

Caterina shrugged, she sought the sun beyond the sliver of light that rose from the sea off Corsica. She was hungry but her bad temper had bothered her all night running up her legs as if it were a frog. And now in the warmth of the morning she was trying to relax. To chew even a breath of air would have made her feel agitated again, down there, behind her navel and certainly a little higher up where her young heart was suspended and besieged amid currents of pain, pride, shame and disappointment.

The royal flagship of the Genoese fleet rocked lazily opposite the Fortress of Monaco with prow and stern kept in place by heavy anchors of Pisan lead. And the Fortress of Monaco too was well anchored ashore to confirm that old saying 'Monaco is a rock'. The sea lapped around it delicately, slowly, smoothing its ankles, polishing its sides.

Old Bice offered Maria Caterina di Brignole a roll from which tender leaves of basil stuck out. But the princess of Monaco refused the fresh breakfast telling Bice to eat it herself.

Bice did not have to be asked twice and like a finch began to peck at the roll greedily while Maria Caterina ordered Admiral Orazio Lercari to go and fetch her a spy-glass—the most powerful one on board the galley.

The admiral bowed to Maria Caterina and called the cabin boy Piscin. With a kick to the bottom he sent him flying off to fetch his German glass, a jewel of brass and lenses, which he had managed to get from Geneva in return for a keg of nicely matured salted tuna.

Piscin returned with a blue velvet cushion and bowed to the admiral then disappeared backwards into a coil of rope. Orazio Lercari busying himself with his jewel, opened the case, wiped the lenses with the hem of his cloak and offered it politely to the white hands of Maria Caterina di Brignole. Maria Caterina sat in her easy chair and pointed the glass at the Fortress of Monaco.

The windows looking on to the sea numbered twenty-one. The first had its shutters closed, the second half-closed, the third wide open: there was a coming and going of little cups, trays, coffee pots, plates of sweetmeats, cooks in white hats, servant lasses in coloured starched caps. She saw open mouths singing among little clouds of pink smoke, a delicate ballet of men-servants and maids in white and blue liveries who opened the morning with gaiety and above all were opening it for that ... that ... Maria Caterina di Brignole found herself poised between searching for an insult and for a compliment. She was unable to choose between head and heart and so uttered only the name: Onorato III di Grimaldi, prince of Monaco.

Maria Caterina lowered the glass, shut her eyes, breathed in, hoping to find a breeze, but encountered the strong smell of olive oil from Albenga and the pleasantly irritating odour of basil from Pegli, coming from the remains of the bread and oil which Bice, that greedy thing, held in her teeth.

'I am going back,' said Maria Caterina di Brignole. 'We cannot,' Admiral Orazio Lercari replied with unctuous firmness, worried about his German glass, which he saw precariously balanced on his sovereign's shapely knee.

'And how long must I stay here, on this uncomfortable ship, sea-sick, love-sick and sick with rage?'

The admiral had no reply. He was an admiral, his duties were very different from those of an ambassador or High Chamberlain. He was not one of the breed of toadies, specialists in undoing Gordian knots. He was a warrior, by Saint George. A sailor. He could have blown up the Fortress and all the gentlemen who lived there, that he could have done.

The admiral replied with a tone of voice that was slightly offended at the judgement passed on his vessel, one of the finest in the Genoese navy, one of the finest in the whole Mediterranean: 'We are waiting for advice to reach us from Genoa.'

He had sent a boat with six oarsmen and a whip. He had personally chosen the diameter of the bull's-pizzle and the sailor who was to wield it. If the six of them did not manage to strangle him by the time they were off Noli they would be back in the course of a week with some disciple of Machiavelli capable of resolving the regrettable dilemma which was keeping them at anchor opposite the Fortress of Monaco.

'Let us wait,' sighed Maria Caterina. 'Let us wait,' the crew sighed in chorus.

Maria Caterina had married Onorato III di Grimaldi, prince of Monaco, by proxy on 15 June 1775, and already somewhat chagrined at having had to say 'yes' to a man who wasn't there and then to another one though it was none of his business, had set out with a trembling heart. But her disappointments were not over: having reached the port of Monaco she had not seen her loved one come to meet her. Nothing. Onorato had not even made the effort to take a boat from the mole to come and fetch her. Elegant, brown, handsome and scented, he had stayed on the mole waving a hat with pheasant feathers and lounging in a red cape, uttering things like 'Uh, uh, hey, welcome, my patience is at an end, come here.'

What? Maria Caterina had said to herself. Come here? You come, take a skiff, a boat, anything you like, but make the effort, you weren't in the cathedral in Genoa, at least come on board. To and fro, to and fro, that day nothing was done: she remained on board and he on the mole. A fine first night, most people thought, including Maria Caterina and Onorato. But etiquette is etiquette advised Monaco's counsellors; Onorato as reigning sovereign had the right and the duty to wait for his bride on land.

Maria Caterina thought of the schoolroom deceptions, of all the lies Magda Viale, who had taught her literature, had told her about sweet Provence and the troubadours, the pain of love and courtly delicacy, chivalry and the heart caught in the vice of graceful verses. All lies if that bumptious sovereign, lord of a rock, a few lemon trees and a few olives, behaved as the lowest wharfinger from the alleyways would not have behaved.

Thus for a week the galley remained rocking in the slight currents off the coast waiting for that subtle, delicate, thorny question of ceremonial to find a dignified solution.

Bice had suggested shutting an eye and disembarking; Maria Caterina would have shut both eyes and thrown herself in to swim but the admiral had recalled that they were on a Genoese ship with all those banners and coat-of-arms of a Great Past. They could not strike their flag in a puddle.

For a week they had been waiting with great pride. And meantime, morning after morning, the ceremony of deceptions and temptations repeated itself in the same way. At about ten, great peals of trumpets and fanfares, then a flutter of banners announced that the prince would descend to the mole. Packs of greyhounds came down the alleys of the Fortress preceding carriages and litters.

At eleven Onorato on a black horse arrived on the mole to repeat his rigmarole: 'Uh, uh, hey, welcome, my patience is at an end, come here.' And there was a flourish of plumes and lace, a display of smiles and dance steps. Things went on like this, unflaggingly for three or four hours, then shrugging, sending a kiss in the direction of the galley and of his bride who hung over the ship's side, eating her heart and her nails, he went back up with a cry that sounded like a nightingale's song: 'Till tomorrow, till tomorro.o.o.ow!'

Bice had tried to undermine her young mistress's pride: like a bawd, she had suggested taking a dinghy from the poop secretly and setting out for the shore. In that way, she had told her, it would have looked like a madcap act, a caprice of love and no royal far less nationalist pride would have come into it. Maria Caterina had refused; a princess is a princess for all that; she can hardly carry on like the lowest of her ladies-in-waiting who doesn't mind dropping her knickers just to get the man she wants. Bice fell silent, she bit the last mouthful of bread and oil and went towards the poop: knickers or no knickers she knew exactly what she would have done, without so much ado and so many diplomatic complications.

Maria Caterina stayed at the prow, her glass still balanced on her knees, her eye gazing ashore. 'I want to write,' she said. And Admiral Orazio Lercari shouted to Piscin to run and fetch the writing-case.

Piscin flew off and returned with Chinese paper and the pens of goose and guinea-fowl feathers.

Maria Caterina prepared the coloured inks, cleaned the writing table, made up her mind how to send a message to her Onorato along the lines: 'Let us make the best of things and think of the two of us for now summer is on the beaches and among the pine woods of Aleppo.' She stared at the sheet and the words refused to come down from her head and along her arm: the rice sheet remained pink and immaculate, against the light it showed flights of herons and royal brothers and sisters, pagodas and junks. Maria Caterina beat her brains, forced her memory to fish up words and turns of phrase. But it was as if a knot had formed along her arm and no thought could cross it. So she gave up—she made little boats and launched them from the bulwark at the prow for them to find the tracks of the current which might bear them ashore and into Onorato's hands.

On the tenth day the sailors of the galley *Doria* muttered 'ouf'. They couldn't stand these interminable days any longer. They had washed down the ship ten times and repainted it five times, sewn all the sails and polished the brasses and the ship's silver. They asked to be allowed to think of themselves and the admiral, fearing a mutiny, permitted them a few distractions. One swam, another began to fish, one gave flute lessons and another dancing ones, one set up a roulette table.

The Admiral, Bice and Piscin kept a severe distance from the crew's recreational goings-on; they formed a screen for the shoulders of the young woman from Genoa which were bowed by the pain that by now had grown over her like a creeper.

With the German glass Maria Caterina had picked out Onorato's windows, they were the seventh, the eighth and the ninth. It was there that in the morning the trays of pastries, the pots of coffee, the baskets of cakes, ended up—in those rooms where she should have been lying in sheets perfumed with lavender waiting for them. She cursed her pride and Onorato's, she cursed royal etiquette and, sighing, asked the admiral if it was not a good idea to send a second boat to search for the first. The admiral agreed and a new crew was lashed to the oars overseen by a huge sailor from Chiavari with a whip.

On the thirteenth day the two boats returned. On board they had Camillo Spinola, a most able minister in every art of compromise, diplomatic ceremony, impossible missions.

He came on board and asked to have a bath. Then he summoned to the edge of the bath the admiral, Piscin and Bice. He asked Bice to wash his back, Piscin to give him a shampoo, and the admiral to tell him how things stood. Then he asked to breakfast with the princess stressing that he wished to have sea-urchins, limpets and fresh oysters. That morning he prevented Maria Caterina from being present at Onorato's usual performance and on the next two days as well he ordered the whole crew to pay no attention to the land.

From the Fortress they noticed that something had changed down there on the vessel, above all when they learned that some sloops had sailed to Menton and Roquebrune to buy fresh vegetables and barrels of water. Worried, Onorato summoned the Grand Council and asked: 'Am I running the risk of losing a wife?' Onorato out of good taste avoided saying what they were all thinking, that is: without having yet possessed her. The Grand Council said that on board there was old Spinola, the cunning fox of a thousand intrigues, and therefore something was to be expected, if the prince had it in mind to play for high stakes, troubles would come.

Onorato had become worried, he looked out from behind the shutters at the indifference with which the galley now considered the land; there was no life on the side facing him, everything went on the opposite bulwarks, down there it was a continuous party, with singing and dancing, banquets with toasts and splashes. It looked as if the Genoese had taken over his waters as a place for holidaying. He could stand it no more.

He convoked the Grand Council again and said: 'Let there be negotiations without giving the impression of wishing to negotiate.'

In the Grand Council lots were drawn to see to whom it fell to play the shameless part and the dice said Tristo Biamonti, already a tried master of deception at certain courts in the territory around Nice. Biamonti took the oars and went to the poop of the *Doria*. He began by saying (and it was agreed) that 'an ambassador is not to blame for bad news' but meantime they did not even offer him a glass of water. Then they let him cook for two hours under the bowsprit, splashing dirty water on his glossy shoes, until they brought him into Spinola's cabin. He had to keep patient, hear it said that the situation could not be more embarrassing, annoying, not fitting in a young and civil principality. Biamonti proposed to cut things short and Camillo agreed. They were like the Pisan thieves, cat and dog by day, Siamese twins by night, so there was no need to waste words. They put on the order of the day the question of how to save face. They plunged into a giddy impasse until in unison, they timidly asked each other a question: 'What if we met halfway?'

To get halfway, since there was the sea between the mole and the ship, they agreed that a gangway would be built. Thus an ecological disaster began. By the order of Onorato, woods of Benedictine olives, almost a thousand years old, and square miles of pinewoods were cut down. To avoid this disaster Bice proposed bringing the galley alongside the beach but the admiral was against it. The people of Monaco stripped the mountains from Belenda to the shore and shaved the coast line from Menton to Fontainville and built a huge gangway. They used rose wood and lemon wood to cover the planks and the handrail. They arranged it in such a way that the gangway measured a hundred metres so that it could be divided equally in two and where it came to fifty metres they tied two turtle doves with a white ribbon and a blue one. At that point, under the doves' wings, after eighteen days of waiting, Maria Caterina di Brignole and Onorato III di Grimaldi, in times past lover of the bride's mother, would finally meet.

And so it was. And although the gangway of olive, pine, rose and lemon wood smelt as sweetly as a paradise the marriage was shaky. One way or another Maria Caterina Grimaldi fell in love almost at once with the Prince de Condé who was passing through the principality on his way to a game of pelota. But this time too it was a long drawn-out affair because she had to wait for Onorato to die before being able to join Condé. The poor thing managed only when she was past seventy. But that is another story with a longer bridge, which spanned thirty-three years of waiting.

Pia Fontana

Phobia

'Life's not exactly brilliant, but I suppose some people have it worse.' That's how Rina consoles herself every time she's feeling depressed. This is usually the case on weekday mornings, especially at a quarter to seven on dark winter days when she has to stand around stamping her feet on the station platform and waiting in the fog for the train that will take her to work. She pulls her scarf up over her nose—since she suffers from bronchitis and a delicate throat, the cold is her worst enemy—and she paces to and fro while she waits for Carla to arrive. Carla is another early-morning commuter like herself. Unlike Rina, she invariably arrives at the last moment, running up the steps of the underpass two at a time.

Three factory workers are waiting at the end of the platform. They're always there before seven too, on these dark winter mornings, arriving before Rina, with their quilted jackets buttoned tight and their woollen caps pulled down. They stand in silence with their hands in their pockets as they wait on the deserted platform. When it's foggy it's impossible to see them, but you can be sure they're there. The railwayman gives Rina a friendly greeting. He hardly knows Carla, because Carla always arrives at the last minute. Sometimes they exchange a word or two:

'Still here, eh . . .?'

'Sure . . .'

As the station tannoy announces the impending arrival of the local 7.18 commuter train, they both stamp their feet in the cold. Carla and the train generally appear on the scene more or less simultaneously, and from the same direction.

It's cold on the half-empty train. Best to keep your coat on. Best to keep your mittens on too. Rina pulls down the edge of her scarf to reveal her nose and mouth. She sits away from the window to avoid the icy draught that's coming through. She sits forward and crosses her legs, while Carla, who's still not fully awake, falls right back to sleep without a word. The train leaves, picking its way through the allotments of cabbages and onions next to the station. On the seat someone's left behind a magazine—slim, pocket-sized, with a coloured cover. It's called *Wake Up!* There's a picture of a young man wearing a red jumper and staring off the balcony of a tower block. He looks terrified. At the bottom, in big letters, it says: 'PHOBIAS—OUR MYSTERIOUS FEARS.' Rina reaches over to pick it up. She's got forty minutes to kill. Carla is fast asleep, with her head to one side and her mouth half open.

'Phobias: Exaggerated fears of some specific thing or situation. Phobias are divided into *common phobias*, which are exaggerated fears of the kind of things that most people are frightened of, such as death, and *specific phobias*, which are fears of things which are not in themselves frightening, such as lifts, or open spaces.' (*The Complete Medical Guide*, F. Miller)

She looks over towards Carla. Rina's afraid of spiders. Is that a phobia? Carla on the other hand is scared of snakes.

'The fear and panic generated by a phobia can be a terrible thing. In the United States almost one person in ten—about 22 million people—suffers from some form of phobia.

Wake up! Print run 10,610,000 copies. Published in 53 languages.

In this edition:
  A Lawyer Puts God to the Test
  Crossword
  What Kind of Clothes Suit You?

The ticket collector nods to Rina as he passes by. He doesn't ask for her ticket—or for Carla's either, because she's asleep anyway. He's been working this line for six months now, and he knows his passengers. Rina on the other hand has been travelling the line for the past six years, and she knows not only this ticket collector, but also the dozen who preceded him. Carla grunts every now and then as if she's suffocating in her sleep. Then she turns her head abruptly the other way, without waking up.

On page seven there's a box with a yellow background, with a list of the principal phobias:

aquaphobia: fear of water
acrophobia: fear of heights
agoraphobia: fear of open spaces
astrophobia: fear of storms
cynophobia: fear of dogs
claustrophobia: fear of enclosed spaces
demonophobia: fear of demons or the devil
haemophobia: fear of blood
microphobia: fear of germs
misophobia: fear of getting dirty
nyctophobia: fear of the dark
ophiophobia: fear of snakes
pyrophobia: fear of fires
thanatophobia: fear of death
xenophobia: fear of strangers or foreigners
zoophobia: fear of animals

Rina is surprised to find that she suffers from at least half of the phobias on the list: she's scared of water, she's scared of heights, she's scared of storms, she's scared of dogs, she's scared of the devil, she's scared of blood, she's scared of germs, she's scared of the dark, she's scared of snakes, she's scared of fire, and she's scared of death. At night she sleeps with a light on. During a storm one time she ended up hiding under her bed. She only swims in shallow water, and she always checks now and then to make sure she hasn't gone out of her depth. If she sees someone dead or injured in the street she'll turn her head away. The previous summer, in the mountains, she'd been paralysed by the sight of an innocent grass snake crossing her path (she thought it was poisonous). She also suffers from vertigo, which is why she never goes climbing. And if people start talking about ghosts or the devil in her presence, she gets annoyed and asks them to change the subject.

But so what? Rina looks out of the window. The countryside is still shrouded in fog, but it's beginning to give way to the pallid grey of morning. The bushes by the side of the track are edged with white threads of ice. Carla is still fast asleep, sprawled on the seat with her legs apart and swaying with the movement of the train.

'Rina,' says Carla (when she's not asleep she's got an explanation for everything), 'you have to understand, there's a big difference between being scared of something and having a phobia. It's like the difference between bronchitis and pneumonia.' They're fighting their way through the jostling crowds at the Central Station. Carla is up ahead, suddenly wide awake and fending her way through the crowd. Rina follows along in her wake.

'What you've got is fears, not phobias,' says Carla, turning back so that Rina can hear. Even though they're no more than a yard apart she virtually has to shout to make herself heard. People are coming from all sides, some of them carrying parcels and some big bags and suitcases; there are porters and their trolleys all over the place, getting in everyone's way.

'I have fears too, you know. For a start, I always worry I'm going to get poisoned. That's why I hardly ever go out to eat, and when I do I only eat things that I can check for myself. Salads and so on.'

Just before getting off the train Rina had put the magazine she found on the train into her handbag. With its title protruding, it seems to issue an order to the world: 'Wake Up!'

'I agree . . . Wake up!' A man's got tired of being stuck behind her, and he pushes rudely past her.

'I can't stand cabbages either, but that's not a fear or a

phobia. That's just because cabbages are disgusting.' Carla is shouting again, to make herself heard. As the breath leaves her mouth it hangs in the air as a small white cloud.

People are jostling and bumping into one another as they pour in from all sides. So many people are jammed onto the escalator that you stand a good chance of being knocked over. Rina suddenly feels dizzy. It must be the cold. Or the fact that she hasn't had breakfast. Or all these people around . . . She holds onto the moving handrail as the escalator takes her slowly down. Her head is spinning; she feels weak at the knees. She rests one arm on Carla's shoulder on the step below her. She feels like she's about to faint.

'Claustrophobia,' says Carla, as she takes her by the elbow and steers her towards the nearest bar. 'Fear of crowds and enclosed spaces.'

Pier Vittorio Tondelli

The Station Bar

It's been cold and pissing rain for days now, and the icy showers mean that the best place to spend the evenings is at the tables of the station bar, with its feeble grey lighting, its mouldering neon signs, its railway smell, and the yellow-red dust that stains the windows. Hanging out, just hanging out, perched on the bar-stools, and bored, just bored. Lousy bloody winter, night after night at the station, talking, playing cards, with a full glass in front of you, and all your friends just hanging out too, and how else are you going to get through December? Just make sure you've got a full bottle and plenty of dope.

During the winter, by afternoon the station forecourt is already blue with the headlights of buses pulling in through the fog and offloading hordes of schoolkids and students. On days like this you arrive early, about five o'clock; but when the weather clears a bit, with the wind whistling down the tracks and blowing rubbish down the streets, and the mountains, in the distance down south, standing out against the sky, then you go later, when the only people still kicking their heels on the station concourse are a handful of conscript soldiers and the occasional drunken prostitute, and the kids have gone, and with them the sound of chattering and laughing and giggling over their teenie-mags, and the girls with their fingers already calloused from so many Saturdays and Sundays and afternoons doing the sewing for their mums. But this evening the station concourse is bustling and alive with the sound of people, like the foyer of some big theatre.

Josie comes here every day, regular as clockwork, tripping

along and shaking out the long mane of hair that he tucks up under his Peruvian beret; he takes a quick look around the station and picks his way deftly through the small groups of spotty students who come in from the surrounding countryside to study at the technical colleges here in town, and who have stocky legs and thick thighs, and bums that are so rounded and solid that it looks as if the muscles packed into them are about to burst out of their blue jeans. They used to come in on Sundays too, on coaches that would trawl round the country-side and ferry them off to the local nightspots, but the bus service was suspended because on the return journey there would always be bras and panties flying all over the place, and sex sessions on the bench seats at the back of the buses, everyone screwing, even between the males . . .

Josie walks through the middle of them and into the corridor that leads down to the waiting room and then to the station bar at the end. Through the window that runs the length of the corridor he looks towards the tracks and sees the young lads standing on the platform waiting for the local diesel service, hopping from one foot to the other like they're doing a jogging session, and jostling each other, and laughing behind the scarves that they've pulled up over their mouths and noses. He stops to light a cigarette. He peeks into the waiting room, more or less by force of habit; many's the time he's scored on those benches . . . these cracked walls could tell a tale or two—stories of blinding piss-ups, and violence, and beatings, and paranoias that last for days on end without eating or pissing, curled up in the corner, wrapped in his jacket and imagining that he can see people flying through the window in the corridor, and trains all flashing by like lightning, shattering the silence of his trip, and the walls seeming to stretch out all around, and then the inane chatter of the social worker who comes to take him away—'You'll be all right, you'll live, you're young, you'll manage, you'll find a way . . .' What a load of crap. Fuck off and leave me alone.

On the bench, a lone tramp is eating a husk of parmesan with some bread, taking care not to waste a single crumb. Josie looks at him. The tramp licks his fingers and wraps the leftovers in a piece of tin-foil which he then puts into a cigarette packet and tucks into the pocket of his black overcoat. Josie passes him by and continues down the corridor towards the light of the station buffet which appears through the glass door at the end. He rubs his eyes as he goes in, and orders a cappuccino at the cash-desk on the left. The bar-tender comments sarcastically: 'You're up early today.' Josie gives him a passing greeting. 'Seen anybody?'

'Only the tall one tonight. He was in a while ago . . .' He looks around. He can't see him. 'Never mind, I'm sure he'll be back.' He turns the steam handle and the milk bubbles and hisses.

'Did I tell you to boil it?' Josie grumbles. 'Mind what you're doing.'

The bar-tender pours the frothing milk into the cup. Josie takes a sip and wipes the froth from his beard. 'Was he on his own?'

'How should I know? He asked for you and then he went off looking for something . . .' He looks up. 'Oh, here he comes again.'

Josie checks the big mirror in front of him and sees Bibo coming over. He turns round, and Bibo comes up and gets an arm round his shoulder. 'Jesus, Josie, I've been waiting for a bloody hour. I've got fifty thousand lire on me . . . Get a move on, I'm busting.' He looks at him and waits for an answer. Josie looks at him impassively. 'I've got fifty thousand, I said, and it's burning a hole in my pocket . . . Come on, man, don't fuck about . . .'

Josie takes him by the arm. 'Listen, don't start shouting the odds with all these people around. Let me finish my coffee first . . .'

'Hang on—have you got the stuff or haven't you? You're not going to fuck me about, are you? I mean—you are carrying, aren't you? You aren't going to keep me hanging about and then tell me you're not carrying? If you've got fuck-all, then tell me and I'll take the train and find someone else, I don't give a shit . . . Seriously, though, you have got some, haven't you?'

'Calm down for a second! Are you going to be all right on your feet?'

Bibo stops. He turns away from the bar and chuckles. 'Jesus, of course I can manage. I'm not drunk, you know . . . What d'you think's going to happen . . .? That I'm going to fall over like a bag of shit? I've got the fucking money, never had so much money on me all at one time!'

Josie smiles. 'Just as well,' he thinks.

They head over towards the bar stools in the old self-service that's been taken out of use. It's at the other side of the counter, so they have to go down the whole length of the bar to get to it, and this means meeting people. Including shitheads. There's Molly, for instance, leering a big hello, still drunk from the night before, and asking them for a hundred lire. They tell her to fuck off and call over the bar-tender to bring them two Camparis and a couple of pastries to cheer themselves up.

Molly is sixty if she's a day, and she sits at a corner of the long stretch of tables. She's got an old cardboard suitcase next to her, all tied up with string, and stuck on it a sticker from Lugano, but she's got fuck-all inside, just in case someone comes and tries to rob her when she's pissed and fast asleep. So she carries her wardrobe by wearing it—one jumper on top of another, one pair of trousers on top of another, so that when she's sitting down she looks more like a tub of lard in her old black overcoat and the faded headscarf that she always wears. She's got no teeth, and always seems to have a fag-end sticking out from the corner of her mouth. On her feet she wears a pair of black hiking boots with yellow laces and worn rubber soles, and they're too big for her because she bought them extra-large so's she can wear at least four pairs of socks inside. At this precise moment she looks like she's pissed paralytic, sitting there with a glass of Folonari in front of her and snoring quietly with her head slumped forward. Every now and then she shifts position and makes as if to scratch her whiskers, but she's not sleeping—as usual she's wide awake, with one hand on her suitcase and the other stretched across the edge of the table in the hopes that some mug's going to give her some money.

Molly and Josie aren't the best of friends, because there's an unresolved matter of a hundred thousand lire which Josie says she stole from him, that time when she disappeared off for ten days or more and nobody knew where she'd gone, and they all thought that maybe she was dead, passed out in the wine shop in Via Bassi. But when she came back to the station bar, even the most dimwitted among them could see that she'd taken off to Lugano, because she had a Lugano sticker on her manky old suitcase, all bright and shiny, and her just fucking stupid. There was a tremendous row, with Josie grabbing her and kicking her and spitting in her face, but then Johnny arrived, and sorted the whole business out by giving Josie a hundred thousand, but Josie was still angry about having been ripped off, and as far as he was concerned the money didn't settle the matter. But Molly always denied the whole weird story, and always said 'Nae way . . . It's niver true . . .', in her Mantuan accent, which is even more slurred because she's got no teeth, and when she talks she sounds like an open sewer with her never-ending refrain of 'Gi's a hundred lire . . .' which she must have picked up from some old tramp somewhere. So bad blood remained, even though in the station bar grudges never last long, because life is life, in other words one shithouse after another, and when you have to swallow shit day after day, after a while you get used to the taste of it, and you even begin to want it.

Josie and Bibo were sitting on their bar-stools, smoking and knocking back the drink.

'Listen, Josie, I've got the cash here. I want at least two deals off you, and the sooner I get them, the sooner you can have the money, and then I'll disappear, and you won't see me again. OK? . . . Come on, what's keeping you?'

Josie looks him in the eye. 'Nothing doing. I've got nothing, for the moment . . .' Unruffled.

'What? You mean you've been keeping me here on cold turkey for nothing, you've got fuck-all to give me?'

'Like I say, nothing doing at the moment. I'm cleaned out. Try again around midnight and you can have as much as you want.'

Bibo swears and downs the rest of his drink in one gulp. 'OK, see you later,' he says, getting up. 'Why the hell didn't you tell me straight away and get it over with?'

Josie lights a cigarette. 'I was trying to tell you . . . Look, I tell you what, for fifty notes, I'll give you three.'

Bibo stops in his tracks. Raises three fingers. 'You're not kidding me on, are you?'

'Listen, Bibo, when have I ever tried to cheat you? Jesus, we started out together; have I ever done the dirty on you? When have I ever given you a bum deal? I love every hair on your head, friend. Serious business. We're friends, OK . . .?' he chuckles.

'OK,' says Bibo, but now he's off to see if he can find someone else, because now he's got cash in his hand he's got to spend it. He'll be back again the next day looking to score, although where the hell he'll get the money from, who knows . . .? But he'll turn up anyway.

Josie's eyes follow him out of the bar and down the corridor. At the end of the corridor he sees the outline of a white raincoat. It stops for a word with Bibo. Josie lets out a muttered curse and is about to slip off the bar-stool when the raincoat enters the station buffet, goes over, reaches out a hand, and says, 'Hi there, Josie!'

Another muttered curse, this time swallowed. Shit! 'Well hi, Johnny, what's new?'

'Let's sit down, OK?'

Josie nods. They sit down at a table not far from where Molly's sitting. 'Do you fancy a smoke?' says Johnny. He pulls out a packet of Lucky Strike and hands one over. He goes to give one to Molly too, because she's been leaning forward ever since she saw him come in and is grovelling so low that she's almost banging her forehead on her glass. But Josie raises his hand and takes the cigarette out of Johnny's hand. 'Don't give anything to that slag.'

Johnny laughs. 'OK, let's talk about us. How's it going? How are you doing for stuff, these days? Good? Bad . . .? Come on, what's the word?'

'Hmmm . . . Johnny, get this straight. I haven't seen a decent score in this shithouse for a month, and you know it, because you've got the dealing circuit under your belt, and there's fuck-all we can do about it. If you want to put the screws on the

Calabrians, that's up to you, but either way, whether you win or they win, you won't find anyone of the old gang round here any more. All disappeared, wiped out, gone . . .! So don't fuck about asking if the bad times are getting the better of us. What's it to you, eh?'

A ring of cigarette smoke rises to the ceiling. 'Forget it, Josie. By the way, you haven't forgotten our other little business, have you? Do you remember how much it is?'

Josie sighs. 'Five hundred, Johnny. You ask me every time you see me, for fuck's sake!'

'That's just so's you don't forget.' He stubs out his cigarette. 'Do you think you can get the money together tonight?'

'If I had five hundred thousand, you wouldn't see me for dust!' Brusquely said. Johnny parts his lips in an attempt at a smile. 'Like Molly?' Josie mutters a curse again. Touché! Hit the nail on the head, there . . . Nobody messes with Johnny. Not if you're sensible. Josie knows the rules of the game—never run off with other people's money, or at least never come back if you do, and however far away he ran now, he'd never survive without the station bar, he'd be right back there the very first time he hit a spot of bother. In any other town, he'd have to make new contacts, and that would mean trailing all over the place, spending sleepless nights for weeks on end; he'd have to make the acquaintance of new cops, the insides of new police stations, start everything over from the beginning, with all the beatings, the kickings and the fear. No, Josie's not the sort to run off just like that. He will one day, but only when he's sure that he's got it in him to survive without the station bar. For ever, whatever hard times he runs into. Once he leaves, never to come back again. Cut out and blow.

'Honestly, Johnny, I've got nothing on me tonight,' he says at last. 'Absolutely fuck-all.'

'OK, OK . . .'

'I saw you talking with Bibo. Did you give him anything?'

Johnny gives him a hard look. 'You don't think I carry the shit around with me, do you?'

Why doesn't he just fuck off . . .? Why does this arsehole have to come round bothering us at the station bar? Between you and me, who exactly does Johnny think he is, with his fluttering Burberry mac? What's he after? What the fuck do you think you're playing at, Johnny?

'Tell you what, though, Josie—one of these days we're going to have to get this money business sorted out, in your own interest as much as mine.'

'OK, OK,' he interrupts. 'Johnny, I know that. I also know that I'm paying you interest. So why make an issue out of it? I owe you the money, and as soon as I get it I'll give it to you. It's as good as yours already. You can count on it, eh? You know you'll always find me here, you know where I live, so what does it cost you to give me a bit of extra time . . .?'

'Well it was you who said there's hard times around, not me. All I'm saying is that tonight it's six months to the day . . .'

Josie bursts out laughing. 'Fuck, it's its birthday. Let's celebrate, Johnny, what do you say? We can have a party for the anniversary of the money I owe you. You're a wild man, Johnny!! Come on, let's have a drink. You can pay. The drinks are on you.'

Johnny gets up, sticks his hands in his coat pockets, and hisses some lethal comment. Something perfect, just right for the moment. 'I wouldn't laugh if I were you . . . You think it's funny, eh . . .? You wait and see . . .' They look at each other, with an air of seriousness. 'One month, Josie. One month and not a day longer. OK? Here, have a fag on me.' He chucks the packet across the table, and gets a last look at Josie's face. 'See you soon.'

Up your arse, you fucking pig. Josie takes a cigarette and lights it. Molly cackles; nobody needs to tell her what's going on because she understood perfectly. You can't keep secrets in the station bar. But she curses Johnny because he never gave her a cigarette. She swears behind his back, gobs into her hand-kerchief, and then watches him as he emerges from the place with his short, tight steps and his buttocks clenched as if he had an urgent case of the runs [. . .].

Josie goes out onto the station forecourt. The fog's come down so thick that you can't even seen the edges of the square. He sees the passing silhouettes of a couple of people, and over to one side there's the 'Vigilantes', the two night security guards sitting in their Ford. The courtesy light is on inside. Probably listening to the radio and smoking. At the wheel there'll be William, who's fiftyish with a big beer gut; one time he let off his gun in the station bar during a row, and they suspended him from duty, and it looked like they'd got shot of him for ever, but then the next year he came back acting flash again, and ordering drinks without paying, and making as if to reach for his Smith and Wesson, like he wasn't a man to be messed with, so everyone started calling him the 'Sheriff', and he loved it, like being called 'Your Excellency', 'Your Honour' . . . May you rot in hell, Sheriff William! Josie goes back to the station concourse, and sits on the bench. It won't be long before Guerrino arrives—about half an hour, assuming that the train's on time. Then there'll be enough stuff to deal in for at least a month, and life'll get a bit easier, and it'll be like the good times are back again, and there'll be plenty to go round. Whammo, and we'll all be in heaven , . . come on, Rino, get here real fucking soon, you angel!

And while Josie is sitting there killing time, Bibo comes in again looking wiped out and sits down in front of him. He looks a wreck and just about collapses in a heap. 'Hey, Bibo, what's up?' says Josie, taking him up in his arms. 'What's the matter, old pal? Did you miss me, did you? What's the matter? What happened?' He pulls back to look him in the face, but then he feels him stiffening as if he's about to pass out, so he makes him sit down, and when he finally takes a close look he sees that Bibo is just about done for, although he's still holding up one hand with the fifty notes clutched between his fingers. Fuck, he really is on cold turkey. Hard bloody times. How goes, Bibo?

Bibo pulls himself together a bit and tries to sit up, breathing heavily.

'I'll tell you what happened. I made it from the square to here. Fuck, I made it, Josie, I won't let the bad times get the better of me . . . fuck the lot of them!'

'Hang on, because Rino will be here soon. Hang on, and it'll pass. If you're not up to it, why don't you call someone . . . How are you doing with the CIM?'

'In the shit, if you really want to know,' Bibo fumes. 'They want me to sell my soul for a bit of fucking methadone. They go on about how you have to say you'll behave yourself: "I'll stop seeing the same friends . . . I'll move house . . . I'll go away and never come back . . . I'll find a job, and I'll never again be the same fucking person." ' He stops. They fall silent for a moment. Bibo seems to have recovered. He continues: 'But it was a good bloody circuit, more or less you could scrape by, in times like these . . . Then I nicked ten packs of methadone. Fuck, man—there they were, fifty little tubes, just sitting there, a dead cinch to have them away, and so I did. Too fucking right! Someone called her from the other room, and I was straight in there, quick as a flash—put them in my pocket, and off out the window. Fuck—two hundred notes-worth, easy as piss, and now I could score some decent stuff, and go sell the shit stuff to the bums in the Bar Sozza; so I jumped out of the window, like I said, and bang, I ran straight into the Sheriff, bang into his big beer-gut. And he gave me a fucking bruise right here, look, with the butt of his gun, and then he punched me round the head, and took me back in, and then they found the packs, and my little scheme was up in smoke, shit fuck and bollocks, and so was the two hundred notes . . . last I've seen of that . . . I tell you, I could feel them, right there in my hands, all cool and crinkly . . . And now, gone . . . Just like that . . . Shit! Would have been nice, wouldn't it!' Josie chuckles. He asks if he wants a bit of smoke, to keep his end up, or a Campari to cheer him up. Bibo replies that he can wait—they'd best be off to Platform 3, because any minute now their dealer would be arriving.

The train pulls in at the platform, looming up through the dark fog with a whistle and its wheels clattering over the points. They station themselves at the top of the two sets of subway stairs, one at one end and one at the other. Bibo's the first to see Rino. He runs to meet him. Josie follows. He nods a greeting. Nice to see you. Then he see Rino's face is clouded, and even from a distance he realizes that something's wrong, badly wrong.

'Nothing doing, son . . . What can I say . . . Skippy promised me, the cunt, and I gave him a deposit, no problem, everything was OK, but then he rang me today and I went to meet him, and it turns out they picked up his courier, in Verona, so what can we do, they arrested him, you know how it is, it doesn't always go smoothly, maybe they were keeping an eye on him, so anyway, well, nothing doing, not for the next few days, fuck-all.'

Bibo doesn't know what to say. He turns pale. He had the money in his hand; he had his armband in his jacket pocket all ready to jack up; but instead there's nothing doing. Only emptiness and cold. Josie curses, kicks out viciously at a pile of cardboard boxes, once, twice, three times. He curses again, angrily. He clenches his fists. But Rino's right, there's fuck-all to be done about it. Best to go back into the warm. Back to the bar-stools in the feeble half-light of the station bar, and chill out.

There they are, like whipped dogs, with Bibo looking white as a sheet and getting whiter by the minute. He says if he gets another squeeze he'll shit himself, because he doesn't have the strength to control his muscles. And he's getting more and more turned in on himself and useless, and Josie knows that any minute now he's going to blow a fuse, because it's two days since he last had a hit, and he's not going to last much longer. 'Rino, what are we going to do if Bibo blows out?' he mutters. Rino doesn't reply. He just drinks his grappa and says: 'Take him to hospital.'

'Fuck off—that'd be like hell for the poor bastard. He hasn't passed out. He's just cold turkey, that's all. Just cold turkey.'

Meantime Bibo has begun to sweat. He's wiping his forehead, over and over again, and looking at his damp hands, and stammering that he feels hot and that he's shivering, and can't keep his back straight. Josie takes him under his armpits and hauls him up. 'Let's put him on a bench. At least he can lie down for a bit. I'll go and see if I can find some stuff. I won't be long. You keep an eye on him, OK? If you see him passing out, fuck off out of it. Leave him there, just go, 'cos otherwise it means trouble for all of us.'

Rino leaves the bar, with Bibo staggering like a drunkard.

The Calabrians are still sitting there drinking and passing the time of day with Vanina and Liza and Molly. Josie sits in a corner. He watches as Salvino raises his glass.

'What's wrong with your pal?' they ask.

'How should I know . . . maybe he's got problems . . . probably tired . . . stoned . . . no idea . . .'

Salvino pours Josie a drink and waits for him to finish it. He looks at him, and Josie meets his eye, and what he sees is one of those looks that are the death of anyone who's ever seen them, because when he looks at you like that you just know that you can count on him, absolutely, whether it's for small-time wheeler-dealing, or the big stuff. 'Come on, let's take a walk.'

They get up from the table. As they reach the door, Josie speaks. 'I need to score, straight away. How are you for stuff?' Salvino shrugs his shoulders as if to say 'Come along with me.'

On the west side of the station, beyond the toilets, there's a big open space with sidings, a kind of shunting area, leading to a sorting shed. Further on, beyond some more sidings, you reach a second space, a lot smaller than the first, where there's a few passenger carriages parked up. There are four carriages in the yard, the kind without compartments, where you go straight in and sit on hard wooden benches that are as cold as marble. They appear intermittently out of the mist, in the light coming from the flashing neon sign of the bowling alley at the back of the station, on the other side of the feed-road leading up to the road bridge, and the effect of it is that the carriages seem to come and go in a dim yellow light.

Salvino knows which of the carriage windows is open, and pulls it down with a jerk. He waits till the neon sign flashes off, and climbs in. Josie follows him. They sit down, facing each other. Salvino gestures to him to keep quiet and freeze while the security guard does his rounds. They watch as the beam of his torch probes the fog and pokes around between the rails and the piles of sleepers and the purple lights of the lanterns by the points, and then disappears off towards the sorting shed.

'OK,' says Salvino, 'now we're OK. I'm going down the end for a moment, to get something. You roll the joint.' He tosses a small piece of hash into his lap. Josie pulls out his papers, and rolls the joint while Salvino rummages around in the dark at the end of the carriage. What the hell's he doing? Then Salvino returns with a sleeping bag and a grimy blanket. The carriage is freezing cold. Josie smiles to himself. OK, here we go. They lie down the length of the gangway, side by side, gazing at the roof of the carriage, while the yellow light from the bowling alley comes in through the windows and seems to pulsate. They light the joint. As they pass it to and fro, Josie explains: 'I want heroin. If you don't have any, I'm off. No point hanging about.'

Salvino takes in a deep breath, closes his eyes and holds the smoke down in his lungs. Then he breathes it out, all in one go, right to the end. 'Relax.'

'All right, how about now? Sooner the better.'

Salvino passes him one envelope, then another. Josie sits up abruptly. He sniffs it to check the quality, pulls up his sleeve, opens the stuff, tightens his armband, and shoots up. Salvino watches him from the floor, with a spaced-out look in his eyes. He's stoned. When he sees Josie pulling out the needle, he undoes his fly and pulls his cock out. He's got a hard-on. He starts masturbating as Josie comes over next to him. Now that they're close to each other, Salvino touches Josie on the arse. Josie turns round and gets down. He shuts his eyes. *OK, you fucking Mafia creep, now do what the fuck you want! I'm all yours!*

By the time Josie reaches the waiting room where he left Bibo and Rino, it's already late. The only signs of life on the station concourse are the menacing figure of the Sheriff, an itinerant Moroccan sleeping in one corner, and the ticket clerk behind his armoured glass. Even the waiting room is deserted. Josie sits down on his usual stool in the bar, not thinking of anything, and sets about demolishing a beer and a toasted sandwich. The immigrants have gone off, taking Vanina with them. Only Molly is left sitting there, like she's got bricks up her arse. Plus a couple of young lads dealing hash, and some old men. Someone touches him on the shoulder. He looks up.

It's Liza.

'Hey, Josie—your pals are waiting for you in the toilets, so what are you doing hanging out here?'

'Do me a favour, piss off, will you . . .'

'Come on, off you go! Chop-chop! Come on! ' She propels him out of the station bar.

Inside the toilets there's nobody to be seen. Josie curses. He turns towards Liza angrily. Then he hears a groan, and goes towards the half-open door of the last cubicle in the row. He opens it. Inside is Bibo, with his eyes out on stalks, and Rino holding him under the armpits and cursing. He's undone his trousers. 'For fuck's sake, Josie, why did you have to dump him on me? He's shat himself, he's got the fucking runs . . . Look, the cunt's shat on me too!'

'Relax, relax!'

'Well do something. Have you found the horse?'

'Yeah, sure . . .' He holds up the envelope of heroin. As soon as they can get it into Bibo's veins he'll be right as rain, and then they'll be able to take him somewhere, or get onto social services so that someone else can see to him, or maybe just put him to bed. But meanwhile Bibo has started groaning and babbling. He's getting stomach cramps and says he can't control his guts and that if they don't hold him up properly he's going to fall down the pan and drown in his own shit. He's convinced he's going to die. *Rinoooo, hold my arm, for fuck's sake, I'm falling!!!*

Josie gears himself up to deal with the situation. He pushes Bibo's sleeves up, but then curses. 'You've got no veins, for fuck's sake, Bibo, you've got no more good veins!' Rino shouts at him to get a move on, because he can't stand it for much longer. 'Don't just stand there—do something!'

Josie tightens the elastic round Bibo's arm, but he still can't get his veins up. His arm is a mass of livid marks, and further up there are yellow blotches of congealed blood. Nothing to be done. So he grabs his cock, and begins to work it up and down, trying to masturbate him, trying to give him a hard-on. And all the time Bibo is sweating and drooling and shitting watery shit all over the place and begging them to keep him away from the hole in the pan. He's sliding down, slowly sliding down, for God's sake . . . he's covered in shit up to his waist, and he's digging his nails into Rino's arms . . . and Rino curses and looks at Josie, where he's got Bibo's cock in his hand. 'What are you doing? You're fucking crazy, man.'

'Shut up, idiot!' he shouts. 'Piss off and get the syringe ready!'

Liza peers round the door and lets out an 'Oooh'. 'Stand by the fucking door,' Rino shouts, 'because if anyone comes in, we're fucked!'

Liza covers her mouth as if she's about to spew, and backs off. Josie pulls Bibo up by the hair, holds him towards him and buries his face in his chest. 'The fucking thing won't get hard . . . Hey, Bibo, come on, make an effort. Are you hearing me? That's a mighty cock you've got, Bibo, and it's getting bigger, it's getting hard . . . Put yourself behind it, Bibo, you bastard! I've got it in my hand, I'm rubbing it up and down. This is your cock, baby. Just think of all the cunt you've had with this prick of yours . . . all the cunt in the station bar . . . and they loved it, the slags . . . Remember how they drool and squirm when you stick it up them . . . screw them with your great hard cock . . . up and down you went, Bibo, just like now, in and out . . . Come on Bibo, get it up, for God's sake . . . what's happened to your little pistol . . .? Remember how you used to go wanking for the old boys, eh, Bibo? Remember what you used to do for the old tossers . . . how you used to show your cock off in the park, how you used your prick, how you used to do it with the dirty old bastards! You used to put on a good show, Bibo . . . with the dirty old bastards . . . you and your cock, Bibo! And they'd be drooling and showering you with hundred-lire pieces, and you'd pick them all up . . . All that money, Bibo, all thanks to your mighty engine . . . Hey, Bibo, this is your cock here, baby . . . Look how it's swelling up, Bibo . . . gettting bigger . . . You're a king of the fucks, Bibo, the best . . . You're screwing now, it's coming up, getting bigger, getting wings, Bibo, it's big, it's hard, it's fat . . . Up and down, for fuck's sake, come on! Up and down, Jesus, remember how they used to drool . . . how the women used to suck you in with their cunts, this cock of yours, and you used to whack it right in, balls and all, and they'd go all fucking wobbly and start moaning. Do you hear them, Bibo? "Come, come! Now, now, come!" Go on, Bibo, we're there, it's getting hard, it's hard, it's in orbit! It's a rocket! Come on, well done!!! Bibo!!! You're flying now, you're on your way, fucking brilliant, Bibo . . . Shaft it, Bibooo!!!'

And then, in with the needle, zac!

Over on Platform 3 Guerrino's going back to Bologna, and Josie's there to see him off. He waits for the train to slip away down the icy rails across the plain. He looks over at the red, rust-stained neon-lit windows of the bar and sees the rancid shadow of Molly, coughing her guts up and drinking her cheap white wine, with one hand firmly on her suitcase . . . Bibo hunched on a stool, with his head buried in his arms, more or less out for the count. Josie goes out onto the forecourt feeling done for. His head's aching, he feels disgusted. Then he remembers Salvino . . . he'll be breathing down his neck from now on . . . but he'd had no choice . . . Fucking stupid hard times, these . . . poxy times . . . You can't even score yourself a decent joint to get you through the day . . . and you're always having to deal with shitheads . . . Johnny and his raincoat . . . that cunt of a 'sheriff' . . . and the old witch, always there, always with her suitcase sitting next to her, even though she never so much as shifts her arse off that fucking bench . . . why don't you just fuck off, you old slag . . .! But when all's said and done, who gives a shit about Johnny, and the whole gang in the station bar . . .? I want to survive . . . OK, so I've been in the shit since the day I was born. It doesn't matter, though, because something's bound to turn up . . . something will turn out right, and it doesn't matter what happens now, or the day after tomorrow, or the day after that, because one of these days things are going to change, and I'll find myself on my own two feet and I won't have to deal with all these fucking tossers at the station bar, and I'll find myself a good woman, and I'll have kids, and I'll pack it in with the drugs, while I've still got some veins and a bit of money left, and a bit of arse to trade, because, because, because . . .

In the station forecourt the fog is clearing from between the streetlamps. Josie sets off home, staggering slightly. Almost morning. The next night he'll be back at the station bar as usual

. . . or maybe he'll leave this city, and everyone in it, and he'll leave Bibo too. Right now he doesn't realize that he's so tired, with so much fear and anger to get out of his system, that his legs feel like the wooden crutches of some poor invalid of a long-forgotten war.

Marina Mizzau

How to Make a Martini

'Two Martinis, please.'

The barman poured us two glasses of vermouth and added a drop of gin to each.

'That's not how to make a Martini,' said my friend. 'It should be the other way round.' He gave the impression that this was a sort of generally accepted principle, in an attempt to distance himself ironically from his own statement, but people aren't always sensitive to these things.

By way of clarification I supplied the smile that my friend had forgotten to add, but it was not reciprocated. 'Well anyway, let's say some people do it differently.' I qualified my friend's statement, because I felt that this was the kind of thing that starts rows.

'That is how you make a Martini,' said the barman, a note of annoyance in his voice, but also of entreaty.

'Not necessarily,' I observed, slightly hurt that my offer of conciliation had been so peremptorily rejected.

'They're right,' said a man sitting at a nearby table doing some figures, who appeared to be the manager of the bar.

'That *is* how you make a Martini,' the barman repeated and by now the tone was simply of annoyance.

'On the contrary. That's the way *you* make it,' said the other. 'In the best bars they make it with all gin and just a touch of vermouth. Everyone knows that.'

'Anyway, they're fine the way you made them,' we said, because things were starting to get out of hand. But it was obvious that there was no such easy way out of it.

'A Martini is made the way I just made it,' number one retorted, addressing his remark to number two. 'If they want it some other way, I'll do it, but then it won't be a Martini. I've been making them for twenty years, I should know.'

'In that case you've been making them *wrong* for twenty years,' replied number two, and the way he said it was as though he had been waiting twenty years for the chance to say so. Then, in order to make his victory the sweeter, despite the risk of giving number one a break, he called to a passing third party: 'Hey—how would you say a Martini should be made?'

Whether fortuitously or not, the third party came up with the required answer: 'Two thirds gin and one third vermouth. Everyone knows that. I'm surprised at you even asking.'

Number two was visibly happy with this reply, and with the last bit in particular, because it gave him the chance to turn a defence of himself into a further attack on number one: 'It's not me. It's Gianni. He says a Martini should be only vermouth.'

'I never said only vermouth,' said number one. And then, not content with having set the record straight, he plumped for outright perjury. 'I said half and half.'

One half-lie having been matched with another, the matter might have been considered settled—half gin and half vermouth, half victory and half defeat. But number two wasn't giving in so easily.

'What do you mean, half and half?! In Harry's Bar they do it properly: they put the vermouth in the shaker with the ice, they shake it, and then they tip out the vermouth and pour in the gin. That way you're left with just the flavour of the vermouth.'

'A Martini is vermouth plus gin. Otherwise it's not a Martini,' number one decreed. He had calmed down by now, but would still brook no disagreement. Since he'd been left with no way out, he was retreating into dogma.

'Just the flavour of the vermouth,' repeated number two, almost crowing.

By now number three was rising to virtuoso heights. 'What they actually do is wave the closed bottle of vermouth over the top of the gin,' he said. 'The bottle has to be kept closed.'

It was an old joke, but everyone laughed, ourselves included.

Unfortunately nobody laughed in quite the right way: number two and number three passed up the opportunity of laughing with a sense of self-irony at the enormity of what they had said, thereby inviting number one to a moment of cathartic solidarity, and preferred instead to laugh in celebration of their complicity in having made an idiot of number one; number one was laughing sarcastically at the absurdity of what number three had said, and we were trying to ease the atmosphere by laughing in such a way as to convert the others' laughter to a higher plane of meaning, but it was obvious that we were not succeeding, because everyone was continuing to laugh in ways that were contradictory and therefore wrong.

'In America they probably do it the way you say,' resumed number one. So far from giving ground, this was actually a statement of manifest contempt.

'That's right. Perhaps it's the American way,' I said, trying to carve an opening through his contempt in the hope of finding space for mediation.

'Real Martinis are made the way I make them.' This was number one again, and his insistence on shunning linguistic relativism suggested a degree of essentialism that some might say was the start of the whole wretched business.

'And in Italy many people do it the American way,' I thought it necessary to add, in order to round off my intervention.

At this point number one's wife intervened. 'Of course he's right,' she said, referring to her husband and turning to the assembled company. 'It's obvious.'

'You haven't the first idea what we're talking about,' shouted number one. 'What do you know about Martinis? Nothing!'

'Fair enough . . . How do *you* say a Martini should be made?' number two asked, with a view to bringing her into the discussion, having presumably sensed that there was some fun to be had here.

But while the question had been directed to her, it was obviously risky for all concerned. As regards number one it was obvious that there were historical antecedents which meant either that he couldn't expect too much support from his wife, or that for some reason he preferred not to avail himself of her help. So he moved to preempt her involvement.

'What does she know about it?'

'All right, then, what do *you* reckon?' she inquired cautiously, and from her caution you could see the likely outcome of whatever it was she answered. You could also see it from the fact that her husband was obviously intent on stopping her answering.

'You know nothing about Martinis. Or cocktails,' he said.

'Well, on balance I would say that there are probably two ways of doing it.' Number three seemed to think that things were getting out of hand.

By now it was too late for any possibility of mediation. 'The way you two say it should be made,' said number one, increasingly revealing his ignorance of the pliable definitional qualities of language, 'is not Martini.'

'Well, actually, it's the only way,' shouted number two.

'The only way among civilized people,' added number three, suddenly repenting of his moment of generosity.

We had already finished our cocktails, but we couldn't bring ourselves to leave. It was as if we felt that certain disaster would follow in the wake of our departure.

Enrico Palandri

PEC

Four months had gone by since Gregorio had submitted his
application to the central office of public certification, as
required by law. As usual, he had left it until the last extension
of the last deadline and for hours, amidst a throng of other
latecomers, he had elbowed and sniffed his way past aged and
youthful bodies of either sex, going from one counter to the
next until his application on official paper had at last been
forwarded. Forwarded! he thought silently as he edged his way
closer to the glass partition, how apt a term! Over on the other
side of the high counters, out of range of the odours of us
citizens crowded together, you clerks in your spacious rooms
seem to have all the time and leisure in the world on this
summer's morning: you joke together, consult together,
question us when we finally get to speak to you and lavish your
advice upon us, we who don't understand the purpose of these
papers, what's missing from them, whether we have all that's
needed, whether they're all in order! Do you have your
residence certificate? your birth certificate? your certificate of
discharge from local military headquarters? and the three
authenticated photos?

It's all here! You don't throw yourself unprepared into such a
fray!

The clerk had reluctantly gathered up Gregorio's file and
passed it on. Down there in the dark heart of the state, they
would now have begun to prepare that document for him. In
the meantime Gregorio had been issued with a small pink
counterfoil, similar to a cloakroom ticket, and he had returned

smiling to the street, thinking to himself that after all, this new document was necessary, the clerks were doing their job, the world was spinning as it should. After the pounding of elbows, he was rising like a well-kneaded dough on a window sill in the euphoric breeze of a benevolence full of illusions.

He and his file had already gone beyond the counter, he had overcome the bureaucratic hurdles which ensure that the fringes of society are kept prisoners of confusion, he had registered with the law, he was on the right side, as his pink slip of paper attested. Comforted, he thought of the place he had allotted to it in his wallet among the film club membership cards, so that he'd be sure to have it with him always, for with that little slip of paper he could survive his flat being burgled or even burnt down. If he was ever robbed, he could hand over every single penny to the thieves just as long as they gave him back his little pink slip, which would be of no value to them anyway. Such thoughts were greatly reassuring: it was as if he'd been offered a handhold on a galleon during a storm, when up until the day before he'd been kept on deck, easy prey to the sudden waves. With enlightened detachment, he thought appreciatively of the fact that offices nowadays condescended to provide citizens with a counterfoil which testified to their successful completion of an obstacle course of office counters and to their humility in submitting to them, so that even before one actually possessed the new document, one could feel oneself, as indeed he felt himself now, to be on the right side of the law.

It was said that today's queue would truly be the last for those who had waited in it. The documents served, in fact, to obtain a plastic card which, thanks to a microprocessor, was capable of storing an enormous amount of data: from registry information to health records, criminal record, current accounts, detailed information on one's career, just about everything. And it was no bigger than a credit card!

It could be used from a public phone box to pay bills or buy a car, it could function as your curriculum vitae and, like all telecommunications these days, it was accepted all over the world. It also emitted a brief, personalized musical phrase and

Gregorio, who was a music lover, had requested that he be assigned a certain refrain from a very cheerful violin concerto.

After a brief experimental phase in a provincial northern city, the card had become obligatory and had been given a pompous-sounding name which perfectly evoked the nature of the obsolete and inefficient bureaucracies which the card was designed to replace: 'The Authorized Certificate of International Public Existence.' However, people more readily called it PEC, from its shorter English name, Public Existence Card.

But Gregorio hadn't received his card yet; all he had in his wallet was that four-month-old pink slip, which attested to his good faith but didn't allow him access to the card services and which was already associated with some embarrassing memories: like the one of that unhappy evening when, after agonizing indecision, he had at last agreed to go dancing with his colleagues.

His mind only partially befuddled by alcohol, he had allowed himself to be dragged into various smoke-filled bars and driven recklessly in cars at speeds well over the legal limit, woefully presaging the moment in which they would all be stopped by the police. So that, when a patrol car had forced them to draw in to the side of the road, and while his colleagues carried on laughing and swigging from a bottle, taking turns to display a quite awesome, but as it turned out, justified self-confidence, Gregorio, though perfectly aware that such an utterance would lose him their friendship, whispered: I knew this would happen!

Of course, it was all right for them to stand there now and breezily feed their PEC card into a little gadget—with which Gregorio was unfortunately not familiar—and watch it flash enthusiastically. While he, with his little pink slip, had to make excuses, feed his data little by little into the patrol car computer and wait in vain for the SUBJECT EXISTS panel to light up, explaining to the officers that perhaps the data hadn't yet been inputted to the central electronic data bank, that, in fact, this was certainly the case, otherwise he too would have had his Public Existence Card by now instead of that stupid pink slip!

What a pathetic spectacle, he had exclaimed heroically to his colleagues with all the dignity he could still muster, 'Go on ahead, I'll catch up with you later at the Flashing Flesh.' He'd been taken to the station where he'd drunk a cup of strong coffee with the police officers while the three of them waited for someone to verify his existence manually at head office. When at long last, they'd let him go, he hadn't been able to face rejoining the party, feeling that he'd already endured enough public humiliation for one evening.

But while there's life there's hope, and beyond the dark tunnel of his present anxiety, Gregorio still eyed the card machines with an inner benevolence in which, however, there was now increasingly a hint of covetousness, intolerance, impatience.

Down there in the dark heart of the state, was this wretched PEC card being prepared or not? Perhaps a clerk has fallen asleep, but he'll wake up, sooner or later . . . But couldn't he perhaps also have lost all Gregorio's documents? Maybe burnt them? Or thrown them all in the wastepaper bin to impress some female colleague? Things like that happen every day!

Often, in the midst of a crowd, he would murmur to himself, 'Oh you who insert your PEC cards into the machine and get money back in exchange, oh you lucky winners of the jackpot!' By this time, Gregorio was even jealous of the terrible 'Two by One', a game that had caught on among almost all PEC card users, despite its being swiftly declared illegal. It was a sort of gambling game which could be played from any phone box that accepted the card, but which he, as he solemnly promised to himself, would never, ever have played.

By now, like everyone else, he was familiar with the rules of the game: you called up a data bank with your card and, by selecting 'Random 2×1' you would be paired up with another player. Then you would choose a field of play: it could be health, profession, age, current account, criminal record, etc. The player took turns to bet on the value of their hand, as in a game of poker, while the computer compared the data of each and awarded points accordingly until one of the two players withdrew. The winner then had the right to open one of his opponent's files and take out something proportional to his advantage as established by the computer: it could be money, a diploma, an amnesty, anything, and he then transferred it to his own card.

Instead of the PEC card, Gregorio received a letter from the Ministry of Public Certification declaring that his pink counter-foil was suspended. He took another day of leave from work and went along to the Office of Public Certification. On the way, he bought a newspaper (something which people were reluctant to do in public these days, for fear of appearing old-fashioned), and on the front page he read with dismay the headlines: 'Yet More Trouble with Non-existents!' The article was a sober analysis of the situation six months after the introduction of the card.

The advantages were undeniable, on that score all were agreed. No more queues, great mobility, an end to the petty despotism of bureaucrats and consequently an extraordinary decrease in government expenditure. Even the gambling game, the writer went on timidly to suggest, had, after all, worked to reward those who exhibited most enterprise and daring, creating a number of new accumulations of capital which were undoubtedly having a beneficial effect on public revenue.

There had of course been the unfortunate case of Carla Del Greco, reported in the pages of this newspaper (date in brackets), the 26-year-old office employee from Bergamo who had had her eyes removed because they had turned out to be the property of a gentleman in Carrara who had found a buyer for them in England. The case, the writer recalled, had been taken up by the opposition who had tried to exploit it politically, and the whole affair had caused an even greater stir, simply because the deal had fallen through and Del Greco's organs had putrefied in the hospital. The courts had, however, ascertained that the doctors had not been guilty of professional misconduct and, above all, had in no way broken the law. And after all, nobody had forced Miss Del Greco to play "2×1".

In another front-page article, a famous philosopher approached the question from the ethical point of view, under the title 'The Price of Progress'. 'Some people claim that Del Greco is a victim,'—his opening lines had a seductive clarity—'but what are these people really getting at? They are the same ones who used to reproach us for thinking only of our own well-being, and who continue even today to hold out against the technological development of the country. Are they the left-overs of the old Christian humanitarianism? Is theirs the legacy of natural philosophies? Has not the apparent contradiction between the Public Existence Certificate and human life been resolved by the fact that, taken all round, à propos the very thing that Carla Del Greco is now deprived of, she has, as far as her public certification is concerned, been truly deprived? Should we not then conclude that the card therefore works, even in extreme cases such as this? Even in the cases of those irresponsible wretches who fritter away all they have at "2×1"?'

These arguments are all a bit beyond me, thought Gregorio in the crush. If they give me the card, I certainly won't play it away like that!

The clerk can give him no information, he simply confirms that the application has been lodged and that his pink slip is no longer valid. So now what? asks Gregorio. Nothing, you'll have to wait for your notification of existence. Next please! What are they up to, down there in the dark heart of the State?

But Gregorio is beginning to grasp something from the philosopher's laudatory articles on the prosperous future of our society. The non-existent, explains the philosopher, are not only those who lose all their stock contained in the micro-processor through playing their card illegally (so maybe, thinks Gregorio, an avenging God truly does exist), but they are also those honest and hard-working employees of countless redund-ant institutes (Alas! thinks Gregorio, that's me) who appear only symbolically in their current accounts (Poor souls) and who weigh heavily on the now streamlined bank infrastructure.

All these individuals who have never been members of a political party, who have, in fact, nothing to offer (lose) and nothing to ask (win) from a Public Existence Card! For such people, a secondary privilege card will have to be created, something which will guarantee their peaceful extinction. Every step forward has its victims, as history has taught us, and the scientific and technological progress of the West certainly cannot stop for the likes of Miss Del Greco or the humanitarian preoccupations of some moralist. Those on the fringes of our production system would linger as disquieting presences in the centralized PEC system. Their existence would have to be limited within appropriate confines. To distinguish between productive citizens and needy citizens is today a necessity dictated by our model of development.

Gregorio's card has still not come. Sometimes, as he watches the trees and the dogs, he thinks back nostalgically to the now invisible world in which you could still get to know things and other people, the real world that trickles through the fingers like sand in the desert. Every morning he peers anxiously into his letter box to see if, by some chance, his Public Existence Card has arrived.

Paola Capriolo

Letters to Luisa

Dear Luisa,
    My little prison is finished at last. I will not tell you how much patience and what inordinate skill I have needed to construct the twelve cells with their paper walls, and to cut out of each one of them an opening large enough to allow our guest to pass through. I have covered the prison with a sheet of clear paper, making it impossible for him to escape, and enabling me to watch his every movement. There is also a little door, likewise of paper, that leads outside, and which I alone can open or close. As you will have guessed by now, I shall make use of it to provide the prisoner with what he needs by way of nourishment.

But I still have to carry out the most difficult part of the project, in other words the capture, and I shall not conceal from you that the matter arouses some measure of apprehension. For, you will agree, it is quite essential to take him alive. I have been observing his behaviour for a while now, and I know his talent for cunning and trickery. He can climb at an extraordinary speed, and what is more, there is no lack of hiding places here.

All the same, I do not despair of success in the enterprise: in my life, as you know, I have triumphed over much more taxing problems. Or perhaps you do not know. Some day I shall have to take it upon myself to tell you everything exactly as it happened, faithfully, so as to dispel certain misunderstandings that could come between you and me.

All I wish is for you to understand me, and for your affection.

Dear Luisa,
I am happy to tell you that my adversary proved himself to be much less cunning than I had thought. Trusting as a babe, he came down from the ceiling to cling with all eight legs onto the point of the stick I held out to him. What do you say to that? Could you have imagined him capable of such naivety?

I must confess that the ease of capture caused me grave disappointment: you will remember my fondness for risks, gambles, and challenges to the opposing will of men or destiny. You were always a challenge for me, even with the tenderness that you often have showed me, and you remain one. This is why I endeavour still to have you understand me, and you alone. What do I care now about the world's opinion? And why should I lie? Even the spider, shut up in the paper prison, has ceased to weave his deceitful web: he is motionless, resigned, waiting for the end. If he could speak, he would utter nothing but the truth.

But the truth, dear friend, is nearly always tedious, and so I have left our guest to his melancholy musings in order to devote myself to the violin.

I hope you have not given up music: I should consider it the ultimate betrayal. I play every evening, after supper, when the sounds of the courtyard have ceased. My notes have need of silence as fish have of water, as I have of you. For you perhaps, dear Luisa, I could still lie.

My friend,
Earlier today I heard a great upheaval in the courtyard, and this evening, while I was playing, I was interrupted by someone knocking at the door. Through the revolving hatch I received a note, which I read with difficulty, since my eyesight is becoming weaker every day. I could ask to be seen by an optician, who could prescribe the lenses that I need, but I don't want anyone coming in here. In the early days, so

many years ago, I craved it, and would have given any visitor a joyous welcome. No longer. And then what good would it do putting on a pair of spectacles so as to decipher the pointless messages conveyed to me: 'The prisoner is informed . . . From today . . . The new commander of the fortress . . .' With this senseless succession of men, they make believe they can mark out time for me as well, but I could no longer find my days on their calendar.

I have learned to catch flies, using an old wicker strainer. I open the skylights to let some air in, in the mornings, and one of them always slips into the room; from this proliferation of fauna, and from the relative mildness of the weather I deduce it must be spring: April, or maybe even May.

I follow the insect's flight with my eyes, and wait unmoving for it to settle somewhere. Then I pounce on it like a predator and cover it with the strainer. I believe not even our guest could do better.

Capture having taken place, I open the little paper door, and place the victim in the prisoner's room. Through the sheet of clear paper I look on at his savage meal, and each time I think of you, Luisa, of the pure and childlike face you counter to my scepticism. I wonder, if you will allow me, whether you have ever considered how monstrous is the idea of a heavenly spectator watching from among the clouds the mutual laceration of his creatures; impassive, or maybe faintly curious. Doubtless he must be bored to death up there, making do with the paltry pleasure afforded by such spectacles. Just so, I, wearied by endless imprisonment, watch the little fly annihilated in the spider's grip, and you must surely be horrified by the pleasure I take from it, or at least the tender girl I knew once would be horrified.

But why, Luisa, do you refuse me forgiveness, if you can forgive your God?

My dear,
I am still receiving messages from that new commander, even though I have made it quite clear to him, with my somewhat

laconic reply to his first note, that I have no intention of embarking on a correspondence with him. I am so put out that I have decided not to open letters any more; I would open only yours, if you ever deigned to write to me.

I wonder if I would still be able to recognize your handwriting, that neat and graceful script that once was so familiar. The years may have changed it, as they have changed mine; so many things have happened in the meantime, so many images, too many perhaps, have passed before my eyes. First triumph, then ruin, dug a deep abyss that separates me from my past, and only the memory of you can span it now, like one of those long bridges made of creepers that the American Indians would stretch over precipices, and they were fragile in appearance, but held firm and fast for whoever dared to take a step.

You too, Luisa, should dare, should try to understand. Yesterday I heard a woman's voice rising from the courtyard, sharp, vulgarly accented. She was screeching out something about a 'devil', and I realized she was referring to me.

Don't imagine that I am displeased by this: on the contrary. I think the spider too would be cheered if, from his paper prison, he could hear the cries of the little insects that fear him still. Instead he ingests his flies wearily, with no enthusiasm, his *amour propre* as a predator degraded.

I am so much moved by the abasement of this creature that I have decided to catch him another spider. Out of their meeting there would certainly arise a combat to the death, and I own that the prospect of being there is one that excites me somewhat. I would feel like a Caesar, absolute arbiter of life and death, gazing on the bloodied dance of a pair of gladiators.

The trouble would be if the two spiders were of the opposite sex, and instead of fighting should elect to multiply. In which case I think I would free them, so that they could go and enjoy their tiresome domestic bliss elsewhere.

I hope, sweet Luisa, that my tastes do not shock you too much. Music too is a battle in the end, and there was a time when you liked to duel with my violin. I remember you still

as one of the worthiest adversaries it was my lot to
encounter.

Dearest,
For days now I have heard the rain beat against the frosted
glass of the windows, and I cannot open the skylights for fear
of flooding the room. My advanced age compels me to avoid
the damp.

I have scoured every one of the prison walls, but there is
not a single spider to be found. The provision of flies is
becoming difficult too, though as yet the situation is not
desperate, since I had the foresight to keep a dozen of them,
alive, in a glass jar. I replaced the lid with a cambric
handkerchief, allowing them to breathe, and I have made
some little holes in it, through which now and then I drop
some bread crumbs. Thanks to this precaution we are
equipped to face this period of scarcity, sustained by the
hope that the weather will clear before our supplies
completely run out.

I think these flies, already half dead when they reach his
lair, must have little flavour for our guest: likewise, for me,
the more refined foodstuffs which the soldiers pass regularly,
twice a day, through the hatch.

They are solicitous in their dealings with me, and, what
matters more, totally discreet. No one is authorized to enter
the room wherein I am confined, and even my windows are
screened, ensuring that I can see nothing that goes on
outside. Total isolation, for as long as I live, is the sentence I
must serve for my misdeeds, and believe me, Luisa, it is a
punishment somewhat less harsh than it appears. One gets
used to it, there are companions to be found among the
insects, or else among the ghosts.

Admittedly, one could not imagine anything further from
our adolescent dreams. What I dreamt in part became reality,
and other men, mirroring themselves in my dream, found
there the distorted outlines of a nightmare. You dreamt of a
world in your image, a kind of paradise, and even then I
smiled at such illusions, for I knew that paradise cannot be

achieved on this earth. You must admit, however, that there have been some excellent approximations of hell.

I know, poor angel, how much this cynicism wounds you, and how it distresses you that a devil such as I should dare to address you in such intimate tones. But I wonder if the years might not have torn some plumes from your fine wings, or dimmed their candid brilliance. Perhaps those stains, those tiny wounds that opened in your flesh just where the plumes were joined to it, speak to you also of me, of the ever rebel angel, ever fallen. Slowly they will teach you to understand him and to forgive his woeful dreams.

My Luisa,
Forgive me if I have neglected you for some days, but an extraordinary adventure has befallen me, entirely absorbing my attention.

I define as 'adventure', and moreover qualify as 'extraordinary', an event to which in other times I should not have given even a thought. You must make allowances for me: I explained to you before that I have lived for decades in the company of ghosts and insects, with no sound reaching me but for the hoarse shouts of the soldiers, the noise of clogs and cartwheels, and the melodies that I myself perform on the violin.

Imagine then my amazement when suddenly I heard, across the prison courtyard, the unwonted sound of a piano. Someone was playing, where I knew not, a superficial but pleasing passage. It was played neither badly nor well, no, more badly than well, in a fashion that for sure had nothing to do with your incomparable mastery; and yet this music had an extraordinary effect on me, and every day since then I have waited impatiently for its return through the skylights of my prison, which I always leave open in summer, to profit from the warmth.

I wonder where these notes come from, from whose hands. I believe the person playing is from the new commander's house: he himself, perhaps, or more probably his wife or daughter. There is a certain coyness in the style, and a lack of heartfelt vigour that bring to mind a woman. Do not misunderstand me, I beg you; I speak of women in general, with no reference to yourself. You too were coy in many respects, but not when you sat down at the piano.

Listening to this music reminds me of certain young ladies of good family who at social gatherings would agree to 'play something' for the delight or the torment of the guests. I still recall how it amused me to observe the confusion that gripped them when I appeared in the room: their fingers became all of a sudden uncertain, faltering. Sometimes the poor little things would break off altogether, and they would stare dully at the music, as though, at a stroke, they had ceased to be able to read the notes. If then I approached the piano, a furious blush would irradiate their cheeks.

Perhaps the mysterious pianist would also blush if I appeared before her, and she would be unable to continue her melodious exercises. The mirror, where I look as little as possible, returns to me the distressing sight of a grizzled head, a face ravaged by time; but the gaze is undiminished, and in it I still recognize my ancient, terrible self. You too, dear friend, would recognize it, and perhaps, in its presence, you would once again assume that look you had on your face when I saw you for the last time. You did not blush, but a light came into your eyes in which pity and horror were combined. It was at the trial, remember, and you were wearing black.

Luisa dear,
Could you but hear how this amateurish musician presses on the keys, constantly, even when there is no need whatsoever. Her little airs, the insipid little waltzes would be more endurable perhaps if performed with a light touch, and with a measure of detachment. Instead, so it appears, she strives to infuse them with accents of desperate passion, which, in pieces like these, mere divertimenti, produces an effect that is utterly grotesque.

I write all this to show you that imprisonment has not succeeded in making me lose my mental clarity, nor my powers of discernment. But whereas my judgement draws back repelled, a strange perturbation, an inexplicable emotion assails another part of me: that shadowy part, inaccessible to reason, that you, schooled as you are in hazy formulations, would perhaps call my heart, or worse still my soul. Despite my irritation, I cannot stop myself from feeling pleasure as I listen to the notes of that instrument.

I have asked myself why she plays so loudly, and I have reached the conclusion that she wishes to be heard by someone. Now, whoever can this someone be? Certainly not one of her own family—for in that case such a din would prove quite needless—but rather a distant being, one who does not live in her home. You will now have guessed the outcome of this line of reasoning: the someone, the distant being, can only be me: it is for me that the girl so cruelly strains the keys of her piano.

She will have heard me spoken of, it is natural, they will have told her of my deeds. Many times over, I wager, ever since childhood, perhaps leaving out some details unseemly for the delicate ears of a young lady. She knows I live in here, only steps away from her, still girded by the last rays of my glory; how could she resist a temptation so great? Doubtless she has heard me play, and she deludes herself, poor child, that she responds to me by abusing the keyboard in that way.

She deludes herself and she does not, since I have already confessed to you that her music gives me a degree of pleasure. And yet, my Luisa, what can that be, but a shadow of the sublime pleasure that in other days you and I, playing together, could draw from one another?

Dear girl,
Alas, I must give you some painful news. Yesterday, around midnight, our guest expired, from natural causes I believe. I found him turned over on his back, all eight legs clamped around his final prey, which he had not had time to devour.

The funeral will take place this evening, with all solemn rites, and even though you are unable to attend, I beg you at least to wear in his memory the black dress spoken of before, the one I saw you in at the trial. Tell me, were you in mourning for me? I know it, I am sure of it, but I should like you to assure me of it. And I should like you to assure me that it was indeed black, and not in fact dark green as it sometimes seemed.

The late departed companion of my solitude now lies in a small wooden box. I watched him for a little while as the piano played, not the funeral march, but the usual light music.

You know, dear, that in the course of my existence I have achieved a measure of familiarity with death, above all with the deaths of others, but also with the thought of the inevitable end that awaits me. Did you perhaps see me bat an eyelid, you who looked on from a back row when the threat of sentence of death hung over me? No, I did not bat an eyelid, neither then nor ever; in the midst of the dangers of victory and of defeat, face to face with that baleful spectre, I dared always to proclaim myself proud master of my destiny.

But this dead spider in his paper prison, this black tangle of stiffened limbs, is more than I am able to bear. In its presence, for the first time death appears as something horribly senseless, as something that cannot be confronted, because it is faceless, it is unseeing, it is naught but a blind hand that clumsily strikes wherever it touches.

No one will attend my funeral, apart from a few bored soldiers, and everything will take place in haste, and in silence. But this evening, my violin will sound the sweetest of laments for that dead spider.

Dear friend,
I could not help myself. The other day, before the hour set for the ceremony, I closed the little wooden box and tied it with string. Then I placed a chair beside one of the windows, I stepped up onto it and, reaching up as far as I could on tiptoe, I cast the bier outside, through the skylight.

I now take consolation with a new companion. This one is of a different type, he is not black but a yellowish hue, with markings. His body is smaller and his legs longer and thinner. Unlike the other, which scarcely moved, he runs frantically from one corner of the prison to the other, seeking an aperture for an impossible escape. Do you see what vast differences in character you can find even among examples of the lower species!

Even his way of eating up the flies betrays a strange anxiety. He is greedy, impatient, scarcely have I had time to set the insect inside than it is gone, swathed in the embrace of its executioner.

All this amounts to a novelty, and it helps me to pass the time in a pleasant enough way. The spectacle of violent death in itself has something deeply reassuring: it allows one for a moment to banish the thought of that other, anonymous, faceless death.

Anyway, these are my little distractions, the only ones alas, since for some time now the piano has been silent. Certain sounds I have heard lead me to suppose there are guests in the house of the commander. It is odd, though, that no one ever asks the girl to 'play something'.

I hate them all, every last one of them. The echo of their conversation reaches for me from afar, I am sure they speak of me. And of what else could they speak?

I play the violin for long periods, to smother the intolerable buzz of their voices, perhaps even to disturb them. I should like to be able to enter among them, to disconcert the fathers and the mothers by my presence, to terrorize the young girls.

You, I remember, always withstood my gaze, and I never managed to make you break off while you were playing. And to think you are so young, and so shy . . .

Luisa dearest,
My days pass in infinite boredom. Time, as you will know, expands and contracts, and always in direct opposition to our desires, so that there is not a single instant that does not appear to pass too slowly, or else too fast. If I were you I should lodge a complaint about it with that gentleman up there, assuming you are still on good terms.

My time expands, Luisa, it expands beyond measure. The moments go by at an indolent tortoise pace, and I miss the piano more and more each day.

Sometimes it happens, after the midday meal, that an absolute silence descends on the prison, as though everyone were asleep. Then I take up the violin, I go to one of the screened windows and begin to play, in the hope of being heard by the unknown pianist. Sometimes I play for her at night too, when the glow of the torches that light the courtyard is too faint to reach me through the glass.

It is like a call that I send out to her up through the narrow vent of the skylight, or rather, a spider's web I weave to capture her. It may well be that I succeed in persuading her to take up her instrument again, and maybe in making her see that there exists in the world a better kind of music than the one already known to her.

I devote myself to this project with the boundless patience of one who has nothing else to do.

My dear,
The coy little fly has finally fallen into the net; yesterday evening, after her long silence, she began to play again, and the notes that issued from the piano were no longer her music, but mine.

To attract her I was playing a slow seductive melody, the slowest and most seductive that I know. Yes, Luisa, it was indeed that adagio, the adagio of the sonata that we loved above all others. I was playing it, I have to admit, in a somewhat academic manner, naturally not because I have lost my skills as a virtuoso, but to have the girl apprehend me more clearly.

And indeed, after some time, she began to respond.

Her fingers moved shyly, uncertainly, and often it seemed she had difficulty following the score, but, as I have told you, I have patience, a boundless patience, and I shall continue to repeat the piece every evening, until my partner has learned to play it in an acceptable manner.

I say 'my partner', and I almost feel shame at these

words, for I well know that this appellation refers to you, and to you alone. This one will never have the wherewithal to match your exquisite interpretations, nor can there ever exist between her and myself that profound understanding which made of our instruments the double echo of a single voice.

But bear with me, I must make do with whatever I find, and for me it already means a great deal at last to have someone with whom I can play. Are you jealous, by any chance? Ah Luisa, I wish with all my heart for it to be so.

Sweet friend,
My pupil begins to make some progress, although remaining a thousand miles away from perfection. There is now a degree of delicacy in her manner of playing the adagio, and you yourself, perhaps, could listen to her without too much irritation.

You will see, gradually I shall succeed in teaching her my language, our language. Slowly I am drawing her towards regions unknown: the days of ingenuous divertimenti, of sugary melodies are over and done with now. I believe that even if she wished to she could not go back to them.

Unexpectedly, as I toy with my new prey, I find myself in a garb to which I am most unaccustomed: that of the philanthropist. For, you must admit, it has been a genuine act of succour to wrench that unknown creature away from her refined barbarity in order to raise her up to the spheres of art alongside me.

In short, dear Luisa, you will now have to treat me with every honour due to a spider in the odour of sanctity.

Dearest,
The girl begins to repay my efforts with some happy surprises. She no longer seems the same: the traces of that intolerable amateurism that to begin with afflicted her performances are fast disappearing, and, little by little, out of the fingers' touch there is flowering a new sensibility, one more polished, which at times reminds me of yours.

This insofar as concerns the adagio. Whereas, with the first

movement we have hardly begun, and I must try to forget
you if I wish to be forbearing. All the same, her
interpretation is fair, and I observed with pleasure that her
capacity for learning has developed in an extraordinary way,
and in a very short time. If you had not spoiled me, I should
perhaps be altogether satisfied.

My friend,
I realize that lately I have not given you any more news of
the spider, but you must not wrong me by imagining that my
new mission of pedagogy is leading me to overlook the duties
of hospitality. I spend long hours hunting for insects, most of
all in the morning, whether because I have the impression
that the prey is then more numerous, or because music, you
will agree, is certainly not something to engage upon before
luncheon.

The weather is warm, the sky is clear, but it seems to me
that all this is how things have been for a long time now,
perhaps months; the slanting rays of the sun that filter
through the skylight to warm my room now depart ever
earlier, leaving me at the mercy of a shadowy half light. I fear
that summer will soon reach its close, and with it the season
for flies.

Our friend seems not at all alarmed, he goes on eating his
meals with the usual voracity, almost as if he has entrusted
his own destiny to the benign hands of a special providence
which guaranteed him food in abundance until the end of his
days. And perhaps that is truly how it is.

As you may recall, I never had any great inclination for
study, and the tortured events of my life have left me without
any at all. Yet now I should like to be an entomologist, and
to know whether spiders survive the first onslaught of winter.

Luisa dear,
After having happily crossed the hurdle of the first
movement, the girl has mastered the scherzo and the rondo
with quite astonishing speed. We are now able to perform the
sonata quite smoothly, from start to finish. Of course, here

and there there is still the odd flaw, but you will remember what an intricate score this is. When all is said and done, I am able to say I am proud of my pupil. She is most receptive, she manages to make up for the deficiency in her own training with a musical instinct for which I did not give her credit. Gradually, this instinct is being awakened, thanks to my maieutic skills, and I believe that it surprises her just as much as it does me.

Spiders' webs, sweet friend, are woven out of the most impalpable of elements, yet they are able both to attract the prey and to hold it. Thus I with an invisible thread have bound her hands to my hands, her will to mine. I lead her, she follows me. Slowly, with no need of words, I teach her to respond precisely to my every request, to ask precisely at the point where I wish to respond, and sometimes I seem almost to have returned to the happy days when you and I conducted such dialogues together.

My God, Luisa, how like you she is! When we play our sonata I can only picture her as blonde, and dressed in black. And always, she is looking at me with that doubting, painful expression, and she is sitting far away, at the back of the courtroom.

I have never doubted that it was you there, looking at me in that way, while I stood in the dock. I have never doubted it, although my eyesight, even then, was a little poor. She was too much like you to be anyone else. Who but you would have dared to stare at me so long, so unswervingly into my eyes?

But if at that very moment the guards had not taken me out of the courtroom, I am convinced that you too would have lowered your gaze, just as the unknown pianist has made herself docile, submissive to my will. Treading close behind me, she enters into the most cunning labyrinths of the music, into those dark paradises that once were our realm.

I wonder sometimes how you were able to venture through them, all the while preserving your pristine lack of guile. Not a shadow, even then, darkened the splendour of your wings. I opened yawning chasms at your feet, and you flew over them, impervious and sure.

For me you were an exasperating companion, especially when we played together and were like brother and sister, like husband and wife.

This one too, perhaps, would vex me, if I were not made tender by the memory of you. Tenderness is a luxury I can allow myself now, but in moderation: too high a dosage would poison me. Which is why I should sometimes like to banish your memory, I should like you to leave me a little to my solitude.

Dear Luisa,
This girl frightens me. There is something, in her manner of playing, which frightens me. The overwhelming sweetness, the extraordinary resemblance . . . I believe that the spirit suffers thus when joy approaches, and I know not whether to fight against it or surrender.

I beg you, Luisa, pity me.

My angel,
This evening, as soon as you began to play, with that touch so light, it seemed that you were opening wide before me the gates to my happier past.

Little angel, your white wings are the twins of my dark wings, to me belongs your innocence, and to you my cruelty.

I have never doubted that we were the two halves of the same thing, that the hand which strikes and the flesh which receives the blow were the same thing. My Luisa, lift your eyes from the piano, and see with what sweetness the spider tightens its legs around the body of the fly. Do you not feel it too, that everything is fitting?

All is fitting, my girl, all is redeemed, and every thing rediscovers itself in its own opposite. I have never doubted this, I have never doubted it was you, sitting down there at the back, in the courtroom. You dressed in black, you with white wings. Of what else do the piano and the violin speak, but this mystery and its double face?

Of what else did they speak then, and we had not yet understood, and we believed ourselves to be far apart? When the brother did not recognize the sister, and the wife denied her husband?

Look: the little fly has vanished in the spider's embrace.

Beloved girl,
I no longer know who guides and who is guided. Our sounds fuse and mingle, and last night the sky lit up every one of its lamps in solemn celebration of our union.

Might you have been troubled by the lightning flashes? Might you have been fearful of the dull thunder claps? Of course not, you were travelling undaunted through our garden of notes, you were fluttering, small winged insect, above the chasm that is yours and mine, that is my cruelty and your innocence.

Look, twin, how each thing fuses with each other thing, how each one guides and each one lets itself be guided.

Lovely angel,
After these long days of silence I began to despair of hearing your voice again. Let there be thanks to both you and the cold air of the evening, which has brought it back to me.

Yet in that sound there is something different, something strangely remote. Your gaze, from under the light veil of your hat, was fastened to me, and yet it seemed to evade me.

Angel, why do you answer me no more? I beg you, say something to me in that liquid voice you have, some words of love on your black and white keys. I wish to go on being mirrored in you.

Sweet Luisa,
The violin is weary of playing alone, and the spider devours his flies with little appetite. Why this silence? Why do you abandon me now, after having brought me to the edge of the final abyss?

Madam,

I write to you again, after such a long time, to tell you of the state of my health.

I am too weak to play, and ever since you abandoned me I find no pleasure in the violin. The soldiers persist in thrusting on me huge jars of flies that they pass through the hatch twice a day. I still eat one or two, now and then, but with little appetite. I no longer even have the strength to run from one corner to the other of the paper prison to seek an exit.

I lie on my back almost always, my legs in the air, and now, stretched out on my cot I write you this final letter.

I shall force myself to get up and go and put it in the drawer, along with all the others. It may be that after my death someone will have it delivered to you, assuming that they manage to find you, and that you have not yet left this world to reach the heavenly dwelling place to which you once aspired. There for sure you will never be likely to meet me, and so I bid you goodbye, my cruel and innocent half, for all time divided.

Sandra Petrignani

The Old Man in the Garden

Wendy pushed the half-open gate and went in. Parked outside in the sun was the hearse. Some men were standing in front of the raised door of the hearse talking and drying the sweat with big handkerchiefs. She quickly got under the shade of the trees. She put down her suitcase and took a breath. She ran her hand through her hair. She had got there in time. Her grandmother was still in the house. She listened to catch the sinister sounds of the hammer. She imagined other men like those she had seen outside talking round the coffin, busy shutting the lid, driving in long nails. Instead—silence. Only chirping and the movement of leaves. She had not been back at the house for four years but everything was as it always had been. Here time did not pass. Like ten, twenty years ago. Maybe the hiding-place was still there. As a child she had discovered that one of the big stones in the flowerbed could be moved. With a little effort she could shift it, a little hollow appeared in which she went and placed strange things found in the garden—bits of pottery in which she sensed an aristocratic past, specially pretty stones. She darted towards the hiding-place with an agility born of surprise but suddenly she stopped. Her grandfather was sitting on the low wall. Smartly dressed, even wearing his waistcoat with the watch-chain that sketched a parenthesis between his waist and the little pocket, he was fanning himself with his hat. He was staring in front of him, his mouth open to breathe better, his big hand with the swollen veins firmly planted on his knee. His neck stuck out skeleton-like from the fastened collar of his striped shirt; it looked like the neck of dead and plucked chickens. Any suit was always too big for him. His bifocal glasses with their thick lenses gleamed; they reflected the gentle movement of the leaves, which shifted to let brief rays of sun filter through from time to time. He was not really sitting—rather leaning. He had no other way of sitting. He was always 'on the edge' of things—not only chairs. He had never felt at ease in the world; he was afraid of being a nuisance. And he was indeed a nuisance. Her grandmother continually complained about him. Because he was incapable of leaving the house and so did not go anywhere with her. Because he could not endure the least change and they couldn't even have the divan in the parlour recovered. Because he had an obsession about ants getting into his plate and so had thought up a system for protecting the kitchen table—a system which constantly put her grandmother in a bad temper and was at the centre of her principal outbursts. He had placed four metal dishes full of a poisonous white powder under the four legs of the table. Every so often a few ants appeared, black on white, and stone-dead. Then her grandfather, highly pleased, showed her grandmother the results of his hunt. He shook the dish under her nose before replacing the powder, which was speckled with little lifeless bodies, hardly bigger than grains of sand, with clean powder. Her grandmother screwed up her face in a grimace of disgust and said: 'Get away.' She was fat, slow-moving.

Her grandfather continued to fan himself gently; he gazed at a spot on the ground, then examined the wall of the house not more than three metres away from him, a crack in the wall, a little creature clambering up it. He was looking with amazed concentration, a resigned attention. Wendy remembered that her grandmother was dead. That was why she had come back. She thought of the body lying on the bed, of the relatives round it. She must be installed regally in the bed just as once 'the priest' had been installed under the blankets to warm the sheets. Her grandfather had made it. It was a huge contraption, a wooden structure, a kind of sledge. Her grandfather was afraid that the pot of charcoal might set fire to the material and therefore had built a particularly big 'priest' so that it would hold the blankets up well away from the source of the heat. As a little girl, when she went past her grandparents' bedroom she tried not to look in. But she always saw 'the priest' out of the corner of her eye. It looked like a fat corpse. Why it was called that no one had managed to explain to her. She did not even know if it were a term recognized in the dictionary or that belonged exclusively to the family tradition. She dreamt up stories in which some priest had been caught in bed with someone's wife; she had quickly slipped out of the sheets and he had remained trapped between the blankets ready to receive the blows of her relatives.

She decided to speak. 'Hello,' she said.

Her grandfather turned round to look at her. His open mouth and his eyes, magnified by the lenses, gave him an expression of astonishment. But he too said 'Hello' as if they had seen each other the day before. He stopped waving his hat and hung it on his other knee. Now he had both hands firmly on his knees. 'And how is your father?' It was typical of her grandfather to ask questions of no importance to him. In the house Wendy's father was contemptuously called 'the American'. He had separated from his wife before Wendy was born; he had got to know his daughter very much later when, as an eighteen-year-old, she had begun to spend time in the United States to learn the language. Wendy did not reply; she sat down on the wall. 'It's hot,' she remarked after a little, for something to say. 'Is Mother inside?' He nodded, he passed his handkerchief over his bald head with an uncertain, trembling gesture. The few hairs he had left formed a semi-circle round the nape of his neck. He kept them untidily long; they went inside his collar. He blew his nose noisily. They both began to watch a lizard zigzagging from the shade to occupy a triangle of sun. Wendy for a moment felt completely at one with the little animal, she felt the cold of the shady earth under its paws and then the fire of the tiles, she felt the fresh darkness of the leaves and then suddenly the heavy light, which enveloped her like boiling water. But on the low wall it was not too hot. The entwined branches of the fig-tree, of the medlar and of the persimmon, marked out a wide area of shade. Her grandfather violently set

to pruning it, every year at the right time, which called forth an
angry reaction from her grandmother. No one in the house had
faith in the ability of that self-taught gardener; they expected
the trees to be amputated for ever, that they would never regrow
the slaughtered limbs, would never again nurture flowers, never
again would the petals fall to the ground forming a pink and
white carpet to go into ecstasies over. Yet every year her
grandfather showed he was right; the garden became more
dense, more beautiful. Where had he learned it? He did not read
books, he never met anyone. Since he had retired from the
railways, too early for his pension to fall due, he had never gone
out of the gate. He kept a little case ready 'for all eventualities'
—an employee's briefcase full of medicines and a little bottle of
milky coffee. It was the bottle for Giuliani's Medicinal Bitters,
with its dark brown glass. Every morning her grandfather threw
away the coffee from the previous day and replaced it with fresh
coffee. He prepared everything himself, aware of the hostility
that surrounded him. What could that briefcase have done to
defend him from the dangers of the world the day he was forced
to go out? He spent his time in the garden or shut himself in his
study, which no one was allowed to enter—only his grandchild
when she had to have her maths lessons. How on earth was her
grandfather so good at maths? The study was more like a shop
in which someone had jumbled every kind of object together.
To give lessons he cleared a corner of the square table and made
room for his granddaughter. There was a blackboard hanging
on the wall, just as big as the ones in school. There her
grandfather had written his numbers . . . Wendy did not
understand a thing; she had not the courage to interrupt him, to
ask for explanations. She gazed at him, fascinated by his
untidiness, by his stained clothes, by his old slippers, by the
woollen beret he always wore, in and out of the house, summer
and winter. How had he managed to carve out such inde-
pendence among a wife and daughters worried about changing
the towels in the bathroom and putting flowers in the vases
when people came, dazed by a continuous background of radio
and television.

*

Perhaps she should go in. Show herself. Her aunts, her cousins would assail her with questions. Would she be able to smile? her grandfather said something about the funeral. He said: 'We are taking her to Todi.' That was where the family tomb was. He really said 'we are taking her' in the plural, including himself in the group. 'Is the briefcase ready?' asked Wendy, recognizing in her voice an involuntary note of complicity. Then she actually added: 'What about the feeding-bottle?' It had been her grandfather who had called the little bottle of Giuliani's Medicinal Bitters his feeding-bottle, sending himself up. And everyone had always called it that, sending him up. Wendy thought that her grandfather was witty and that there was in his neurosis a kind of joyful ribaldry, of prolonged childhood. But he looked at her shaking his head, almost alarmed, almost rebuking her for wanting to start playing now of all times. He shrugged his shoulders keeping them up for a moment, leaning his head to one side. It was as if someone had seized him by the scruff of the neck like a disobedient dog. Then his shoulders slumped again suddenly. He said: 'What's the point? Too late.'

In fact he showed he had no need of his case. He got into the car with his daughter and granddaughter. Wendy was amazed that no one bothered about her grandfather: no one seemed to notice the change. Her grandfather who came out through the gate, got into the car, let his hand lie on the door handle and stayed like that, fragile and calm. Her grandfather who in church got up and sat down again slightly later than the others, watching his daughters to see what he had to do since he was completely ignorant. He had always boasted that he hated priests, of not having set foot in church once since his first communion. But he did not wish to go to the cemetery. It was decided that he would stay in a relative's house and that Wendy would keep him company. The heat was suffocating in that house. Her grandfather, sitting with his arms on the table, fanned himself with his hat. He had taken off his jacket and rolled up his shirt sleeves above his elbows like a boy. For something to do Wendy had made coffee. She poured some out for him in a big cup with a little milk. He drank slowly. In the silence Wendy heard the noises his throat made as he swallowed it down, the noise when his teeth met. She remembered so many times seeing his dental plate sunk in a wide glass full of pink water. And she remembered her grandfather without his dentures, his skin all wrinkled round his mouth and his lips which had disappeared, sucked back into the oral cavity above the smooth gums. She thought of the thick soups her grandmother had made for him, of the 'vegetable broth' without lumps, of her grandfather who instead of a glass for wine used a bowl, his bowl, so that he could dunk his bread in it easily. She thought of her grandmother and her disgust, of how she looked the other way so as not to see him doing these horrid things. She thought back to when that same morning she had finally decided to go into the house and had seen her grandmother's body, surprisingly thin, small in the big bed. And she had listened to the talk. Her mother and her aunts would share her grandfather. He would go and stay for a time with each of them in their fine, roomy houses, with the formica kitchens and the air-conditioning. 'What about the house?' she had asked, holding back the rest of her sentence, 'the house that is his world, his life.' They had stared at her in astonishment. 'It will be sold,' they had said with a sigh, briskly. They couldn't be expected to turn their lives and those of their children upside down, to move into grandfather's house where you weren't allowed to move so much as a pin.

For a moment she had a fantasy of taking her grandfather with her to America, of settling him in her father's flat. Perhaps he would feel at home in that disorder. He had a fine tenor voice and was an opera fan. At Christmas, when the whole family still used to get together, at a certain point in the evening they asked him to sing. He was delighted but had to be coaxed to do it, he said: 'For goodness' sake—once I did have a good voice but now I am old.' 'It doesn't matter,' they all said, already pushing him to his feet, 'we understand.' Then he agreed so long as it was 'behind the door'. He half-closed the leaves of the door with the frosted glass and hid himself there as if behind a fan. He began to sing 'Un dì felice'. On the glass his moving shadow was outlined, the shape of his beret, the profile of his big nose stuck up in the air, his arm and hand raised high as if to sustain the song. '*Croce e delizia, croce e delizia, croce e delizia al cor.*' And everyone applauded and said bravo and he was pleased with himself: 'I am not all that bad though, in spite of my years.'

Wendy was searching for something to say but he spoke. 'When are you leaving again?' he asked, for once asking the right question and looking her straight in the face. She felt she had been thrown against a wall. She desperately sought a reply but before it there came the words of a pop song rising from the street through the open window. 'I'll leave you' shouted the song and was about a completely different situation—a man and a woman granting each other the reciprocal freedom to be unfaithful. But that cry said the same about her, Wendy; it replied brutally for her. She could not lie to him. 'Tomorrow,' she answered and instinctively lowered her eyes and was ashamed.

Goffredo Parise

Friendship

O ne day towards the end of winter in the mountains a
group of people who knew each other only slightly and
had found themselves by chance on a frozen and wind-swept
peak decided to take a very long and lonely piste which led to a
distant valley. There were ten of them, by a happy coincidence
none of them was really 'advanced', indeed they were all more
or less timid and this made them immediately have trust in each
other.

The ten were: Gioia, a woman with sweet Jewish eyes, full of
something ancient and religious, which was a sense of family,
Carlo, Gioia's husband, tall and blond with four-square
features and almost white, slightly science-fiction eyes. Adriana,
tall and nice, a little anxious to be always nice, but neither too
soon nor too late. Mario, Adriana's husband, with many signs
of fragility drifting across his limbs and face, but with a round
head full of the need for affection which made up for
everything. Guido, the least 'advanced' who skied without style
telling the steep rocky bits 'I'll beat you' and he beat them;
because nearby there was Silvia, a girl-woman with Mongol
features, a burred 'r', whom he had loved (and contemplated)
for many years, of a beauty so great that everyone she smiled at
felt frail and mortal. But Silvia (without Silvia's presence the
ten would never have found themselves together by chance)
loved Filippo, a man who resembled Achilles (but Patroclus as
well) in being 'human' for he had dedicated his life to Silvia. The
eighth was Dabchevich (enough said). Then Pupa, the most
unknown of all, who lived for many months in the mountains,

had yellow eyes speckled with black spots like the sun, skied as if she were flying and in a way that was filled with silence—two things perhaps developed in these parts in her childhood in order to live and look after herself in the snow like the squirrels and the hares. And finally another man who was able to do only one thing in life—that is to say to observe the ever-changing particularities of the other nine and of the weather, hoping that all these things were in harmony with each other and looking for a way to bring it about, without anyone noticing.

They set off from the peak one after the other amid gusts of wind and snow, all—except Pupa and perhaps Guido, who 'had no nerves'—with some fear because the first stretch they had to cross was strewn with rocks which stuck out and the snow, being so thin, increased their speed just at the point where there was a ravine and they had to stop. They met at that point almost without seeing each other but Silvia had seen that man No. 10 had no cap—she slipped from her neck her 'yachting club' scarf (a big foulard of blue silk with little flags from every country) and gave it to him. He wrapped it round his head pirate-wise and set off first (such had been the favour granted by the goddess) into the immense white valley sloping down between the high peaks, which was the second part of the descent. Here the wind suddenly ceased as did the cold, the pace became very fast because the skis sank into the fresh snow giving a grip and the sun lit up everyone's face so strongly that each person had a sense of that beauty. Pupa swung with wide open arms in long Christies leaving a single track (and one for ever unique) which fate prevented the others from following. Gioia said under her breath to Mario who was coming down at her side, 'Isn't it beautiful, Mario?' and Mario because of these words addressed to him experienced a moment of gratitude which she had foreseen; Silvia crouched in a racing pose to get up speed (questions of resistance to the air) and as she did so smiled to herself with much affection and irony; Filippo traced a personal and extremely fast route without wishing to compete with Pupa; everyone was silent or spoke very quietly, only Dabchevich, extremely tall and very excited, overdid things in a way that was Slav or Austrian or Russian and shouted

'Sublime, sublime' whereby he won the affection of them all for ever, then 'sublime' was lost in the mountain air and nothing more was heard. In short they were all so wondrously happy as to attribute the reason for this feeling not only to the pink mountains, to the snow and the sun, but above all to people like themselves who at that moment (a very important moment in their lives) were ten little coloured dots in the valley.

The third part of the descent presented 'considerable difficulties'; there was no avoiding one piece, in the shade and therefore frozen, which bordered on what looked like a chasm and which ended up in a vast bowl in the sun once more with a little Alpine hut. If one had sufficient courage it would have been possible to go down without fear straight over the ice, making a curve in the sun where the snow is soft but at high speed and then once more going straight in the fresh snow to the door of the hut. The women, except for Pupa, lacked it, of the men few had it (Guido had already got to the bottom somehow or other), Silvia stopped, calling for help, Filippo dashed up but she wept, stamped her feet (with her skis on) and did not want to go down; the man with the foulard slipped into a little valley they didn't know about among virgin snow, tumbled over twice without being able to stop himself and thinking of fate, but in fact he stopped against a bush, saw two black squirrels busy scratching away and filled with fear, and remained by himself for a little to rest and to think. But everything went well and when he reached the hut where Filippo was wanting to organize a rescue expedition, Silvia was smiling with her eyes still full of tears.

The fourth stretch was a path on the mountainside with corners where it disappeared from view and where as a joke the man with the foulard allowed himself to be discovered by Guido hugging Silvia. Guido passed and said 'Very funny', Adriana lost a ski and to begin with it seemed very serious, then it was found by Filippo. Pupa, always the first, was waiting leaning on her sticks, tidying her hair with a hairpin in her mouth.

The fifth stretch was a steep descent, a little in the shade, easy too, but by now everyone's ankles were a little tired and there were some falls, none of them serious. But Carlo said to Guido and the man with the foulard 'Follow me, follow my coat-tails.' or else, 'There, turn where I turn', but with very little irony— that is to say with more affection than vanity and meantime the others were already at the bottom of the valley in a wood of young larches. Here they had to walk, pushon their sticks, get hot, take clothes off a little at a time. Silvia slipped off her white sheep's-wool hat with a big pompom, her hair fell over her shoulders and at that moment they entered the hut where they ate eggs, ham, bread with caraway seed, drank wine from a monks' cellar, sent postcards, smoked, went out, took a couple of taxis and the sun set. The moon rose white as snow in the sky which suddenly became black as pitch and they returned home tired.

The next year the ten friends (they had become friends) met again on the same peak, not by chance, and came down along the same piste. To tell the truth not all ten were there, Dabchevich was missing and everybody was a little unhappy about this, in their hearts some of them felt a doubt that his absence might cause a gap—not a very big one but one that might become such if other similar gaps, even little ones, opened up in the unpredictable harmony of the group; but this did not happen because when they reached the second stretch of the descent someone shouted: 'Sublime.' Others still had doubts because happy things don't happen twice (but they do and they don't—there is no rule); it is true there were some differences, there was no blizzard at the beginning, the third stretch of the piste was no longer so dangerous, the man with the foulard had a hat (on the other hand the foulard was no longer there), but they stopped at the first hut to drink a *vin brûlé* which they had not drunk the previous year, warmed themselves in the sun which was much stronger, and swopped a cream which smelt like but alas did not taste like barley sugar; and above all one man said to Silvia in an aside:

'Silvia, I was looking at you earlier—there's something different about you—I mean you are more beautiful but different from last year.'

'What is there about me?'

'I've no idea.'

'Tell me at once. What is it?'

'There is something—is it true or not?'

'It's true.'

'And what is it?'

'I don't know—but it's true.'

Two years later Pupa and the man whom we shall call 'the one with the foulard' came down the same piste in a storm. Stones stuck up everywhere, the piste was buried in snow, they had to side-step down part of the first stretch (not Pupa, the other person, and Pupa watched him with apprehension) covering their eyes with their hands because of the sharp little particles of ice which blew into their faces, then everything became calm, as on the first occasion, on the second stretch when the peaceful valley appeared; the wind died and the clouds, as changeable as Silvia, scattered somewhere leaving the blue sky.

Years later they met up again on that mountainside and in that valley which had made them so happy the first time. Then they stopped meeting at these spots, spent years still as friends, allowing others to take their place.

Sandro Veronesi

A Worthwhile Death

From the age of six Ropiten was taken by his father to the club two evenings a week. His father played billiards for money with his friends and Ropiten stayed there watching them. In the early days he kept falling asleep but then as he grew up he was able to keep awake until the games were finished. He learned all the rules and began to follow the play with great attention. Even if he sided with his father, his evidence was objective and thanks to him the players became aware that sometimes they made mistakes with the scoring. So when Ropiten was fourteen he was given the task of scoring for all the games. At first his father and the others checked that he wasn't making mistakes but soon saw that Ropiten made no mistakes and they could all concentrate exclusively on the game. It was the first time that the club had at its disposal an official scorer for the billiard games—one who wasn't waiting there for his own turn to play but preferred to move the plastic balls about on the wooden frame.

Then one evening Ropiten's father had a stroke right there in the club while he was playing. He was laid on the billiard table and the doctor, when he arrived, saved his life but told him that for him the time for smoking and playing billiards was past because he had a weak heart. So Ropiten's father could not go to the club any more. Ropiten was eighteen and continued to go to the club by himself twice a week to score for the games between his father's friends. They liked him very much and each time, after the matches, they offered him a drink and accompanied him back home. The next day he would tell his father who had won and who had lost, how many matches, how much money, why. Then Ropiten went to work in his father's agency for wools and synthetic fabrics. His father stayed at home in his dressing-gown and gave him advice from his own experience over the telephone.

After a little, even though he had stopped smoking and going to the club or to work, Ropiten's father died from another stroke. The doctor said then it was fate and there is nothing one can do about fate. Ropiten found himself alone carrying on the agency for wools and synthetic fabrics and the work went neither better nor worse than when his father gave him advice over the telephone.

In the evening, twice a week, Ropiten continued to go to the club to score. His father's friends continued to play billiards for money and to smoke, none of them had a stroke and the doctor forbade none of them anything. This seemed unjust to Ropiten. It seemed unjust that his father had died without anything changing at all, not even at the place where he had passed all his time for so many years.

One evening something suddenly came into Ropiten's mind. While he was there scoring it came into his mind that he could cheat. He tried it, he scored more points for one player and fewer for another and no one noticed anything. On the other hand his trick had not been decisive because the winner would have won just the same even if he had not cheated. So next time he cheated with more courage, going as far as to change the result of the game. Once again no one noticed the trick, the winner who had lost put his money on the table and the loser who had won stuck it in his pocket. Then Ropiten realized that no one would ever suspect him.

He began to cheat systematically following a precise rule: when he arrived in the club he took note of which player lit up a cigarette first and whoever it was Ropiten gave him only three points for every four he scored. According to how things went, Ropiten's changes could upset the outcome of the matches or not, but in no case were the results normal. Little by little Ropiten saw his father's friends begin to argue over this question of points. At the end of the match one person began to show that he was puzzled at having lost or at having been beaten by too big a margin; but his adversary immediately explained to him how and when he had lost or had built up the margin. If the latter was not convinced the other called to witness all those present who took sides according to their personal sympathies. And if anyone dared to suspect that Ropiten had made a mistake in the score the player who had benefited was quick to demonstrate that it was not true and some witnesses swore to it. From one evening to another the player who had lost out and the one who had benefited changed over according to whoever had lit his cigarette first and thus, while causing confusion (but not to the advantage of any one person), Ropiten, as scorer, was never suspected. What emerged were only a lot of reciprocal suspicions among the players, distant rancours which went very far back in time, to when Ropiten scored the points correctly and his father was still alive.

Then Ropiten had another idea and at once tried it out. He suddenly stopped cheating in the same way as he had begun. The arguments went on just the same. The results of the matches were once more in order but the players did not stop quarrelling. In fact they went further, they got to the point of insulting each other, of threatening to punch each other, until one evening one of them aimed a couple of punches at the opponent who had beaten him. Two others jumped on him and began to kick him and a cue was broken over the head of the man who ran the club. Ambulances were called and along with the ambulances the police arrived and took everyone's names and three players were taken off to the police station. But it was recognized that Ropiten was not involved in the affray.

So it was that games of billiards were no longer played at the club—not even by his father's friends who had sound hearts and went on smoking but were no longer friends among themselves. Other players whom Ropiten did not know took their places. The man who ran the club, too, stopped working because after the blow to his head he could no longer run the club: he sold the licence and retired to live on an insurance policy.

Ropiten no longer went to score for people whom he did not know and stayed at home every evening in the week watching television; he was bored but at least he could say that his father's death had been worthwhile.

Piera Oppezzo

Minutes Go Around my Head

I run my hands along the strip of woven hemp. My hands which are so alive to me. There's a fine pale sun, the temperature has softened.

I didn't expect it, I am so surprised. My head most of all is surprised. My body's already inside the situation and my head is surprised by this: it was given no warning. It really seems as if the head is everything.

I looked down four floors. The tram windows show reflections. Not the rails. I like the rails a lot. They're so good-natured, so old-fashioned. Beside the trams of course a lot of cars go by, green ones white ones dark red, some blue ones. Yellow taxis. Here and there a motorbike.

There are buds on the trees of the avenue. My eyes take in these things, the eyeballs straining hard, on the point of tears.

I go into the bathroom with this body softened by the softened temperature.

Now the water is running into the tub. I'll take a bath thinking about spring. The water runs, roars. Good, I mean not bad.

While the tub is filling up I go into the kitchen to make my coffee. I drink it then I lean for a moment with my head against the window pane, the small cup in my hand. It takes more than a little courage, more than I've got, for me to start the day. If I think about it.

Then I went into the bathroom again. Down, into the tub, deep in the water. I soaped myself all over, meaning to wash myself properly, even my arms which I always forget. I got out and slipped into my towelling robe. From the bedroom came two short coughs.

I am here alone, in there in my bed there's a friend, he's waking up. He's there. My body has been away from his for something like an hour. Now he'll be awake; his life is starting up again, mine has already.

I go past the room. He has propped up the pillows a little. His eyes are closed. I think about his thoughts. I walk on tiptoe even though he'd told me to wake him if he should oversleep.

I feel the coffeepot; the coffee is still hot, I pour some in a small cup. Being nice. I'm here quite by myself. Then I go into the bedroom still waking on tiptoe. I know he's awake but I feel I'm disturbing him.

I set the cup on the floor, I sit down on the edge of the bed, rest a hand on his. He doesn't clasp it at once. He too, quite by himself? Now he drinks the coffee with his eyes half open. He says hello. He asks me did you get up early? I say I've had a bath and I take off the bathrobe making me sweat, there separate from his body which is naked. His skin is warm and mine is cool. This thing I have breasts and a man only nipples. Like a surface for me to stretch out on top of.

Now again I'm no longer by myself even if it's only a question of time. I'll start again later. While he caresses my hair I caress his hair. I feel myself drowsing. I could fall asleep. Can I?

Loads of people would. They've got time. I've got time too, but I feel in my belly the day that lies ahead and this won't let go of me. Nothing lets go of me. Everything is always on the point of happening, I have to be there, nobody does it for me.

I move my legs. He says you're still sleepy, why don't you have a little nap? His voice is drowsy now. Although I'm quite comfortable I ease myself into a better position. What I want to see is whether I can sleep on top of him like this. Whether I'll cause him discomfort, whether we'll have room to breathe. He shifts his arm slightly so he can cradle my head, he smoothes out my hair, he's happy with this.

He's sleeping. I don't sleep a wink. My body has got warmer, more languid though, but I'm thinking. I'm thinking, remembering. We made love, for that's what you call it, we laughed, who's the first to fall asleep?

Now he's breathing deeply. Our skins are damp. I slide away and keep just my head and one arm on him. The head is important for feeling joined close. When he wakes up I'll only have to nudge it to reach his lips.

The traffic is crazy outside. Brain-numbing screeching of brakes. How will the pedestrians survive? I picture them skittering all over the place to avoid being killed. Bed is safer, the best place for whatever fears, it's always there.

I must have slept for a minute or two. Afterwards I felt I'd had another rest. If only I could really rest the way he's doing. Then wake up slowly dazed just like him. Fallen on to the bed from who knows where.

I've brushed aside my hair which is damp with sweat. Why this perpetual vigilance? I keep watch on myself, I suppose. I'm afraid I'll lose track of myself. Have to search frantic for myself everywhere I can think of. It would be exhausting. And I've got no imagination no sense of adventure either. I've got nothing it seems. I don't have resources, I just have feelings. In this sense I feel I have nothing.

I decide to light myself a cigarette and I raise my head. I reach out, feel the pack, squeeze it, nearly empty. The cigarettes, I need them to have all my wits about me. He's asleep I am wide awake. I can hear an ambulance coming to a stop down on the street. Why didn't I hear the crash happen; I've really slept then. I smile but down in the street they're smashed up, down in the street it did happen, people there got run over.

The cigarette's good. It's the second one. Half smoked I stub it out, crush it. I have to sleep. I lay my head where it was before. My arm too I lay where it was before. I can feel our skins smooth. I want to caress his skin but I wouldn't like to wake him. It's nice having this model of relaxation so near just as my head has got going again. Only stops still when I make love, almost still.

Now I see us looking in each other's eyes and everything was so near and we were smiling and we smiled at one another too.

Now I see his hair tumbling on to me. Tumbling, dishevelled. Then I feel his lips, feel them tiny on my shoulders, on my neck, then words. We listened to music, cigarettes, let's sleep now he says as I fall asleep.

Well and good. Yet it's like always. Living and thinking about it. Stop and go. It's the stops that are overdone. I have too many stops. I mean to do it, I do it to collect my thoughts, to tell myself things have taken place.

If only there were someone to free me from the stops for a longer time. Let's say a whole day, three days would be better, a few months at most.

No I kiss one of his nipples, he breathes a bit more deeply, nothing more than his breathing. He's sleeping soundly, I could sleep soundly too. My body's really ready for sleep. Relaxed by the bath and the loving. It's ready.

He shifts, moves around, takes over my position. Here I am with his head on my breast and an arm on my hip. I smooth down his hair a bit. I go on thinking about having everything in my head, in my head but it's not true. Right now I have nearly everything, a lot in my body. In my body-heart.

This morning is soft as can be. I've chopped it up a bit. Got out of bed, taken the bath, had the coffee. Tried to push it down. Let's say I want to leave a mark on things. Even tidied up the kitchen a bit though there was time enough. Not even that untidy.

I can't move now. If I shift I'll wake him; I'm doing it out of fondness, I'm doing it because I feel like trying.

Like this I felt my head dissolving into the pillow. A noise woke me up. Maybe there are bells nearby, maybe there's a church, it's noon, I've done it. Now that I've done it I'm impatient because only if we're both awake have I done it like him.

Now I'm impatient, it's really time to start the day for I haven't made it start I feel and it's passing, slipping away. I move less carefully, I manage to light a cigarette, I'm really rested too. My heart is racing less, for it was racing hard. It hindered me. Without that hindrance now I calmly smoke. I am calm. I know it won't last, that I'll soon be on the go again frenetic, messy. I make a lot of mess, idleness mess as I roll along with the day.

I'm getting hungry but if I eat alone I'll erase all the morning being together. Like having been at a play and I wasn't on the stage. But I did, almost did what other people usually manage to do. The telephone now. Three times, I get up, on the fourth ring it stops.

I'm standing in the bedroom, he's lying in the bedroom, the telephone didn't get through to him. It always gets through to me. I go towards him. I'm laying an ambush.

He's drawn into himself then he'll plunge into the day. There are so many days. Me standing here robbing the room of its climate of sleep. My body doesn't know what to do.

To get dressed or not. To lie down, lie back where I was before or. But it wouldn't make sense now. It wouldn't be trying any more, I'd be putting something off, that's all. As I'm looking towards the window, the blind that's still down, hardly any light coming in and just as I'm going to reach out he says hello what are you doing? I slept until a little while ago, I slept a bit. So you did come back, he eases himself up. He's got the dazed look I expected.

Then he said what time is it, he said do you want to have something to eat, we could I answered relieved. There was a terrible thudding noise down on the street. So you weren't sleeping I said, yes but I heard. Well then he heard and he wasn't unsettled by the doubt whether to sleep on or to stop sleeping. It's what normally happens if someone's asleep.

Maybe he asks if there's any coffee left while I'm in the kitchen making coffee. I pour it in a single cup, a little for each of us, one cigarette between us. He asks if there's anything sweet to eat, so he doesn't want to have lunch, to catch up with time. He wants to stay with breakfast, anything else will come later. I say let's get up as if we had gone to sleep together and I hadn't done all that toing and froing to stay, to stop myself staying. I'm someone who's always toing and fro ing. My head my body my movements. It's staggering all this stuff that goes on with me and that I'm the only one to know about.

I stretch out flat on the bed. He goes into the bathroom and comes back out. I'm not stretched flat on the bed, I'm waiting for him to come back, the position is a detail. He comes back and his body stretches out next to mine. He's got plenty of time.

He says things, I reply to the things he says, I say things, etc. The things I say are things I want to say but meanwhile I stop myself from thinking that this day is slipping away from me. I started up I stopped short I started up again I'm stopping short.

Now I can't wait to end this coming and going in my head and body. Either he has lunch with me or he goes. Until he goes I have no space, always this question of space.

He knows these things and he doesn't know them. Besides they're my monologue, something of mine. I'm tired of these things that are too much mine. Sick and tired.

He gets up saying let's go into the kitchen. He's forgotten about the cake or else he's realized. In the kitchen we get some stuff out of the fridge. Two plates on the table, some beer, cutlery. When we start eating everything's right, it's lunch time, we're having lunch, we've caught up with time, I feel relieved. Fact is I've coped well.

What are you doing today he asks, I don't know. I don't think he's asking as a way of asking to stay with me. We've got no problem about this. Meanwhile we go on drinking and then we go back to bed because next to the bed is the bottle of whisky.

By now everything's like it was before, about to be. As I swallow the first sip minutes go around my head, I'm drowsy, there's his body next to mine. It's so different being two of us. Meaning me and someone else not meaning me and me. One more thing to do, or not.

I smile and hold the glass against my lips. I realize that this day today won't stop starting. It isn't even this, which is above all in the mind. Now it's that the head has less space, the body's taking over more, whatever I do. More space, expanding. And it isn't just this. It's that there are two heads. They are roads that diverge that converge. All the time.

Elisabetta Rasy

Clerambault's Syndrome

Chocolate. A strong smell of chocolate, like when a bar is unwrapped, or a trayful of chocolates are set down on a table. Not a stale odour, a lingering odour, but a living fragrance, like an essence. It seemed, in other words, that the woman standing at the front door, in the posture of a supplicant, her face perfectly aligned with her body, her body perfectly straight, four-square, used chocolate the way other women use essence of tuberose or jasmine as a perfume. But even allowing the existence, the admissibility of a chocolate eau de cologne, it was by no means the right perfume for that woman.

Anita, who ever since she'd been the household help with Dr and Mrs B.—not more than five or six months, really—had found herself quite often in that strange confrontation on the doorstep, at each new encounter told herself inwardly, as if that brusque affirmation were a comfort, or indeed her safety, that she had never ever met a woman wearing chocolate perfume, and that she had never seen in the whole of her now not altogether short life, eyes and hair like those she now had in front of her again. The eyes were blue, and the hair blonde, at least that's how they would be described on a passport. But it was as if on that blue and on that blonde there had been thrown buckets and buckets of soapy water, water with a double strength detergent, one of those cut-price detergents that takes out dirt and colour, pretty much indiscriminately, in a wholesale hygienic resurrection. Or else, Anita would think at other times, as if it had rained in them, rained in those eyes and that hair, a blustering dusty rain, a rain that was hot and abrasive.

Now, though, Anita knew how she was to behave, even if she still didn't find it easy. And it had been very very difficult the first few times that the stiff, listless female form had appeared at the front door, or, even more inexplicably, by the gate of their nicely secluded little house, that was so well tucked away among the little streets of that elegant, distant, almost inaccessible suburb, a place which for Anita had been extraordinarily hard to get to, and then to find her way around. By this time, though, Anita no longer had to ask the woman polite questions, she had only to say, being as firm as possible, 'There's nobody at home.' And since the chocolate woman filled her with terror at heart, and since she was very unsure about this whole business, she stressed each of the sentence's six syllables as if she were addressing a foreigner, and then, in the face of the stranger's unwavering look, repeated it over and over again, until there issued from her mouth nothing more than an unnatural sound, a singsong lament at once both cruel and abject.

At the beginning Mrs B. had been reticent, unclear. Then on the third or fourth appearance of the unknown woman she had come to Anita in the kitchen, and, as she heated up the water for tea, had broached the subject with a weary, or possibly exasperated, 'I meant to tell you.' The lady of the house had told what was at first an unbelievable, or certainly ridiculous story. Then, though, to Anita's doubting ears it had seemed that in the vehemence with which it was repeated, in the long list of anecdotes and details, and most of all in the fury, in the fury that grew in the lady of the house at every dot and comma of her speech, at every pause of breath, and more so in the hatred that the unfolding of the story caused to explode, to swell in the voice of its teller, it had seemed that right and wrong, good and bad were shared out, divided in a just counterposition, as in every true story, thought Anita, as in every story worth repeating.

Clerambault's syndrome, Mrs B. had said at a certain point, her voice now lost in labyrinths of rancour, and it had been the seal of science, the conclusive proof. Clerambault's syndrome, Mrs B. had explained, from the name of a French doctor, the psychiatrist C.G. de Clerambault, who in 1942—and at that point Mrs B., herself also a psychiatrist, had spoken to Anita with great sorrow, and above all without any condescension of status or knowledge—had pronounced that a woman who experiences and cultivates an imaginary love affair suffers, this is exactly how he had put it, from a specific psychotic condition, thereafter identified as Clerambault's syndrome. In other words, a genuine illness, Mrs B. had concluded. Her task, in that kitchen conversation, was not easy: not only did she have to justify the appearances of the unknown woman before the incredulous eyes of Anita, but before the suspicious eyes of Anita she had to put forward reasons for her own powerlessness—in the face of these appearances—and above all the powerlessness of her husband, Dr B. Insofar as it was obvious in everyone's eyes, Anita's, Mrs B.'s and of course the unknown woman's, that he was the one, that thin, hardpressed, and perpetually ill at ease 45-year-old man—such as Anita saw him as he went out in the morning and returned in the evening, which was as much as she ever encountered him—was the keystone of the whole business, the point of perspective, the focus. And he was blameless, said Mrs B., or rather, only to blame in having been ignorant, at the time of his meeting with the chocolate woman and, despite his profession as a therapist in a psychiatric hospital, of the studies of his astute colleague Clerambault. Because things, Mrs B. had explained, drinking quick sips of tea, shaking her head between one sip and the next as if in the grip of a sudden tic, things had happened like this.

Ten years earlier, D. had turned up at Dr B.'s hospital; a young woman, with a number of children and a husband no less fond of her for all he was engrossed in his work, who was suffering from a pronounced generalized anxiety that alternated with depression. The woman had quickly been referred to Dr B., who was then experimenting with the possibility of small therapy groups for less serious patients. A few sessions after D. joined, Dr B. had decided to dissolve the little group, and to discontinue that form of experimental work, because, in his opinion, nothing of any significance was happening in the group. It was then that Clerambault's syndrome broke out in D.; a sickness, and here Mrs B. became even more ill at ease than her husband, for which there is no cure, as the man who discovered it explained, and which is fated to last until one of the two parties involved should die. Imaginary love, no, outright persecution, Mrs B. insisted, outright invasion.

From then on D. had laid siege to Dr. B. with no truce, with no respite. She paid constant visits throughout the months when the man had still been working at the hospital. Or else with constant telephone calls, one telephone call after another, up to fifty in one day, at first greeted with amusement by the hospital switchboard, then with sarcasm, finally with exasperation. And when Dr B. had taken up his new job, the one he now has, in a big industrial institute in town, and when D., after checking in every way possible, had become convinced of his departure from the hospital, the inexorable pilgrimage had begun. Every four or five days, according to some inscrutable schedule, the female figure with its strong perfume of chocolate and its tear-filled eyes and hair would materialize at the front door, in search of the doctor.

Like now, in the shimmering April afternoon, silhouetted in the doorway, mute and insistent, immutable, impervious to time and season, attired with meticulous and featureless care, unalterable, a rebuke to all that passes, that changes, that does not repeat itself.

But her husband, her children? Anita had asked, not just on the day of the kitchen explanation. The children, Mrs B. had answered, are far from being unaware of the situation; they think the mother has a lover, a real lover I mean, a normal sort of thing, she had hissed, and the husband, the husband would rather not think about it; besides, D. still keeps the house clean, shops, cooks, looks after the children, and is even less anxious than she once was, according to the husband, although just as neat and tidy as ever. But don't imagine, Anita, that their surrender was an unconditional one; they fought, and with every means possible. If Dr B. has deemed it best, more expedient, never to appear, not even once, before D.'s blank gaze, his wife has faced that gaze many times. And she hasn't just faced the gaze: she has spoken for hours, she has asked her own father to be there, she has telephoned the woman's husband—but the woman's husband is hard to find, and then he's elusive or busy, reluctant to talk or about to go out—she has even thought about the police (but what could she say, that there's a woman, in love with her husband, who's bothering her? . . . if only she made threats, did damage, like other women affected by Clerambault's syndrome, things would be different . . .) and then, then one day she actually threw a bucket of cold water over her head from the window.

But nothing, nothing makes a jot of difference. D. is convinced that Mrs B. isn't Dr B.'s wife at all, that the doctor doesn't have a wife at all. Quite the opposite, and this is the crux of it—of the syndrome, says Mrs B. in a voice that now seems to Anita to be really breathless, and of the calamity which has stricken the family: D. is convinced that Dr B. loves her. That he loves her, and he has loved her for all these ten years, that he in fact was the first to love, the first to send out unmistakable signals in the small, dark, therapy room; scant gestures without meaning at first, but then, by their repetition, by their relentless persistence towards her, becoming clearer and clearer, more and more explicit. And so now, while he is really to blame in letting the whole conspiracy bear down against them, even now, despite his inexplicable fear and obvious powerlessness, he, D. believes, goes on loving her and sending her signals. She is able to decipher them with certainty. Some by now are almost too apparent, like the way she is greeted at the supermarket check-out, good morning, morning—good morning, madam, in conformity with the required civilities. And those cartoons too, that cartoon strip that appears in the paper every Thursday, holds no more mystery now. Somewhat harder, D. has divulged, are the signals that appear to her in the sky, the shape of certain clouds at certain times of the day, the patterns of bird flight at dusk. The signals in the sky, sometimes, still belong to the devastating realm of mystery. But everything, everything else, according to the crazy woman who now makes not the slightest response to Anita's dry utterances, and who above all shows no sign of going away, everything else is imposture, mystification.

But Anita now knows that she only has to wait, to put up with the constant tinkling of the doorbell, after she has closed the door, and every so often to go back and open the door again to the petrified body to stop the tinkling for a moment or two, until it's four o'clock. At four o'clock, and it is pointless doing it any earlier, because that would just be cheating, Anita will inform her that it's four o'clock, and she will say she has to go and fetch the children from school, but to tell Dr B. she has been there, and that of course she'll be back. That she, Anita, is to make sure she gets her name right, and she is to write it down, to make a note of it there, on that table set against the wall of the hallway, directly opposite the door. There, she has to leave her name written down just there, there and nowhere else. She is to swear it.

It is just after four o'clock. Now D. walks along the silent little avenue of the distant suburb, several hundred yards, as far as the stop for the bus that will take her into the centre of town, to another stop for another bus. It is very hot this April, and there are no clouds in the sky. Precisely in April—or maybe not, but in a month like it, a luminous warming month—in the little hospital room, beside the window, Dr B. had offered her a chocolate bar, it's good for you, he had said. And since she didn't take it, and she had stood there unmoving, staring at the brown stuff, the doctor had put a piece of it into her hand, and then, since she kept on holding it in her hand, with it sliding and starting to melt, the doctor had taken her hand, and both the hands together, the doctor's and hers, held against each other and maybe slightly intertwined, had reached her mouth, and the chocolate, through the slight pressure of the male hand, had gone inside it, and then even deeper inside it, and then had slid down her throat.

Claudio Piersanti

Little Alberta in Flight

Two blackbirds, as fat as pigeons, were scratching about in the corner of the garden. A lot of sparrows, in scattered ranks, were scratching about in what remained of the hardened earth. The sky was grey and it was cold—almost cold enough to move one to tears. It was as if a breath of wind were coming from the distant North Pole or perhaps from the Himalayas, at least from some remote and unknown place. It was this feeling that made the cold almost move one to tears—like the visit of a stranger. It is precisely here, I thought, among our cars, just here that this light archaic wind has descended. On the roofs long decorations of ice shone and from the drain-pipes hung dry ghosts of water.

It was a wonderful January morning. I was passing the time looking out of the window because I was waiting for Margherita, who was coming back after a long stay abroad.

As always she was even later than she had vaguely hinted ('early morning'), speaking of flight connections as if they were a game of infinite possibilities. Perhaps she had stopped off in London, perhaps in Belgium, perhaps even in Moscow. But all the permutations translated themselves into the hint 'early morning'. Let's say between seven and ten. But at midday it was already 'late morning' and Margherita was late. As the hours passed the air, already bone-dry, was accumulating electricity and I had the feeling that lots of tiny electrical discharges were tingling on my skin as well.

Between me and Margherita there was no formal agreement, we had only a past of very amusing encounters. Sometimes we had made love but we had hardly ever talked seriously—that is without laughing a little. One day she found herself being offered a good job in Australia without having ever asked for it. So, astonished but without any bitterness, she left for Sydney at the beginning of an extremely hot May to come back permanently to Italy only five years later on that January day I was describing.

For the occasion I had lit the fire and dusted off a good bottle of wine. Margherita arrived at sunset and found me half-asleep on the divan. I did not manage to reply to her in a sensible way, I was giggling—certainly because of having drunk too much wine. But I was also confused by an inexplicable vision. There were two Margheritas: an adult (the usual Margherita) and a little one.

'Where have you come from?' I asked, paying no attention to her double.

'From Melbourne—of course.'

'I knew that.'

'We stopped off at Moscow and managed to see Red Square, didn't we?' Her double did not reply but made odd faces. 'You must speak Italian.'

'Noooo,' replied the little girl.

'It isn't true that children can be bilingual. Alberta doesn't speak any more—she has forgotten everything she learned.'

Meantime she had slipped the coat off the little girl, who, pleased with herself, showed off her dress.

'About Alberta . . . I had no idea.'

'I didn't tell you in my letter—that's true. If it's a problem for you to put us both up . . .'

'A problem?'

'I didn't write to you about it because I didn't know how to . . .'

'She's quite big,' I commented, 'you could say she's quite big, isn't she?'

'She's almost four,' Margherita explained. I began to laugh and she did the same. 'It's true. I didn't lose time.'

Alberta was not interested in our chat. She climbed on to the divan and hid herself in a little cushioned fort. She wanted to be alone. She was very independent, Alberta, and never gave the lie to this first impression.

That evening we dined almost in silence, Margherita and Alberta were tired from the journey and their appetite showed it. Alberta dissected her portion of chicken and made a lot of strips out of it which she arranged in a beautiful geometry on her plate. Finally she built four little towers with the purée and began to destroy them with blows from her fork, pitilessly.

'What a pity,' I commented. 'All that work.'

'Yes, what a pity,' Margherita echoed me. And as she talked to me about the difficulties caused by her enormous amount of baggage—it too travelling about the world—the little girl laid her head on the table and fell asleep. As if she had been the one to drink the bottles of Brunello.

But Margherita and I too were exhausted, our eyes were half-shut and the rings under our eyes dug hollows in our cheeks. I accompanied them to their bedroom (or rather I accompanied Margherita who carried her sleeping daughter) and immediately went to my own. Once again Margherita had surprised me. I dreamt of her that night.

I would never have found the courage to ask Margherita the stupid question 'Who is the father?' but within me hypotheses and fantasies about that unknown man flourished.

I tried to subtract Margherita's features from her daughter's face but what was left was not much with which to form a portrait. The down-turned mouth and the dimples in the cheeks—these were the salient features that made Alberta different. I noticed them the following morning. I had got up at nine and was making breakfast in a leisurely way—that morning I didn't need to be in school till eleven.

Alberta came and sat beside me without even saying Hello. She was expecting me to get everything ready and that was what I was trying to do.

'Do you take a little coffee in your milk?' I asked her.

'Yes,' she replied with assurance.

'There you are. Very little—but it's real coffee.'

'I speak Italian, did you know?' she confessed at the second biscuit.

'I can hear that,' I answered. Alberta said no more and after drinking her milky coffee began to play on the carpet. She was interested in two corks. She placed one on top of the other and then knocked them down. When she was tired of knocking them down she laid one alongside the other and covered them with two tram tickets. Then she lay down too and pretended to sleep. Every so often she raised herself and arranged the paper blankets on her corks.

I left the house at ten and set off on foot for the school. There was a little sun but the wind was icy and it got in everywhere. I had plenty of time to prepare in my head my lesson on Schopenhauer and in any case it was my tenth time round with him. I thought that for ten years nothing new had happened to me. I was feeling fine but I was bored. The students exhausted my need for social intercourse and I had got used to passing my free time alone. It tired me to meet my old friends; I no longer found them interesting. I read the philosophers whom I had to explain to the students and little by little had got together a good library. My secret prayer had become this: 'Lord, don't let me become a bore.' Isolation increases this tendency, which is in each one of us, as I very well knew. At this point in my existence Margherita reappeared. I fell in love with her right away; I hadn't loved anyone for too many years.

When I stroked her hand and led to her to understand what I felt she began to laugh. She took my hand and kissed my fingers one by one.

'It's not the moment,' she said.

'There will be another moment, I hope.'

'You know that Alberta adores you?'

'If it's true I'm pleased.'

'Her father is called Enzo.'

'Is he Italian?'

'Yes. I didn't even want him to know her. Enzo is a shit.'

'I'm sorry.'

'You're sorry?'

'No—maybe I'm not so sorry.'

Then Margherita talked in a way that really made me feel sorry. She had found a little flat in an apartment block and was thinking of going there as soon as possible.

'The important thing is for you not to go away because you're afraid of being a nuisance. The house is big and you can stay as long as you like.'

She smiled and kissed my fingers again. She must have learned that in Australia, she never did it before. Within me I was begging her to stay: 'I love you and the little girl, please send for all your luggage and do up the house as you want. Live here with me.'

Saying these things to Margherita, even only in thought, I had to try to maintain a certain sense of humour. She is the kind of person to whom you had to announce even the end of the world without tearing your hair.

However Margherita was not in love with me. She had other things in her head, I saw. It had happened to me too to receive a declaration of love and to feel only astonishment and disappointment. But to know for sure that I was not loved back by Margherita wounded me greatly and something in our relationship changed. I took to spending more time shut up in my study which is a little long and narrow room with a window at the end which only opens a bit. I prepared my lessons but above all I read.

I took up Kant again whom I love greatly. Margherita had decided to stay on while she waited for a real house; Alberta too liked it here and never intruded. Sometimes I brought her a picture book, sometimes we went out together to have a hot chocolate.

Alberta fell head over heels in love with me. I noticed this one morning when I was leaving to go to school. She went out on to the landing with me. She was in her knickers, barefoot and uncombed. She hugged me round the knees and looked at me the way I would have liked Margherita to look at me.

'You're very pretty, Alberta,' I said to her. Her eyes were shining. I bent down to give her a kiss.

'I love you,' she confessed to me.

'Me too.'

'But I really do.'

'So do I—really. As soon as I'm back we'll go and have a chocolate with cream. But please, don't come in your knickers.'

She looked at herself crestfallen. I had been an idiot. I told myself a hundred times. I was incapable of loving them, my fellow-tenants. Perhaps I was unable to love anyone. In the street I noticed that it was a terrible day from the point of view of the weather as well. It began to rain almost at once and soon the rain turned to sleet. I felt I deserved the little icy whip-lashes that struck me in the face and did nothing to shield myself from them.

The crisis was about to burst. The spark was a cigarette. For some days I had started smoking again and was smoking even in the dining room where Alberta passed much of her time. I made the air unbreathable—a transparent metaphor. I felt towards my guests a sullen rancour which humiliated me, made me feel guilty. I would come out of the study meaning to be polite but the moment I saw them I was struck dumb. I would sit down and begin to smoke. One afternoon I looked attentively at the cigarette I was smoking. A disgusting dark-brown slime had formed which ran from the burning tip towards the filter. I touched it and felt it was slimy. I sniffed at its bitter smell. I don't know whether it was the touch, the sight or the smell, that produced the effect; I went pale and began to tremble with cold.

Margherita put me to bed and covered me with a duvet and some blankets as well. Then she made some tea and brought it to me steaming. It did me good, that tea, like a miraculous elixir. Margherita and Alberta were sitting at the foot of the bed and were looking at me. Alberta seemed alarmed.

'A drop in blood pressure. You collapsed,' commented Margherita, smiling like an expert nurse.

'It would be better if I didn't smoke any more,' I said. The cold had gone. I saw that I was no longer in love with Margherita. I saw her as she always had been.

'Are you better?' asked Alberta.

'Yes.'

'So why don't you drink some chocolate?'

'Later.'

'Shall I make it?'

'Yes.'

They both went off to see to my chocolate. Naturally I didn't need chocolate but it pleased me to think that someone was taking care of me. I was touched. Also because I associated the chocolate with the end of my passion for Margherita. I was not waiting for a simple cup of chocolate; I was taking part in a ceremony. For a month I had desired Margherita and had never looked at her without hoping for a kiss. How the hell doesn't she see, I said to myself, that it would be wonderful to kiss; we have done it before and it was never so wonderful as it would be now!

But she was taken up with her work, which had started recently, with the little girl, with the house she had at last found and which needed a lot done to it and with my house as well, which had been enriched with things in good taste and which had never been so alive and so tidy. Now that I no longer loved her I felt better and again felt liking for her. I got out of bed and joined mother and daughter in the dining room. The odour of chocolate was spreading through the house. I felt weak and calm. Alberta welcomed me with a little dance and gave me a present of all her toys. Dozens of little animals, some that squeaked and some that didn't, a little piano, a little bag of corks.

The winter passed pleasantly and the days began to lengthen. We often went out, the three of us together. Trips into the country and to the parks, some ice-creams. The work on Alberta and Margherita's new house was well advanced: from their windows you could see the park and both were happy about that, although Alberta would have liked there to be certain birds with unpronounceable names in those trees. She wouldn't give in. When we were walking in the park she often cried out 'There it is'. Usually she was pointing at a blackbird or a pigeon.

Between me and Margherita completely normal relations had been re-established, and every so often we kissed. Alberta had got into the habit of sometimes sleeping with me. She would join me in the middle of the night or else in the early morning hours. She took up a little corner of the bed and did not move. One morning I woke at dawn convinced I had been sharing the bed with Alberta. Instead I was alone but in a good mood because it was a fine clear morning. I went into the kitchen to make the coffee and found Alberta there. She was sitting on the carpet in front of the window. She had no clothes on, she had thrown her pyjamas across the room. She was looking at the trail of an aeroplane and was imitating its trajectory with a toy car but going in the opposite direction. She was making a noise with her mouth, a very fair imitation of the noise of a jet.

Francesca Sanvitale

The Electric Typewriter

The rainy September cast a low, melancholy, beautiful light. Day after day it caused feelings of detachment and separation, even despair, especially at sunset.

For hours Carlo hadn't moved and had passed the idle afternoon without enjoying the September light. His gaze had shifted from the bookshelves, and slowly moved from one object to another. Like one wretched, depraved, or obsessed, he had stared at the orderly piles of newspapers and magazines on little benches and tables, separated according to a personal work method, and gazed at the flowers in the rugs, the elaborately decorated borders. Everything scrutinized in detail but without thought.

He had been trying to pursue, gather, differentiate and thereby destroy a fog behind his eyes that came out to cloud his glasses. This fog had a peculiar characteristic: it dissolved backgrounds and perspectives and outlined things in dusty lights.

For more than a month he had calmed his aggravating restlessness by devoting the entire afternoon to the observation of his studio and he no longer felt the need to go out.

Iris would come back soon and he was waiting for her. His eyes stopped searching the shadows and were cast outside himself, like an object in a surrealistic painting, towards an imagined door. Everything would return to normal in his sight and in the room as soon as Iris turned the key in the lock. As always she would slam the door carelessly and break into his space. She would open a window and lean out, exposing her fat hips, crying out, 'Air! Air!' She would observe with disgust the ashtray full of butts. She would hurriedly question him ('How many pages?' 'Have you finished?' 'How far did you get?').

Out of habit Carlo would not answer. From the kitchen would come the smells of garlic and onion that he found reassuring. The work day was over. In other times, which seemed far away but were not, they would see friends in the evening, go to the theatre or a movie.

He had turned sixty-two the day before. Many said he was a great writer, but not too prolific. He had noticed that after sixty almost all writers, for one reason or another, become great writers. The public is lavish with its praise and then forgets all about them.

He gazed at the books, the objects of various size and value, pictures, rugs, armchairs, divans, and observed that this was what remained of the many words used which formed neither emotions or memories. They had materialized there around him as if he had been the manager of a small, agoraphobic business for forty years.

For him and Iris almost forty years of artistic activity had transformed themselves into a series of objects contained in that middle-class apartment and in the small seaside apartment. His stories were born one after the other with relative ease, and he was convinced that they were always significant. Iris had said repeatedly in the face of his uncertainties and anxieties: just write and don't think about it too much. It's all right, it's all right. You are an artist.

And the future? the future? This had been the past: an introduction, indeed a necessary introduction. He was sure that the future would be different in the sense that he finally would grasp something that he had only vaguely sought inside himself, he would plunge into the surging depths that exist below human surfaces. Maybe he would sell the two apartments. Maybe he would move abroad. Maybe Iris would die.

Iris kept saying with love or with scorn or with a particular maternal inflection that he was an eternal child. This was the way she forced him in bed to touch the depths of his weakness, and at the moment he understood it she would brush it away with a sleight-of-hand. In a kind of dream, a show *ad absurdum*, he found himself practising a virility without tenderness, only frenzy, and in that kind of game or dream he was the tyrant and she the slave.

Iris was very fat and had become old. She didn't care. She seemed to believe that their nights would never change. She had assumed the role of trainer and in the morning Carlo was ready for the ring of his studio, at the desk, strictly tied to her and to that room, unfit for life or any other kind of woman. He still desired Iris because she allowed him the vices his mind needed. Iris barred any novelty, she obliterated defeats. She prevented a calm reflection on the meaning of existence, but she also prevented thought from sinking into darkness, beyond the curtain of flowing images.

For a month his depression had deepened and his headaches, anxiety, and tiredness had increased. He was forced to withdraw into himself. The doctor and Iris consulted behind his back. He had come to a passage, perhaps providential: he had to reflect, to understand something that had escaped him. Then he could go on.

He was not writing any more. That didn't matter. He was too tired, trapped in a dismal listlessness. His face played annoying tricks, but the doctor said the symptoms were entirely gratuitous and connected with his nerves. The same with the nausea that every once in a while rose from his guts for no reason. He had to let himself rest.

He went out on the balcony and looked to the left towards the neighbouring balcony. Almost dark. The other window was illuminated. He heard the regular, muffled noise of the electric typewriter. Short pauses, followed by a clicking. He sat down, even though the cool wind bothered him. He watched the wind shaking the stems of the long, thin, nearly wilted carnations that Orlando, the next door neighbour, didn't take care of. They drooped over the railing in small dry clusters.

He was aware of the traffic on the street. He listened to the stopping and starting of the electric typewriter. With an idiotic joy every day he tried to imagine what in the world Orlando was writing. It might be a new novel. He had already written two of them, very much like two stories, and not much longer. Competent representations. Pleasant female characters. Plausible dialogue. The stories that Orlando told were easy to understand. Orlando himself was more difficult to understand.

Since he had to rest, Carlo often amused himself by inventing stories to the rhythm of the electric typewriter. He was free to tell himself nonsensical stories, imitating the avant-garde buried before his youth. He drew out and put together odd bunches of images in the surrealistic manner, or composed obscene love songs, or sonnets in the manner of Carducci. It was his solitary and entirely new way to play in the dark silence and also to feel that his mind, like an enclosed reservoir, was full of words that mingled in amazing fantasies even without his willing them. He seemed to have regained a sense of freedom, a taste of childhood, of adolescence.

From Orlando's apartment came a longer caesura than usual. Immediately Carlo imagined in the darkness before him the gigantic ectoplasm of a hand suspended over the keyboard and he waited. He thought only one exact phrase: maybe that clicking will never start up again.

In that case, in such an extraordinary and unprecedented case, the silence would become high, magnificent, charged with emotion. Orlando and he, like two astronauts detached from their spaceship would move away into empty space grasping each other tightly, quickly disappearing, exactly alike and mute. But the clicking recommenced and Carlo heard within it the arrogant superiority of youth.

Orlando lived alone. He wrote articles for a newspaper and was a researcher at the university. A girl named Gina visited him at irregular intervals and lived with him for two or three days. Carlo had never understood their real relationship. One could suppose it a stability that had lasted for years. Or a complete casualness that had kept them apart as it had united them. He spied on them. They kept a rhythmical pace on the street as they walked in step. They dressed alike, faded jeans and nice sweaters, coloured shirts, jackets. They gave the impression of cautious confidence and harmony. They had the habit of stopping every once in a while as they walked and looking into each other's eyes with a slight smile. Gina would toss back her long straight hair with a loose, careless motion, and bending her head would gather it in one hand, bringing it forward over her shoulders.

Carlo watched them as if they were two people to be robbed. Their affectations as a couple, their over-harmonious movements made him feel spiteful. He criticized them: according to him they were showing off on a stage and Orlando would have to watch out because that was not life.

In a certain sense he desired both of them. He allowed himself sexual fantasies or extravagant erotic impulses because he knew he was depressed and wanted to amuse himself. Orlando was thirty, slender as a fifteen-year-old but without the aggressiveness. He went through the world taking his pleasures with a casual elegance and a secret obstinacy. Carlo envied him with an intensity and confusion so strong that at times it seemed like love.

The doorbell rang. Carlo shuffled down the hall and opened the door.

'Excuse me for bothering you. Can you lend me your Collins?'

Orlando spoke with a pleasant urbanity.

Carlo made a brusque gesture, turned on the lights, preceded him into the studio. Orlando's self-assurance was stupid. Why on earth did he have to have that particular dictionary? He bent over with difficulty and his head spun. A whirl, a dangerous dizziness, passed through his brain.

'Here is the Collins,' he said, panting a little. 'I have it by chance.' He was observing Orlando's body: his well-built arms with long muscles, his chest and slender hips. He possessed a supple gracefulness, a suggestion of boyishness with his sudden gestures. His eyes were slightly convex, clear and very still, like those of certain insects.

Orlando looked around, a little unsure of himself. 'I see,' he remarked, in a tone of respect by no means humble, 'that you have the Tommaseo Bellini dictionary in the first edition of eight volumes!' He made a slight gesture towards the volumes.

Carlo said nothing. There was a pause. Orlando began to say

that he would be leaving for New York the next day. 'On a scholarship for one year. I wanted to say good-bye because I'm leaving my apartment. I'm sorry I didn't see more of you.' He stopped. He frowned and added, 'Naturally it was unavoidable. It's hard for anyone who writes in the province . . .'

Carlo gave him an uncomprehending look and interrupted him: 'The province? What has the province to do with it?'

'I meant Italy. The real game is happening somewhere else . . .'

He smiled.

Silence reigned. Carlo straightened some newspapers. 'One can write anywhere,' he mumbled. He was about to add something else but Orlando was heading rapidly toward the front door. 'I'll bring it back right away,' he said in a high voice. Shrill, a sort of warble.

Carlo was alone again. He turned off the lights. Over Orlando's bed was an Escher poster. In the living room a few pieces of light wood furniture, red and black director's chairs. Basically the boy was almost poor and, compared to him, lived like an ascetic. He didn't own a house and earned little. He owned only an electric typewriter. But Orlando made him angry: he didn't realize the complexity of the problem, he didn't even understand that he was dealing more with an enigma than a profession. Or both? At this point he became angry with himself also. That happened to someone suffering from nerves: small exterior events, little upsets resulted in inner disturbances. Orlando was going to New York and consequently Carlo wouldn't be able to know what turn that life had taken. This bothered him, annoyed him very much. In six months of being close neighbours they had talked only foolishness, letting the two women take the lead in their rare encounters. Did he like Conrad? Did he like James? Had he read, for instance, *Kiss of the Spider Woman*? What was the plot of the novel he was writing? and *his* novels? what did he *really* think of them?

He didn't hear the clicking any more. A particular silence fell over the house and over him.

The lock turned and in a moment Iris was in the studio.

'Well,' she said at once. Her voice left no doubt of her

invasion. 'Still in the dark?' She turned on the light and began taking in everything with her inspection. 'Nasty weather outside. It seems like winter. Better to stay in the house.' She threw a newspaper on the desk. 'The interview came out. The photograph of you doesn't look bad. If I were a young reader it would give me wicked thoughts.' She giggled. She took the ashtray.

'What is there to eat?' Carlo asked.

'Nothing, why?' She broke into one of her typical laughs. It would be a special dish, then. She went into the hall exclaiming, 'I can't wait to take off my shoes!'

For a moment he thought of following her, of taking her by the shoulders, of making love quickly, before supper, as they used to do when they were young. He sat down and lowered his head in his hands. Again the doorbell as he tried to rouse himself from his torpor. Orlando was already back with the dictionary and was looking at him quizzically. 'Aren't you feeling well?' He stepped forward to hold him up or give him support, but Carlo shook his head, overcome by anger and drowsiness. 'Certainly not,' he managed to say in a kind of whisper. 'Nothing is wrong, nothing, do you understand?'

Orlando moved back to reestablish the space he had violated.

'Just remember!' Carlo believed he was shouting, 'just remember that you don't kid around with words!' But he only thought he was shouting and he had lost the thought again. That wasn't what he wanted to throw in Orlando's face to waken him from his conventional faith.

The only words that came to his mind were even more senseless: have you read Tolstoy? Have you read Stendhal? and Dickens? and De Quincey? and Dickinson? and Chekhov? and Goethe? and Dostoevski? and . . .

He was forming a kind of litany in his head that numbed him as though he were counting sheep to go to sleep. He closed his eyes.

Orlando stood there stock still, in amazement, looking at him. He barely murmured, 'I wanted to say good-bye, excuse me.' Nothing happened. Carlo's heavy body folded over in a slow-motion faint and his eyelids opened and closed as if he had swallowed poison. His eyes were rolling wildly.

Orlando backed away in little steps. 'Signora Iris,' he murmured again. 'I don't think Signor Carlo feels very well.'

Iris came out unconcerned and shook her head. 'It's nerves, depression,' she said.

'I'm so sorry,' whispered Orlando. 'I'm sure he'll feel better soon. Please give him my best wishes.'

Carlo heard Iris and Orlando talking and saying good-bye. He heard him go out. He heard the noises that punctuated his afternoons: the turn of the lock, the click of light. He felt that he was sinking into a deep hell: perhaps it was really the well he had dreamed up, the darkness that leads to consciousness, to the horror that right words come from. He had avoided it all his life and he wasn't sure he wanted this ordeal. 'Iris,' he shouted, 'Iris! Iris!'

A menacing silence fell. The shadow assailed him, forced pain on him. What was this empty room of knowledge that, like a twin to torture, his nightmare symbolized? He thought confusedly of Orpheus, of Pamino, of efforts, of hard labours described in fables and was about to grasp the meaning of what he was seeking, as if it were something struggling to enter his heart with simple clarity. Perhaps they were the true words, the unforgettable stories. 'Iris!' he shouted again. He stood up staggering, nerve-racked and shaken by so much emotion. Suddenly he vomited.

The doorbell rang for the third time. Iris ran to the door and opened it.

'How is he today?' the doctor said as he entered.

Iris dried a tear with the palm of her hand. 'He seems worse to me.' She spoke softly to keep Carlo from hearing. 'Much worse. But he doesn't realize . . . he has never realized anything . . .'

The doctor clapped her on the back. 'Cheer up, Signora,' he said good-naturedly. 'Let's go and have a look at him.'

Daniele Del Giudice

Dillon Bay: A Military Tale

Getting that far had been fairly easy, within the allotted time and with casualties contained. Every so often, one of my men had stepped on a mine; a bluish smoke would then plume up from the ground and the soldier would stop, turning to look at me as if to say: 'I'm sorry.' The sergeant would bring out his notebook and record the man's death; the latter would brush the soot off his fatigues and resume walking. I had told them all that when a minefield is crossed at such speed and there's no time to use the mine-detectors, the only thing to do is fix in your mind an image of the pathfinding missile's trajectory. A matter of linking its pathway to some landmark or other — maybe a tree, the crest of a hill — and running straight towards it.

We had made our way between some tufts of juniper and sparsely scattered trees, and were running bent double, less from the likelihood of being within range of enemy artillery than from the roar of our own low-flying fighter planes. They were right on top of us now, for they happened to be our cover; flying so fast that first we saw them go overhead, with the red glow of their exhausts, then we heard the blast of the jet engines, by which time they were already on the hill raising showers of earth and stones, then they vanished sideways. This was another reason we couldn't advance any faster, and we had to make cautious progress; not so slowly as to fall behind schedule, not so fast as to reach the hill before the aerial cover ceased, running the risk of real bombs overhead. All said and done, it had taken some concentration but it hadn't been difficult.

At the bottom of the hill now, we were waiting as the drivers brought the four jeeps into the field with the weapons supplies, and the electronic and radio equipment. They were heading in across the clearing, slowly, one behind the other; I was leaning against a tree, with my arms folded, staring at the lance corporal in the first jeep; he drove hunched forward against the windscreen, his tongue protruding slightly, maybe from the effort of concentration, maybe so as to see the mines in time.

Beside me the sergeant was sitting on a tree trunk, a blade of grass in his mouth. He was scanning his notebook, calling out the names of the half score of soldiers slumped against one another in a circle around him, and every so often, after the name, he would add, in an undertone and with his eyes still lowered: 'Deceased'. The only final resting place of these fallen men was his notebook, where our mission was broken down into halts, route-features and staging-posts, each with its corresponding tallies. There was nothing to stop me from re-using the deceased soldiers, and besides in reality none of us had ever had anything to do with death. I was commanding a patrol that renewed itself perpetually, a patrol of engineers whose nature was immortal.

When the last jeep had arrived, I asked the operator for a photo-visualization of the hill. I watch the soldiers uncovering the keyboard, then testing the radio contacts; they go about it with bated breath, as if they aren't entirely sure that the equipment will work once they are in a combat zone. In the background, on the other side of the valley, our high-speed tanks roll away, rippling across the grass, towards objectives I can picture to myself, far from here. From now on we are utterly alone, in a landscape burnished with tones of yellow and green. Doubtless we'll check the survey map, and I shall have bearings taken; we'll identify imaginary presences, strike targets that are no more than a blip on the instruments, occupy the reading of two coordinates, and set off the red rocket that must be somewhere on this hill. Far less than our competence allows for, but done just like the real thing.

'Open the last envelope,' I tell the lieutenant. He feels for a loose edge, alongside the lettering *Light Knowledge*, the title of the exercise. I wait in silence; in fact I'm wondering who chooses these names, what connection they have to our operations. After all *Light Knowledge* could mean knowledge of light, the light of knowledge, shining knowledge, weightless knowledge.

The lieutenant handed me a large folded sheet of paper, with just two lines in the middle in block letters. Every word was clear, but I couldn't grasp the meaning of the whole. In essence, the first line instructed us to climb the hill, go down the other side, reach the 'objective and effect its deployment'. The second line mentioned the provision of 'technical support'. There was nothing else either about the objective or the support; the former was called 'Dillon Bay', and we had no inkling what it was. The latter was a total mystery.

By now the soldiers and the sergeant are beside me; they look at the sheet of paper I have in my hands, they look at the thin perforated tape curling round and round beside the operator. Only their eyes move. There's a wordless, almost instinctive way in which they all sense whether something is right or not, and they fill in the time trying to connect the parts to a whole; it is consistent with their natural trust that I should have the answer to every problem, and, as a function of my rank, should know virtually everything.

I avoid their eyes; handing the paper to the sergeant to file away, I say: 'Are there any handicaps at this stage of the mission?' He makes a show of checking the schedule, which he must already have read from start to finish: 'We're on the final stage, and everything gets harder from now on. No outgoing radio contact. Just telex-mapping. What's more, your requests will be processed as negative.'

'Negative in relation to what?' I ask.

The sergeant looks at the schedule again: 'I don't know, captain. Are you expecting supplies?'

'Look, I've no idea what to expect.'

He tries a more circumspect approach: 'The thing is, if you

don't transmit orders to the contrary, and, because of the radio
silence, you can't any more, the supplies will come through.'

I could feel they were all a bit tense and I wanted it dealt with.
I told the sergeant to read out the orders, which he did. When
he'd finished he asked me at once what Dillon Bay was, and the
technical support. From inside the jeep, the operator spoke
quietly: 'There it is, on the screen.' He was reversing the tape,
and the perforated dots in the paper rapidly turned into green
horizontal lines, level variants, altimetric quotas, hilly gradients
and reliefs, luminescent figures, vegetation symbols with a
continuous zigzag line leading up to a star with the name
'Dillon Bay' next to it. I looked at the coded figures for our
mission; the speed with which they appeared, along with the
patrol personnel's names and ranks, always conveyed a comfortable sense of detachment, an ironically solid diminution of
uncertainty. 'We're to effect the deployment of a star?' asked
the lieutenant.

We were able to decipher all the symbols, including the
parallel line that appeared then disappeared alongside the
winding road and that showed where we would be visible to an
eventual enemy observer and where, too, we would have
natural cover; but none of us had ever seen a sign like that on a
military map, shaped like a star.

Ever since I've known the ultimate focus of our mission, in
the guise of a peculiarly nebulous and peremptory order, I've
been trying to picture an objective, working through possibilities by a process of elimination. I know that, as we speed
along up the white road, behind me in their jeep the lieutenant
and the sergeant are engaged in the same speculation. I'm aware
that right now the sergeant's mental apparatus is ticking away
hard as he thinks: 'It's not a bridge, because there's no river
here. It's not a railway either, because there's none shown on
the map. Unless it's a road-bridge, but the road ends just where
the star is.' I know that the lieutenant is wondering: 'Can it be a
silo? No, even in a European exercise like this they don't let
anybody near those things, they're out of bounds.' I know too
that the men are curious, but only up to a point; right now
they're more interested in the fun they're having with the jeeps,

skidding round the bends or racing the engine uphill, like the corporal driving mine. Of course while I'm imagining what the others are imagining, I'm unable to concentrate on my own ideas, to envisage scenarios, to think ahead, to grasp instinctively what I have to do, to do what they all expect of me.

We were going across a hill shelled only a short time before; I should have seen toppled enemy batteries, corpses flung right and left, positions blasted apart, an astonishing dislocation of space that must come in the wake of these things. There could even be pockets of resistance, and for this reason I'd kept back the jeeps, ordering the lieutenant to operate the console on his vehicle whose function was to show up in codified outline on the screen any heat-detected human figures within a radius of several miles, this exposing them to us. We were advancing through a grid of bouncing signals, alien perceptions; but we had the advantage of better and quicker vision. It was a lovely September afternoon, with a keen chrome yellow light; it gave transparency to the green of the maples and the chestnuts, to a wild, unthreatening vegetation.

I could hear a tinny pattering noise; it sounded as if it came from the jeep's engine, and my first thought was of a malfunction. Then I turned and looked at the soldier who was beside the radio, leaning over the transmitter with his back to me and the headset on. I reached out, slowly; I unplugged the earphone socket. The soldier fell back as if I had struck him and the music erupted out of the speaker. He looked at me with an air of surrender; I looked back at him without a word.

We sped along in a pleasant wind, now nearly at the brow of the hill; as we swerved round the bends I observed the little column of jeeps following mine, their aerials waving about.

Coming round a hairpin bend, the corporal brakes suddenly; I brace myself against the windscreen, the radio operator has nothing to hold on to and lands on top of me. We wind up with the jeep at an angle on the rim of an almost perfect semicircle which has swallowed up three quarters of the road; the other half of the circle is completed in the wood, edged with incinerated bushes. The soldier between the two seats says 'Excuse me' and tries to get up; the corporal has got out and runs back to warn the others. I take a closer look at the blackened crater made by one of the firebombs from our aerial cover.

We had ground to a halt. The sergeant backed the jeeps slowly around the edge of the hole; he bent right down, got up again, peered up at the support beneath the wheels, and slapped hard at the mudguards within an inch of his head.

I set out downwards on foot, with the lieutenant and a couple of men, leaving the road and cutting straight across the hilltop. The crest of the hill was a wasteland, very windy, and at the peak we had no cover at all. The lieutenant and the men ran ahead to see, then they stopped suddenly, hung against a limitless horizon. I arrived just behind them and I too looked down, in a howling wind. Seen from above like this, in the circular totality of its apices, vertices, and superimposed triangles, it could really be likened to a star, but also a compass-card, with its points directed towards each one of the mountains surrounding it. Whatever analogies might be drawn, there was no mistaking what we were looking at: a fortress. A squat geometric mass. It was the only non-natural form as far as the eye could see; white; a kind of massive machine stacked on apparently flat ground, with mountains around it on every side but one, the gorge being a natural passageway. There was no sea hereabouts, but anyone would have agreed that 'Dillon Bay' was an apt enough name.

'So is that the objective?' asks the lieutenant.

'Yes. I think so.'

'And you know what we're to do with it?' he asks with an expansive gesture, as if to a large audience.

I shrug, my only answer an intake of breath. The two soldiers look at the fortress as if it were a spaceship. The lieutenant fixes his eyes on a point somewhere between me, the soldiers and the fortress. I take no notice, I concentrate on my imagination. I say, 'Let's go down and see.'

The descent in the jeeps was slow, for the road got narrower and narrower with tall grass that got caught in the axleshafts. Once I'd told the sergeant that what we had to 'prepare to deploy' was a fortress, he wanted at all cost to come in my jeep.

settled in the back, squashing the radio operator; he shouted into my ear to be heard above the noise. He listed the things we should have to do once we got there; he wondered if they were really the things we had to do, and how we should manage to do them with the resources we had. Then he went back over the lists, always starting in a different place. He complained, saying: 'Why didn't I bring the manual?' looking about him, as if he might find it in the jeep. He kept shouting, asking me if I could hear him. I answered: 'Yes,' without turning. He said: 'You're very young, captain.' I was embarrassed by his breathing down my neck and into my ear. With every bend the fortress became more impressive. I felt the road would never end.

We've been looking at it close up for several minutes, stock still in front of a gateway now bereft of its bridge, cut off by a deep moat that was a tangle of undergrowth. It is less white than it seemed at first; greyer, more streaked. Now and then we step back so as to get a better view of it; each one of us is struggling with a mixture of emotions and nobody feels like talking. Military transmissions come through on the radio, which we have left on in the jeep, but none destined for us; communications between planes and tanks, between command posts and positions, far off, where everyone else is together.

I order two men to throw across a rope bridge; then I tell the sergeant and the rest: 'Come on, we'll walk round it.'

We keep to this side of the moat, on an earthwork that follows the outline of the ramparts. We walk round a line of alternating projections and recesses, jutting and plunging angles, and longer stretches of concavity or convexity. Nearly all the bastions are breached at the top, as if they had rammed into something: the wall has come down in places, with little landslides of stones covered in thistles and foliage run riot. There are no crenellations, but a rounded, more modern parapet, an outline whose inner structure slightly protrudes, like someone taking aim under cover. The sergeant looks at everything, working out figures, making estimates. He writes on sheets of paper he has attached to a clipboard. He says: 'I don't know how much they can get through to us, but we'll never manage it.'

The base must have been a dodecahedron, on which they had laid another dodecahedron, but some degrees out of true, and this simple distortion multiplied the sides, so that the abutments of the one filled the spaces of the other. There had been added at intervals triangles that stuck out from the body of the fortress. It had an unquestionable charm; there was something solid, still and powerful, softened by the crumbling edges.

'It reminds me of an engraving from the Romantic period,' said the lieutenant. 'Right. Let's go inside,' I answered.

We have split up, and the sergeant busies himself peering in at dark, damp interiors; we see him vanish and reappear on the far side from us, followed by soldiers whom he orders to check out this or that. From time to time he seeks me out on the open space at the centre of the fortress, shouting something from far off, tossing his head. The lieutenant and I walk over surfaces that slope down, overgrown with grass and moss. We enter structures set at odd angles, with hardly any windows, just arches and vaults. Walking under one of these I realize that everything is smaller than normal, though proportioned overall like a stage set. We ascend, descend, go through passageways, our sense of direction lost. It isn't a building, it's a machine: corridors and pathways are pipes, curves are couplings, stairs are gear-wheels, powder magazines are combustion chambers. I felt I was at the heart of a cannon.

After one last ascent, we come out on top of the walls. From up there I gazed at the surrounding mountains, a desolate dark green; the sun was entering the V of the gorge, slicing the walls like a blade, striking the stone sundial that only now, as we turned to see where the ray ended, did we perceive on a small tower.

'What a strange thing,' said the lieutenant, 'a sundial that works the wrong way round. I mean, with light, not shadow.'

I nodded, without speaking. I was thinking of how this must happen day in, day out, in the total absence of watchers, with no one to see it. I thought of the fortress having a kind of dignity.

We were all outside again. We were drinking hot tea and

orange juice, sitting in the jeeps or slumped against the mudguards. Each one of us followed his own concentrated train of thought.

'Personally, I'd concentrate on the artillery,' the sergeant says, as if concluding an argument that could go no further. 'Reinforce the gun emplacements, lower the parapets for automatic missile launchers with surveillance and tracking radar. We could set up a base for supplies and communications and a command centre in the block houses in the square. Put a metal bridge across the moat. Set up a couple of ramps inside for moving the gun parts up to the turrets; if light aircraft sends us a helicopter we'll use it as a crane. No lime, no cement. We'll use vertical supports, do it all with scaffolding and tie-beams, it's the only way. You know we can't do any on-the-spot checks, we have to rely on calculations and judgement. Then we'll see how it stands up under fire and if all goes well we'll go home.' The sergeant accompanies each item on his programme with emphatic gesticulation, his hands slicing the air vertically or encircling vast expanses of sky in horizontal waves. Finally he says: 'What do you think?'

'Excellent,' I reply.

'Yes' interjects the lieutenant, 'I've been working things out more or less along those same lines.'

Whether he had or not I don't know, but I realize that the only thing we can do is to regard the fortress as little more than a base; 'preparing to deploy' meant, for the sake of time if nothing else, overlooking the rationale of its structural form, taking what it had to offer, making a rapid functional organization of space for ourselves, leaving it as it was before and bringing our stuff inside. I try to picture it as it will soon be: crumbling a little, its interior crossed with traction cables according to our own purposeful geometry, written into the fortress's own purposes, but quite extraneous to them.

'As far as the installations are concerned,' I tell the sergeant, 'that's fine with me. Only, I don't think we're going to have all that.'

'Well, we can make do.'

We're waiting for the technical support. The sergeant

outlines a few sketches for the bridge anchorage. The lieutenant has started drawing too; his eyes flit between the fortress and the paper, focusing particularly on the creepers that fall from the ramparts like overflowing water. From an operational point of view my ideas have been clear from the start, but I'm unsure about the total picture. To take my mind off things I look up at the sky and the buzzards high above me, or else I scan the ground for four-leafed clovers. It is always the same; it isn't a matter of what I see, there comes a moment when I sense the four-leafed clover is there. If I were to look for it carefully I would never find it.

The helicopter showed up on the instruments long before we heard it. The sergeant said: 'There are the supplies!' I had coloured flares lit and ordered the men to stand by. An instant later the helicopter drops straight into the gorge like a crossbar between the mountains, slides out above us and touches the ground with a slight wobble.

Hunched down and holding onto my beret, I head towards it. An NCO runs forward waving a sheet of paper.

'Sign here!' he yells.

I yell back: 'Sign what? I'd like to check the supplies first.'

Without turning, he motions to something behind him; a figure beyond the tail rotor, motionless in the midst of the corrugated grass.

The NCO insists: 'Sign, please.'

'Why?'

'Because we've made it here. And on schedule,' he answers.

I sign a scrawl without looking at the paper, trying to make out who it is over there. The NCO runs back on board the helicopter, which lifts its skids off the ground and rises in a wide arc, clearing the line of sight between me and the figure with his back to us, who is looking at the fortress and holding a bag in his hand.

I go towards him thinking he'll turn. Since he doesn't move, I veer sideways, halting on the edge of his perspective on the fortress. He is a tall, thin man, his hair snow-white and receding slightly. He has an elegant profile, and his posture is dignified even in the rather baggy camouflage fatigues with their folds still fresh. I look at the rank and name above the breast pocket.

'Sir?' I say.

He doesn't even move his eyes: 'It's amazing, don't you think?'

I look at the fortress: 'Yes. We liked it very much too.'

'Are you the commanding officer here?' he asks without shifting his glance.

'Yes, I'm Captain . . .'

He cuts my words short, stretching out a sideways hand: 'Colonel Roselani.'

I shake a large, gnarled hand: 'We were really expecting some technical support.'

'I'm your technical support, Captain . . . Marni,' he says, finally wheeling round to look at me with two impeccably grey eyes.

The others have stayed a short distance behind; they inspect the colonel and his bag as if they were somewhat doubtful, and the sergeant glances one last time at the helicopter up over the mountains. Then they salute.

'Have you been inside yet?' the colonel asks, answering the salute with just a nod.

'Yes,' I say; 'we've done a recce. Then we felt we'd rather be outside.'

He gives me an oblique look: 'Yes, I can understand.'

The lieutenant inches forward: 'We've also drawn up a plan of action.'

'Action on what?' the colonel asks, slightly narrowing his eyes.

'On the fortress,' answers the lieutenant. 'Under these conditions there's not much that can be done, and then it depends on the weaponry, and . . .'

'What weaponry?' the colonel cuts in.

'Listen,' I say. 'I received the order to effect deployment of an objective. This objective is the fortress. I haven't the faintest idea what they want done with it. I haven't the faintest idea what supplies will be sent to me.'

He smiles: 'But Captain, you won't be receiving any supplies.' Then he adds: 'Come.'

He walks towards the rope bridge. The sergeant runs ahead of us and rests his hands on the slackened cables as a steadying measure. He says: 'We'd thought of a Baecker bridge too, here, under the gateway.'

The colonel blinks, and says quietly: 'The word is barbican.'

When we get to the end of the bridge he turns, leaning towards the lieutenant, who has started to follow us, and says: 'No. Just the captain for now.'

We walk round the courtyard; he looks at the casemates, the loopholes and galleries, and inside the bastions, as if they corresponded to a mental image he had, as if he recognized them. Then he stares at me and says quietly: 'You've understood. Why didn't you tell your men?'

I shrug: 'Because I wasn't certain.'

His gaze sweeps round the fortifications: 'It's clear that there's nothing at all for you to put in order. There's no need for you to move a single stone. What you're to do is put yourself in readiness.'

'Yes, I thought it had to do with something like that,' I say, without looking at him.

He wasn't one to dwell on terminology. He walked in a relaxed way, with an animal ease, without affectation, and as he walked and talked to me, now and then he would jerk his head: 'That's an oreillon', 'That's a breech', 'That's the scarp wall,' 'That's the cavalier,' 'Those are dentilations,' 'That's the mantel-wall.' The names described planes or curves, vaults or arrises whereby the fortress was folded into space, and small raised or lowered constructions, each with a purpose of its own: for shielding men, for storing supplies, for a bird's eye view, for firing. Only, it was as if these appellations derived from a single nucleus. The different parts of the fortress were named after the devices with which it had been constructed: the gorge was the gorge outside, between the mountains, but also the inward-facing neck of a bastion tower; the cavalier was an attacking enemy, but also a kind of casemate straddling the walls to repel him; pincers were pincers, but also a military formation, and also the literal meaning of the tenaille, that low, arrow-shaped wall set outside the bastions, which he was now pointing out to me. In short, it seemed to me that this poverty of nomenclature corresponded to a period in which the standard against which things were measured was the human body, for everything, images as much as proportions, and it was to that body, whether in its defence or its destruction, that everything led back.

He said: 'Yes, in a way it's true. They saw things more or less like that; in their terminology the bulwark was the head, the flanks were eyes, the artillery placements were arms, and the passages for sorties outside were legs. They would say of a particular place — a mountain peak, a valley floor — that it was sick; they thought of it as having a defect of nature, and that a fortress was needed to free it from this indisposition.'

He has me look out through a loophole and gestures towards the landscape: 'Can you imagine which sickness ailed this place?'

I look at the mountains, at the dense vegetation that thins out more and more all the way down to the clearing where the soldiers are at a standstill around the jeeps, at the distant gorge, at the now more deeply tinted sky. I say: 'No. I can't, I have no idea.'

'A pity,' he answers, walking on.

He climbs the stairs with a regular stride, tirelessly; he scans small details, like the masonry joins, the height of elevations, the load-bearing stress on a rising spiral; he takes notes but he doesn't linger, just as if each detail confirmed what he had expected, and this confirmation wasn't that important anyway. When we came out onto the walls he turned inwards, holding the fortress in a single glance. He said: 'It all began with the arc of a compass. Then the problems started: what should go inside? A pentagon? A hexagon? A figure with even more sides? The more sides the figure had, of course, the more angles there were; the more angles there were the more obtuse they were; the more obtuse they were the more the walls were unassailable as a result, less susceptible to impact.'

He glanced at me quickly, then went on: 'All they did was dispute the relative merits of the acute angle or the obtuse angle, many sides or few, long sides or short sides, curved or quite straight. Every outside angle created dead angles inside, out of range of concentric fire from the walls. Enemies could slip in down there, they were under cover there; they raised ladders, piled up earth mounds, dug holes in the walls, placed explosives. Making a fortress wasn't easy, it wasn't an easy conception; and each formal misconception ended up as a military debacle.'

I followed the colonel along the ramparts. He talked, but without pointing things out; his hands were in the pockets of his fatigues and he spoke consistently in a tone of confidentiality, as with a very personal story about which he had reached reiterated conclusions. 'I don't want to bore you,' he said, halting for a moment; 'but you should realize I've come here with a specific purpose. I should like to guide you to the point where understanding ends, imagination ends; I'd like to guide you to where the senses take over.'

I smiled and said: 'Yes. But I too have responsibilities, and time is getting short.'

'You needn't worry,' he answered. 'There's nothing more for you to do, except what I am trying to make you do. There'll soon be a detachment here with orders countering yours; you were to be prepared, they are to fire, but in the end it's an exercise and we're all on the same side. They'll fire a few shots from long range then "Light Knowledge" will be over as far as we are concerned.'

I think of the men down below. I imagine their puzzlement, their questions. Even if the whole time here there's been very little noise, I now find everything quieter. I catch a glimpse of the sergeant looking up, his arms folded; his eyes scanning the top of the ramparts to follow our movements.

The colonel has walked on, gesturing towards a point in the middle of the courtyard, though without turning to look at it: 'The lines all started from there, from that centre, opening out like rays, towards the exterior, towards the vertices of the triangles. Other, external lines linked up these vertices with one another; they were lines sketched on the plan, but then they became target lines, lines of fire. So the outcome of mathematical perfection was converted into ballistic trajectories, into cannonfire. If the angles were wrong, if the form lacked balance, they couldn't turn the cannons, they couldn't skew them downwards or sideways and there came a time when the enemy would be beneath them or at their backs or very close, to the point where he would now be out of range. A straight line badly drawn on the plan meant a bayonet in the belly, a bullet between the eyes. Circle arcs, bisecting lines, tangents, figures inscribed one inside the other: to begin with they only had the circle and its centre and everything was possible, but once they set down the first figure all the rest followed. They made two upturned triangles overlap and the result was a star, they joined up its points and the result was a hexagon; in the empty spaces between the points, a mere by-product of the drawing, trapezes came into being, and it was those gaps which attracted the attackers. The fortress began to develop outwards, in waves, conversely replicating its form; or it began to develop inwards, in the same way. The fortress began to throb with life.'

The sun has disappeared behind the hills and the light comes in reflections, rays piercing the pale blue mass. The colonel's words reach me in the same way: I don't know whether it's the smile with which he tails off every statement, or the overall tone of complicity, but the thoughts seem to take shape on his very surface, and they hang there pendant and separate, like droplets. I make an effort to attach them to what I can see: the outline of the bastions, rounded so as to reduce the impact of projectiles, the massive stonework accentuated by pointed arches, the spots of green where stubborn moss forms tiny beards.

The colonel lightly touched my arm: 'You should think of all this as a totality of relationships, you should try to experience it like that. Once the form was established, that's to say the size, the initial extent, the rest became subsidiary multiples. The fortress itself was in its way a large multiple, a multiplicator of force and time. Its weapon was delay, its force in the slowing of things, in the dilation of time, in extending its duration to the point of disarming it. There were armies wanting to go straight to the heart of a territory, they had to be held up.'

He looked at me to see if I was following, then went on: 'I've told you that everything originated from the inside, and this is true; but everything was modified from the outside. It was enemy fire that determined the shape of the bastions: enfilading fire, barrages, volleys, broadsides and direct fire. You must imagine every trajectory, every hit of every kind as propulsion towards the fortress, towards its interior, towards its centre; lines that thinned out the bastions or rounded them or made them more pointed or thicker. Everything contracted, or everything expanded, accordingly.'

He laced his fingers together with the palms held flat, closing them up or opening them out in a broader or narrower V-shape.

I began to see the fortress as a threshold between inside and outside, a moving edge in space, elastic continually stretched back and forth. I began to see the fortress as a less rigid thing.

I told him this. He answered: 'Yes, in a sense it is true. Besides, everything could be reversed from one moment to the next: the enemy could open a breach and come through; what had been conceived of outwards had to be able to be turned round, turned back inwards.'

He pointed out a low, arrow-shaped construction on the far back of the moat: 'Even that caponier was less a vanguard position than for rearguard fire on anyone who had got right under the walls.'

'You see,' he said, drawing a hand across his quite un-dishevelled hair; 'each salient served to defend the indentations. They built walls to defend themselves, closing themselves in; then, however, they had to take up more forward, exterior positions so as to hold that interior; they had to become external, they had to see themselves from the outside, see the fortress as the enemy saw it, while staying within. Each and every part of the fortifications had to have the potential for outward strike and surveillance, but also to be flanked and to flank, to be protected and protect — the most exposed of the walls could be used for cannon cover of the more protected. Each point had to be visible from any other within the circular span. Everything lay in the exclusion of points outwith the lines of sight and fire. It was necessary to thrust forward, well forward, so as to see what was behind and protect it.'

The colonel stopped and once more touched my arm with a delicacy that neither the rank nor the uniform could justify. He said: 'Look, I'd like you to feel all this.' I had the impression he was asking something that went beyond my responsibilities, and that this request embodied both complete control and complete despair. Perhaps this was why, from all that he had spoken of, I picked out the element with which I had most affinity: 'It's strange,' I said 'but I've always thought there was a difference between looking and taking aim. I thought this difference could separate my profession from my life.' Then I reflected on the look as telescopic alignment, on the possibility of focusing in a single vision what is near and what is far away.

He gave a faint smile, as if this was not the reply he'd expected; with a change of tone he said: 'Yes, I understand. but then it was different. A way of looking and a way of taking aim had their origins in almost the same set of calculations. That period ushered in an artificial conception of space that gave primacy to man, that made him its central vantage point, and simultaneously it ushered in the conception of an artificial force propelled through space and intended to kill him. Between ballistics and perspective there's more kinship than you can imagine.'

It is almost nightfall. While talking we had circled the ramparts more than once, and now we were at a halt on one of the sides. The colonel looked across the bastion, resting his hands on a crumbling wall, of which less than half remained. We stayed like this for some time, in a deepening silence, with our eyes staring into the surrounding darkness to which we were becoming accustomed. It's the same darkness, I thought, through which the sentinels will have strained their eyes to make out a movement in the foliage, a glimmer of something; the same darkness in which soldiers posted at the loopholes will have fired blindly, terror-stricken, or sparingly, reckoning the speed of the enemy's approach and of their own reloading; the darkness from which will have rained sudden fiery projectiles, shouts, flares, in an access of tension from which there was no turning back, in a time slowed down enough for death throes; the darkness in which men woken by the alarm inside the fortress will have run up to the magazines carrying munitions, run down to the sick-bays with stretchers at which they preferred not to look. For the first time I thought of this place in terms of its life, and almost immediately in terms of death. I thought of the colonel, his strange elegance, the other war he must have known; I thought of his fear, how his fear must have had a real object at some time, in some place, if now what meant so much to him was something so inoffensive, and in his eyes so beautiful, as a fortress.

I made up my mind to tell him this, frankly. He listened, then he turned and smiled; 'Perhaps this was exactly what I wanted you to feel.' And he added: 'After all, for you an exercise is the only opportunity to give death a little try.'

I smiled too and said: 'Yes, perhaps I could do it. But it would be very different, very far from what I must make myself feel in an exercise like this. You speak of time that could be lost, gained, halted, time that lasted a whole night or a dawning day and dwindled to an end, with uncertainties and reversals. But I must make myself experience a second; I need to be able to seize it and dilate it, and see and feel and touch the thousandfold information it contains, the thousandfold decisions, the thousandfold definitive and irreversible choices, among them my death, which for sure would last no longer. My fortress is the size of a second, and everywhere in space, with neither inside nor outside, with a boundary I can imagine only for convenience sake, always displaced somewhere else. It is a second containing millions of connected and disconnected particles, particles guided, aimed; containing conventional moves and counter-moves to a depth now within the bounds of calculation and imagination. Sometimes I think that this vast second is so saturated with all possible foresight, with all possibility, that we are now in search of another, a higher level, a higher space, a faster speed, to begin again the computation of moves and countermoves. I wish all this did not exist, but I have learned to live this way, and to die this way too, "a little," as you say, without anything happening. Sometimes I think that we are leaving this second behind, risking going forward, or turning back. Maybe this is why they sent me to learn about a fortress.'

There was a long silence, a pause in which neither of us spoke again, although at one point the colonel stared at me, holding the silence. We focused once more on the darkness of the valley, and the colonel said: 'You know, I hadn't been to Dillon Bay before either. It's the first time I've really seen it.'

I heard a hubbub of voices from the other side of the walls; I looked over the angle of the bastion and I saw the men down there, gathered round the red blink of the instruments. The sergeant waved his arms up at us, signing to us, shouting something I couldn't clearly make out.

'Yes, they're on their way,' said the colonel, pointing to the hill. Then he went on: 'I had never seen this fortress, but I knew it inside out. I had the original plans, and from them I was able to work out the exterior views. I drew them myself. I would keep adding things then removing them. It's odd, but it's just as I had imagined it, exactly as I expected it.'

From beyond the hill there was the sound of loud diesel engines, revving for the climb, and now we could hear them getting closer. The colonel looked at the hilltop, his elbows on the little wall, and said: 'Must be a French detachment. How do you manage with French, Captain?'

'Fine,' I answered, smiling. On the stairs I heard the steps of the sergeant and the men coming up.

'It's one of Montbaum's fortresses,' the colonel said; 'one of the last he built. He was Dutch, he spent half his life working out a virtually impregnable system of fortifications, and succeeded with fortresses like this one. There was no way of taking it, and it wasn't just the design, it also had to do with countermining. The walls were full of gaps, ballast chambers; even if the enemy sappers mined it with explosives only one part of the wall would come down, but the bastion would hold. So he spent the second half of his life studying how the fortresses he'd built could be destroyed.'

The sergeant came up behind me, a little out of breath. He said: 'Here I am, Captain . . .' I nodded, without turning to face him and the men. All of us stood silent in the darkness, watching the hill; we heard the engines going into bottom gear, we saw safety lights glimmering among the dark foliage.

'Dillon Bay was perfect,' the colonel said. 'And as with all perfect fortresses, nobody ever attacked it,' he added, watching me with a broad smile.

I nodded without replying. I was beside him, the sergeant and the men behind; we were all still, at slightly odd angles to one another, tensed towards the darkness, separate yet united by circumstance.

He said: 'Let's go.'

He turned, but the movement was hesitant, as if he was looking for something. He pressed his hands against his fatigues, and in the valley, a second later, I heard two long drawn out explosions, two blasts of automatic fire, singular, distant. I saw the incredibly large grey eyes, I saw the hand reaching for support in the air.

There was a sudden brilliance, a burst of light; searchlights from the hill punctured the darkness, framing the fortress all at once. We were in a white light, dense as a sound that isolated us from the surrounding darkness; in a liquid, dazzling glare, in a glacial luminosity that seemed less a reflection from the fortress than emanating from its stones.

We were huddled over the colonel. We enacted fast, useless movements. Each gesture was as though detached from its immediate perception, each thing before our eyes dilated into a parallel simultaneity, and after crossing infinite levels it would adhere immediately to itself, to that thing it was: the position of the body, the folds of the fatigues, the white hair against the stone.

We stayed like that for a while, silently, without looking at one another.

From beneath the walls shouts of greeting reached us, loud at first, then more and more hesitant, cautious.

A reconnaissance plane came over the hill, flying slow and low over the fortress. Attached to its wings were two phosphorescent smoke flares, two orange streaks against the dark sky. Our exercise was over.

About the Authors

Nanni Balestrini was born in Milan in 1935. Known both as an experimental writer of prose and verse and as a cultural and political activist, he played a leading role in avant-garde writing and publishing in the sixties. His involvement with the extra-parliamentary left in the seventies resulted in terrorism charges (of which he was subsequently acquitted) and a long period of self-imposed exile from Italy. The extract translated here is from the novel *La violenza illustrata* (Einaudi 1976); using one of Balestrini's favourite techniques, it is a montage of newspaper reports of the death of Mara Cagol, one of the founders of the Red Brigades. His most recent novels are *Gli invisibili* (Bompiani 1987; tr. *The Unseen*, Verso 1989) and *L'editore* (Feltrinelli 1989).

Paola Capriolo was born in Milan in 1962. She has published three volumes of fiction: *La grande Eulalia* (Feltrinelli 1988), a collection of four short stories which includes 'Letters to Luisa', *Il nocchiero* (Feltrinelli 1989) and *Il doppio regno* (Bompiani 1991), as well as a collection of children's stories, *La ragazza dalla stella d'oro* (Einaudi 1991).

Gianni Celati was born in Sondrio in 1937 and is now based in Bologna. A critic and translator as well as a writer of fiction, Celati published four novels to critical acclaim in the 1970s (*Comiche*, Einaudi 1971; *Le avventure di Guizzardi*, Einaudi 1973; *La banda dei sospiri*, Einaudi 1976; *Lunario del paradiso*, Einaudi 1978). After a long period of reassessment, he returned to fiction in the mid eighties with the publication of *Narratori delle pianure* (Feltrinelli 1985; tr. *Voices from the Plains*, Serpent's Tail 1989) and *Quattro novelle sulle apparenze* (Feltrinelli 1987; tr. *Appearances*, Serpent's Tail 1991), from which this story is taken. He has recently edited an anthology of contemporary Italian writers, *Narratori delle riserve*, for Feltrinelli (1992).

Vincenzo Consolo was born in Sant'Agata di Militello, in Sicily, in 1933 and now lives in Milan. He has published six works of fiction, including the widely-acclaimed *Il sorriso dell'ignoto marinaio* (Einaudi 1976), the stories and essays included in *Le pietre di Pantalica* (Mondadori 1988), from which this piece is taken, and, most recently, the novel *Nottetempo, casa per casa* (Mondadori 1992).

Daniele Del Guidice was born in Rome in 1949 and now lives in Venice. His considerable reputation is based on two novels published in the eighties (*Lo stadio di Wimbledon*, Einaudi 1981 and *Atlante occidentale* Einaudi 1985; tr. *Lines of Light*, Viking 1989) and on some shorter pieces among which 'Dillon Bay' is pre-eminent.

Pia Fontana lives in Venice. She was the first winner of the Calvino prize with some of the stories which were subsequently collected in *Sera o mattina* (Marsilio 1989). She has also published a novel, *Spokane* (Marsilio 1988).

Primo Levi was born in 1919 and died in his native Turin in 1987. Some of his best known works draw directly on his experience as a prisoner at Auschwitz and on his subsequent career as a research chemist: *Se questo è un uomo* (De Silva 1947, new ed. Einaudi 1956; tr. *If This is a Man*, Orion Press 1959), *La tregua* (Einaudi 1963: tr. *The Truce*, Penguin 1965), *Il sistema periodico* (Einaudi 1975; tr. *The Periodic Table*, Michael Joseph 1985), and the essays of *I sommersi e i salvati* (Einaudi 1986; tr. *The Drowned and the Saved*, Michael Joseph 1988). He wrote two other novels; *La chiave a stella* (Einaudi 1978; tr. *The Wrench*, Michael Joseph 1987) and *Se non ora, quando?* (Einaudi 1982; tr. *If not now, when?* Michael Joseph 1986) as well as numerous essays (notably *L'altrui mestiere*, Einaudi 1985; tr. *Other People's Trades*, Michael Joseph 1989) and short stories, some of which have appeared in English in three collections to date: *Moments of reprieve* (Michael Joseph 1986), *The Mirror Maker: Stories and Essays* (Methuen 1990), and *The Sixth Day and Other Stories* (Michael Joseph 1990). His *Collected Poems* were published in English by Faber in 1992.

Rosetta Loy was born and lives in Rome. In addition to the collection of stories *All'insaputa della notte* (Garzanti 1984) from which 'The Wet-Nurse' is taken, she has published four novels to date: *La bicicletta* (Einaudi 1974), *La porta dell'acqua* (Einaudi 1976), *L'estate di Letuchè* (Rizzoli 1982) and *Le strade di polvere* (Einaudi 1987; tr. *The Dust Roads of Monferrato*, Collins 1990).

Marina Mizzau lectures in psychology at the University of Bologna. She has written numerous essays on literary and psychoanalytic themes, including *Eco e Narciso: Parole e silenzi nel conflitto uomo-donna* (Boringhieri 1979) and *L'ironia* (Feltrinelli 1984) as well as two collections of stories: *Come i delfini* (Essedue 1988) and *I bambini non volano* (Bompiani 1992).

Piera Oppezzo was born in Turin and lives in Milan. She has published three volumes of poetry (*L'uomo qui presente*, Einaudi 1966; *Sì a una reale interruzione*, Geiger 1976 and *Le strade di Melanchta*, Editrice Nuovi Autori 1987) and a novel *Minuto per minuto* (La Tartaruga 1978).

Nico Orengo was born in 1944 in Turin, where he works as editor of *Tuttolibri*, the literary supplement of the daily paper *La Stampa*. His novels include *Miramare* (Einaudi 1975), *Figura gigante* (Serra e Riva 1984) and *Le rose di Evita* (Einaudi 1990).

Anna Maria Ortese was born in Rome in 1914, and has lived for many years in Rapallo. Her books, which she describes as 'half fiction, half journalism', include *Angelici dolori* (Bompiani 1937), *L'infanta sepolta* (Milano-Sera 1948), *Il mare non bagna Napoli* (Einaudi 1953; tr. *The Bay is not Naples*, Collins 1959), *Silenzio a Milano* (Laterza 1958, republ. La Tartaruga 1986), *L'iguana* (Vallecchi 1965, republ. Adelphi 1986; tr. *The Iguana* Minerva 1990), *Poveri e semplici* (Vallecchi 1965), *La luna sul muro* (Vallecchi 1968), *L'alone grigio* (Vallecchi 1969), *Il porto di Toledo* (Rizzoli 1975), *Il cappello piumato* (Mondadori 1979), *Il treno russo* (Theoria 1983) and *Il mormorio di Parigi* (Theoria 1986), as well as the collection of stories in which 'On the Neverending Terrace' was published for the first time, *In sonno e in veglia* (Adelphi 1986).

Enrico Palandri was born in Venice in 1956 and now lives and works for part of the year in London. He achieved early recognition with his novel of the 1977 student movement in Bologna, *Boccalone* (L'Erba Voglio 1979; republ. Feltrinelli 1988) and has since published two further novels: *Le Pietre e il Sale* (Garzanti 1986; tr. *Ages Apart*, Collins Harvill 1989) and *La via del ritorno* (Bompiani 1990; tr. *The Way Back*, Serpent's Tail 1993).

Goffredo Parise was born in Vicenza in 1929; he died in 1986. The story included here comes from the first of two volumes of an 'ABC of feelings', *Sillabario N.1* (Mondadori 1972) and *Sillabario N.2* (Mondadori 1982), part of which were translated as *Solitudes* (Dent 1984). His novels include *Il ragazzo morto e le comete* (Neri Pozza 1952; new ed. Feltrinelli 1965), *Il prete bello* (1954; tr. *The Priest among the Pigeons*, Weidenfeld and Nicolson, 1955) and *Il padrone* (Einaudi 1965; tr. *The Boss*, Cape 1967). His complete works have been published by Mondadori (*Opere*, 2 vols., 1987-89).

Sandra Petrignani was born in Piacenza in 1952 and now lives and works in Rome. As well as short stories, she has published three novels to date: *La navigazione di Circe* (Theoria 1987), *Il catalogo dei giocattoli* (Theoria 1988; tr. *The Toy Catalogue*, Olive Press 1990), and *Come cadono i fulmini* (Rizzoli 1991).

Claudio Piersanti was born in 1954 near Teramo; he is at present based in Rome. He has published three novels to date (*Casa di nessuno*, Feltrinelli 1981; *Charles*, Il lavoro editoriale 1986; *Gli sguardi cattivi della gente*, Feltrinelli 1992) and a number of short stories, some of them collected in *L'amore degli adulti* (Feltrinelli 1989).

Elisabetta Rasy was born in 1947 and now lives and works in Rome. Her stories and essays have appeared in numerous reviews. Her first book was a critical study of writing by women, *La lingua della nutrice* (Edizioni delle donne 1978), and she has since published three novels: *La prima estasi* (Mondadori 1985), *Il finale della battaglia* (Feltrinelli 1988) and *L'altra amante* (Garzanti 1990).

Francesca Sanvitale was born in Milan and has lived in Rome since the 1960s. Her first novel, *Il cuore borghese*, was published by Vallecchi in 1972, since when she has published two novels (*Madre e figlia*, Einaudi 1980 and *L'uomo del parco*, Mondadori 1984), a novella (*Verso Paola*, Einaudi 1991), a book of short stories (*La realtà è un dono*, Mondadori 1987) and a collection of essays (*Mettendo a fuoco*, Gremese 1988).

Antonio Tabucchi was born in Pisa in 1943. His first novel, *Piazza d'Italia*, was published by Bompiani in 1975, and was followed by *Il piccolo naviglio* (Mondadori 1978) and *Notturno indiano* (Sellerio 1984; tr. *Indian Nocturne*, Chatto and Windus 1988). Two brief collections of miscellaneous pieces (*Donna di Porto Pim*, Sellerio 1983 and *I volatili del Beato Angelico*, Sellerio 1987) and the long story *Il filo dell'orizzonte* (Feltrinelli 1986) have been translated together in the single volume *Vanishing Point*, Chatto and Windus 1991. Tabucchi has published three collections of short stories: *Il gioco del rovescio* (Il Saggiatore 1981), *Piccoli equivoci senza importanza* (Feltrinelli 1985; tr. *Little Misunderstandings of no Importance*, Chatto and Windus 1988), and *L'angelo nero* (Feltrinelli 1991). He is known also as a scholar of Portuguese literature and especially of the works of Fernando Pessoa, whom he has also translated. These professional interests have in turn been absorbed into fiction in his most recent novel, *Requiem* (Feltrinelli 1992).

Susanna Tamaro was born in Trieste in 1957 and now lives and works in Rome. Her first novel, *La testa tra le nuvole*, was published by Marsilio in 1988, and was followed by the collection of short stories *Per voce sola* (Marsilio 1990).

Pier Vittorio Tondelli was born near Reggio Emilia in 1955. He died in 1991. His first book, *Altri libertini* (Feltrinelli 1980), was a collection of loosely connected stories and was followed by three novels: *Pao Pao* (Feltrinelli 1982), *Rimini* (Bompiani 1985) and *Camere separate* (Bompiani 1989; tr. *Separate Rooms*, Serpent's Tail 1992). Tondelli was also the author of two entertaining collections of occasional pieces, *Biglietti agli amici* (Baskerville 1986) and *Un weekend postmoderno: cronache degli anni ottanta* (Bompiani 1990) and was active in promoting the work of young writers through the three anthologies of 'under 25s' which he edited for Transeuropa (*Giovani blues*, 1986, *Belli e perversi*, 1987 and *Papergang*, 1990).

Sandro Veronesi was born in Florence in 1959; he now lives and works in Rome. He has published two novels to date (*Per dove parte questo treno allegro*, Theoria 1988 and *Gli sfiorati*, Mondadori 1990) as well as numerous short stories and occasional pieces (*Cronache italiane*, Mondadori 1992). His most recent publication is a 'non-fiction novel' against the death-penalty, *Occhio per occhio* (Mondadori 1992).

Translators

The translators of the individual stories are:
Jenny Condie: story by Palandri
Ed Emery: stories by Balestrini, Fontana, Levi, Mizzau, Tamaro,
    Tondelli
Liz Heron: stories by Capriolo, Del Giudice, Oppezzo, Ortese, Rasy
Stuart Hood: stories by Celati, Consolo, Loy, Orengo, Parise,
    Petrignani, Piersanti, Veronesi
Martha King: story by Sanvitale
Tim Parks: story by Tabucchi

Permissions

This page constitutes an extension of the copyright page.

Elisabetta Rasy, 'La sindrome di Clerambault', published in *19 racconti per Rinascita*, edited by Ottavio Cecchi and Mario Spinella, © Editrice *L'Unità*, Rome, 1987, pp. 123–8.

Francesca Sanvitale, 'La macchina elettronica' from *La realtà è un dono*, © Mondadori, Milan, 1987, pp. 199–208. English translation from Martha King (ed.) *New Italian Women: A Collection of Short Fiction*, © Italica Press, New York, 1989, pp. 176–86. Translator Martha King.

Antonio Tabucchi, 'Una caccia', from *Donna di Porto Pim*, © Sellerio, Palermo, 1983, pp. 71–7. English translation from *Vanishing Point*, © Chatto and Windus, London, 1991, pp. 150–6. Translator Tim Parks.

Susanna Tamaro, 'La grande casa bianca', © *Panta* 5, 1991, pp. 117–26.

Pier Vittorio Tondelli, 'Postoristoro', from *Altri libertini*, © Feltrinelli, Milan, 1980, pp. 9–18 and 24-34.

Sandro Veronesi, 'Morto per qualcosa', © *Il manifesto*, 1989.